Dear Perplexed,

What a pushover you are! You want to get a woman's attention? Try ignoring her!

Yeah, but only after you've tantalized her. That thought rang so true that Daffy typed it in next. Then she added:

I'll probably get skewered for this statement, but women like masterful men. Wimps are yesterday's news.

Masterful—like Hunter James, the dark-eyed satyr who'd told her with a straight face that given thirty days, he could make any woman fall in love with him.

Two days, and all she'd thought about was Hunter James—followed by all the reasons she had no business thinking about him.

What you lack is confidence. If you want something badly enough, you have to be prepared to walk away from the table. There's your Rx. Try that. Write back and let me know your wedding date.

ATTENTION: ORGANIZATIONS AND CORPORATIONS
Most Avon Books paperbacks are available at special quantity discounts for bulk purchases for sales promotions, premiums, or fund-raising. For information, please call or write:

Special Markets Department, HarperCollins Publishers, Inc., 10 East 53rd Street, New York, N.Y. 10022–5299.
Telephone: (212) 207–7528. Fax: (212) 207-7222.

HAILEY NORTH

Dear Love Doctor

AVON BOOKS

An Imprint of HarperCollinsPublishers

This is a work of fiction. Names, characters, places, and incidents are products of the author's imagination or are used fictitiously and are not to be construed as real. Any resemblance to actual events, locales, organizations, or persons, living or dead, is entirely coincidental.

AVON BOOKS
An Imprint of HarperCollins*Publishers*
10 East 53rd Street
New York, New York 10022-5299

Copyright © 2001 by Nancy Wagner
ISBN: 0-380-81308-4
www.avonromance.com

First Avon Books paperback printing: June 2001

Avon Trademark Reg. U.S. Pat. Off. and in Other Countries, Marca Registrada, Hecho en U.S.A.
HarperCollins® is a trademark of HarperCollins Publishers Inc.

Printed in the U.S.A.

10 9 8 7 6 5 4 3 2 1

For my Sweet-ums,
who created the most wonderful incentive plan ever.
Here's four for four!

With special thanks for the loving friendship
of four special and incredibly talented women—
Barbara Gross, Ph.D.;
Tricia Hiemstra, M.B.A.;
Amy Powell, M.B.A.;
and Devon Scheef, M.B.A.
Christmas would never be Christmas without you.

And to Kathleen Nance, that genius of genies—
thanks for setting me straight in D.C.

1

Daffodil Landry stared at the semicircle of letters spread on her desk. She had exactly thirty-seven minutes to make the deadline on her column and she'd yet to write the first word.

"Eeny-meenie-minie-mo," she murmured, fingering the only letter postmarked from outside New Orleans.

"Not done yet?" A flash of red hair whipped by the cubicle, then reversed as a slip of a woman hovered just close enough to distract. "Losing your touch, Daffy Doc?"

Daffy summoned her sweetest smile for *The Crescent*'s managing editor. Marguerite had vehemently opposed the idea of Daffy authoring the Love Doctor column, yet when it became a hit, the editor remembered only that it was something she'd said that had sparked the concept.

"I always make my deadlines," Daffy said, slitting open the letter with the Ponchatoula postmark. Perhaps country people had more interesting love dilemmas than the city-bred. After six months of secretly penning the column, Daffy was getting restless. From the bags of mail she'd waded through, she'd learned that lovers tended to make the same mistakes over and over; something she'd certainly found to be true in her own life.

Marguerite continued to fill the doorway, drumming her bright red nails on the metal frame of the cubicle wall. Daffy unfolded the single sheet of pink-and-white stationery and forced her attention to the somewhat childishly formed lettering. From the time she'd spent at *The Crescent*, Daffy had learned that if ignored, Marguerite would flit away to alight elsewhere.

Dear Doctor Love, Daffy read, noting the transposition of her title. Well, it was better than Daffy Doc, as Marguerite insisted on calling her. The name had stuck among the few staffers at *The Crescent* privy to the identity of the Love Doctor.

Outside the brick walls of the paper's offices, of course, the Love Doctor's identity remained a secret. As Marguerite, in one strategy session, had put it, the paper would be laughed out of circulation if the citizens of New Orleans discovered they were lapping up love advice from Daffodil Landry! Unless, of course, a socialite's string of broken engagements, mashed hearts, and public displays of misdirected affection could be considered prime qualifications.

But *The Crescent* had been struggling in its efforts to unseat its rival tabloid, *The Gambit*. A year ago Daffy's aunt Wisteria had bequeathed Daffy a ten percent interest, which gave Daffy some say in operations. So Marguerite had given in.

To avoid any conflicts of interest, Daffy had her editor over at the city's "real newspaper" (where she reigned as society columnist and photographer) sign off on her participation and *The Crescent* ran a trial column introducing Dear Love Doctor.

And now hundreds of women—and men, though they weren't quite so open about it—rushed out for the latest edition of *The Crescent*, eager to see just whom the Dear, but rather acid-tongued, Love Doctor would diagnose next. As Daffy often said to her twin, Jonquil, her own life might be a mess, but she was awfully good with other people's problems. But even Jonquil—or Jonni, as everyone called her—didn't know the identity of the Love Doctor.

The tapping had stopped. Alone again, Daffy blinked and realized she'd read not a word of the letter. A glance at her pavé diamond evening watch reminded her of her next obligation.

We've been dating six months, a dream come true. I've known H for years but never really dated him before. He was always popular in high school and now, well, now everyone's after him. I'm head over heels, but he's starting to make excuses about not being available, due to his work,

4 ~ Hailey North

he says. He's in New Orleans a lot and I've been told he goes out with other women there, but when he comes to see me and tells me I'm his country princess, one look at his big, brown eyes and his sexy smile and I start to melt. I can't bring myself to ask him about those other women. Should I?

Signed,
Loyal But Lonesome in Ponchatoula

Daffy groaned and crumpled the letter. What a nitwit! Well, this letter would do just fine. Her readers seemed to enjoy it when she skewered someone. And with this letter, not only the writer but also its subject, H, made perfect targets.

Six months and he's restless. Daffy poised her hands above the keyboard. Six months was pretty much her limit, too. After that, a guy started to expect you to be there for him, and the men Daffy dated assumed she was as interested in marriage as they were. Mistake. Six months was about the point Daffy found some clever way to sabotage any relationship that threatened to become too comfortable. Otherwise, she'd be forced to overcome her demons and take a risk with one of them.

But that was something Daffy had never been able to bring herself to do.

She was willing to bet this H never had, either. Mr. Popular, eh? Daffy bent her fingers to the keys. She knew all about being the most popular one and how others wanted to cluster around you but never really wanted to know who you were beneath the pretty surface, and soon you got so used to protecting the image you never even looked beneath it, either. No, the nitwit in Ponchatoula was better off without this guy.

Should you ask him [she typed hastily, her own emotions interfering somewhat with her editorial judgment] *about those other women? No, my dear, sweet country mouse, you should not. And why not? Because you should never speak to him again. If he calls, you're not in. If he drops by, the doorbell is broken. This man isn't ready, willing, or able to settle down—with you or anyone. Find a man who wants only you, and you won't have to be lonesome. This relationship is diagnosis terminal.*

Daffy saved the file, hit the Print command, and watched her trembling hands in dismay. She knew she was reacting to her own problems, but she didn't have time to reflect on that influence. She slipped the printout into the plain brown envelope Marguerite insisted on for secrecy, and held it out as the managing editor appeared once more at her desk.

Daffy tucked a strand of hair behind her ear. "Right on time," she said.

"Daffy Doc strikes again?"

"You'll like this one," Daffy said, pushing back

her chair and reaching for the silk evening bag she'd brought with her. "You might want to arrange for extra copies for north of the lake."

Marguerite's eyes widened. "Broadening our readership?"

"The letter was from Ponchatoula." That small town, famous for its strawberry festival and antiques shops, was about an hour's drive north of New Orleans.

Marguerite smiled and Daffy knew she was calculating circulation increases. Tucking the brown envelope under her arm, she said, "And what party are you off to tonight?"

"It's not one of the usuals. It's a fund-raiser featuring some new cyber guru."

Marguerite nodded. "That would be the Hunter James meet-and-greet to raise money for the Orphan's Club. We're sending Jill to cover it."

"Jill?" Daffy couldn't hide her surprise. Jill handled technology, not society, and wouldn't know a fish fork from a sorbet spoon. And Daffy would bet she didn't possess a stitch of evening attire.

"Don't you do your homework? James made a fortune in Web technology."

Daffy let the slap go without retorting. Just because she was the society columnist for the city's daily newspaper, people assumed she was nothing but an airhead, certainly not a true journalist. Normally she would have read all about Hunter James in advance, but she hadn't planned to cover the function, considering it of little import, especially on a night when two other galas demanded her attention. But her editor at the other paper—her primary job—had called her at home only that morning to ask her to stop by the James affair. It was, as the editor pointed out in response to Daffy's grumbling, at a private home only a block down from the Opera Guild House, where she had to be anyway.

"At least Jill will deliver an unbiased report," Marguerite said, her eyes narrowing in a way that made Daffy a trifle nervous.

"Why wouldn't anyone?" Okay, so she took the bait.

"You tell me. Next week." Laughing softly, the editor disappeared from view.

"You tell me," Daffy murmured, summoning an image of her idea of a computer guru. Young, no doubt, with pimples and glasses and pant legs that hit somewhere between his calves and ankle-bones. And worth enough money to make the society patrons of New Orleans sit up and take notice. Because it had to be his money that attracted people's interest—he possessed no lineage.

Otherwise, Daffy would already be acquainted with the mysterious Hunter James. Born into the landed gentry of the city, clutching the proverbial silver baby bottle to her lips, Daffy Livaudais Landry couldn't help knowing anyone who was anyone. And for the past several years, it had been her job to call on that background for the social events covered by the *New Orleans Times*.

Daffy reached the reception area and smiled at

the new girl behind the front desk. She smiled back shyly, her glance taking in Daffy's elegant black cocktail dress. "What a pretty dress, Ms. Landry," she said.

"Thank you," Daffy said, acknowledging the compliment with a slight smile, careful to maintain a dignified distance in keeping with her role as part owner of *The Crescent*. That role explained her presence at the paper and helped Marguerite guard the Love Doctor's identity. She'd once said to Daffy, "All we need is some tart receptionist selling us out."

This girl looked so un-tart-like, Daffy had to hold back her impulse to take the young woman under her wing and shape her journalism career. The two previous receptionists Daffy had met at the paper had fallen into the same category. They wanted to be in television, only they couldn't get jobs in that industry, so they settled for answering the phones at *The Crescent* and hoping a TV producer would stumble through the doors and offer them a morning anchor spot. No wonder none of them stayed for long. Daffy didn't know this new person's story, but she knew she'd probably find out. People always told her things about themselves.

"Are you and Mr. Landry going to a party?"

Daffy stared at the girl. Of course she assumed there was a Mr. Landry. Who wouldn't? Daffy had friends her age who were on their second husbands. She shook her head and glanced at the receptionist's nameplate. "No, Yvonne, I'm going to work."

A few miles away from the mid-city offices of *The Crescent*, in a section of town that might as well have been on another planet, Hunter James tugged at the cummerbund his business partner insisted he wear along with his custom tuxedo for these formal occasions. "Damned thing feels like a girdle."

Aloysius Carriere grinned and said, "You'll get used to it."

"My ass," Hunter said. "Who's tonight's quarry?"

"Tiffany Phipps. She's young, she's smart, and she's worth about ten million."

"Hmm." Hunter studied his friend across the cluttered second-floor sitting room of a Garden District house that belonged to one of Aloysius's aunts, who preferred dogtrotting around Asia and Europe with her middle-aged girlfriend to pretending to live properly with her husband and grown children back home. He and Aloysius stayed at the house when either or both of them were in town. "Is she pretty?"

Aloysius grinned again. "I'll let you be the judge of that. She's coming with an escort tonight, but I happen to know there's no rivalry in that quarter."

"Why do you try so hard to fix me up?"

In response he received a wide-eyed stare. "What's good for the heart is good for business.

And as your partner and investment banker, it would be shortsighted of me to look only for potential investors for WebWeavers who are good for the wallet without considering your emotional well-being as well."

Hunter made a rude noise that pretty much indicated what he thought of his friend's perpetual caretaking. "Stick to the banking. I can take care of my own needs."

Lifting a crystal brandy snifter from a side table cluttered with ivory figurines, Aloysius said, "Oh, yeah, that's right. Hunter, he's the guy with a girl in every port. No problem satisfying your *needs*."

A bell rang, saving Hunter from the punch he felt inclined to deliver to his partner's self-satisfied jaw. He glanced at the fancy porcelain clock on one of the room's two fireplace mantels. A picture from his childhood flashed as he remembered the Christmas his mom couldn't pay the power bill and the two of them had spent the holiday beside the fire in their one fireplace. "That would be Mrs. Jarrigan. She's always prompt."

"And most efficient," Aloysius said, draining his snifter. "Before she took over managing the Orphan's Club, we were running a deficit. Now it's becoming one of the most popular and best-funded charities in town."

"Good," Hunter said, shutting out the chill that had crept into his body despite the unseasonably warm April heat from outside that wafted into the centuries-old house and did battle with the central air. "Every Child Deserves a Christmas," the theme of this year's fund-raising efforts spearheaded by Hunter's company, WebWeavers, Inc., had taken the region by storm.

Hunter descended the stairs, noting all seemed in order in the entertaining area on the ground floor. The rent-a-butler had opened the door for Mrs. Jarrigan, who was now standing in the entryway glancing around as if checking a mental list. Which, Hunter concluded, she probably was. She glanced up, smiled, and said, "Want to come with me to inspect the staff?"

That was the last thing he wanted to do, but he nodded and walked with her through the double parlors and into the huge kitchen in the back of the house. His mother would love this room, but when he'd tried to buy her a new house with this sort of luxury, she'd shaken her head, put a finger to her lips, and told him to use his money more wisely.

It had been about three months after that when he'd come up with the idea for reviving the Orphan's Club. Aloysius had told him there'd been such an organization years ago in the city, but that it had died off along with the onset of taxpayer-financed social services. Hunter wasn't an orphan, but as the bastard son of a teenage mother growing up in a small Louisiana town, he'd often felt a kinship with anyone missing a dad or a mom, and how much worse if a kid didn't have either parent.

"We should have a nice little turnout tonight,"

Mrs. Jarrigan was saying as she ran a practiced eye over the bartenders and waiters poised for action. In the distance, the bell rang.

Aloysius sauntered in. "I'm told tonight's ticket is hotter than either the Yacht Club's to-do or the Audubon event."

"That's because this one is the most expensive," Mrs. Jarrigan said. "To the very rich go the spoils."

Hunter winked at one of the bartenders, a cute young thing who didn't need the assist of her underwire bra to catch his eye. "I still don't get why people are willing to pay five hundred dollars to have their picture taken with me."

Aloysius must have intercepted Hunter's wink, because he said something to the bartender and she left the room. Hunter sighed. Ever since Aloysius had fallen in love and gotten himself engaged, he'd been trying to arrange the same earth-shattering event for his buddy—provided he chose someone Aloysius considered appropriate.

Voices were carrying from the distance. Mrs. Jarrigan dispatched the staff to their respective positions. "Well, that doesn't matter, does it?" she said. "As long as they're willing to and the money goes to a good cause."

"Set point to you, as usual, Mrs. Jarrigan," Hunter said.

"Hop to it, old boy," Aloysius said. "It's show time."

Hunter caught a glimpse of his profile in the shiny stainless steel of a walk-in-size refrigerator.

His beak of a nose dominated his face, in his mind, debating and canceling out any contest of looks. But according to his mother, women fell for dangerous and dark. And Hunter had always conceded his mother must know of what she spoke; after all, she'd fallen for his dark and dangerous father, a man who'd disappeared when the responsibility of a child entered the picture.

"How about you charm the moneybags and I spend the night in real men's clothes?"

"Not to be," Aloysius said. "Besides, there's Tiffany. One look at her and you'll quit your complaining."

They'd neared the front parlor. A cluster of guests stood just inside the door, being offered drinks by one of the waiters. The door opened again, and a blonde with a swingy step made her entrance.

Hunter stared. The woman claimed the entryway, paused, and surveyed her surroundings like a queen surveying her subjects.

She had a long, lean body, but filled out with breasts that the clingy black silk did nothing to minimize. Her blond hair, swinging just beneath her chin, gleamed like the storybook gold woven by Rapunzel, a silly thought that made Hunter realize he'd lost his grip.

"Who's that?" he said as casually as possible to Aloysius, wondering if this woman was the much-touted Tiffany Phipps, and deciding he'd forgive his partner for all his romance-meddling if she were.

Aloysius glanced toward the entry, then back to Hunter. Something of Hunter's enchantment must have shown in his eyes, because his friend grabbed his arm and said, "Oh, no, Hunter, down, boy. I'm your friend, so listen to me. That is the last woman in the world you want to meet."

"You raise my curiosity." Hunter continued to watch as the woman declined the butler's attempts to relieve her of a bulky black leather bag. She accepted a glass of champagne from a passing waiter, and glided into the parlor on the other side of the foyer.

"Just what I didn't want to do," his friend muttered. "Think Tiffany."

"If you won't tell me, I'll go ask for myself." Mrs. Jarrigan was bearing down on them, two well-dressed, silver-haired women in tow. Soon he'd have to charm his audience and deliver the public Hunter James who people loved to love. "Who is she?"

"Promise me if I tell you you'll stay away from her. She's nothing but trouble. I've known her for years and years, and never once has she been good news for any guy."

Hunter smiled at the approaching ladies and Mrs. Jarrigan and out of the side of his mouth said, "Her *name*, Aloysius."

Aloysius sighed and clutched at his hair. "Daffodil Landry."

2

"Daffy!"

At the unmistakable sound of her sister's voice, Daffy turned. Grateful for the interruption—a social-climbing couple Daffy couldn't abide had been bearing down on her, clearly intent on getting their picture into her society column—she hugged her twin. "I didn't even know you were back in town."

Jonni, a mirror image of her own blue eyes, blond hair, and body type, smiled softly and said, "We came back yesterday." She sighed. "I missed Erika, but as usual David was right. Jakarta was no place for a three-year-old."

Oh, yes, David was always right. "Where is Darwin? Er, wait, I've got it—Darren."

"Daffy, you know my husband's name as well as your own." Born fifteen minutes earlier than

Daffy, Jonni had spent much of their lives playing the role of older sister and she knew how to put starch in her normally gentle voice when issuing a reprimand.

"Okay, I'm sorry. So where is David? Did you leave him behind in Jakarta?" Daffy tried to sound contrite. For her sister's sake, she struggled to accept Jonni's choice of mate, but she had a hard time tolerating his superior attitude.

"He's getting us drinks."

"Ah." Daffy thought Jonni, despite her underlying beauty, seemed a little dispirited.

"Anyone new in your life?"

Daffy shook her head. "You were only gone six weeks."

"And it only takes a moment in time to fall in love."

Daffy opened the clasp on her camera bag. She'd allotted twenty minutes for this stop and so far, she hadn't laid eyes on the man of the hour. Besides, Jonni's matchmaking talk always made her edgy.

"Well, if it isn't my lovely sister-in-law."

Daffy almost jumped as Jonni's husband swarmed beside her. He handed a glass of wine to Jonni, delivered a peck on the cheek to Daffy, and took a long pull on his customary bourbon and water. "Writing for CyberScene these days?"

He referred to the section of the daily paper that covered popular technology. "No, David, I'm still just an Uptown girl who dabbles in journalism as a society columnist," she said, quoting David's favorite description of her.

"While waiting to snare a husband," he finished. "Hunter James is much better material for 'Money' or 'CyberScene' than the social pages."

"Do you know him?" Daffy glanced around the room. Across the parlor and inside the dining room she spotted the very familiar-looking back of a man's head. The man laughed and his broad ears quivered. Aloysius Carriere. Well, that made sense; after all, this was his aunt's house.

But who was the dark-haired Casanova beside him, leaning toward the elderly Mrs. DeLongpre and flirting with her as if she had been Queen of Rex only this year, rather than half a century ago? If he was a friend of Aloysius's, he had to be from out of town.

Daffy had grown up with Aloysius. He and Oliver Gotho had been her playmates. Oliver remained her faithful friend, but then, she'd never made the mistake of sleeping with him.

Aloysius—well, that was another story.

"I'm telling you what I know about Hunter James and I do believe you're not even listening." David's bossy voice cut into her study of the mystery man.

"Oh, but I am." She gave him a bright smile and shifted her position so she could watch both David and the hunk across the way.

"I was saying," David said, lifting one hand to the back of Jonni's neck and stroking her idly, "that I don't know him personally but I certainly know of him."

Jonni sipped her drink and glanced around. She'd turned inward, as she often did at these social events, and Daffy longed to take her hand and reassure her. For all she liked to play the older sister, Jonni needed protection a heck of a lot more than Daffy ever did.

"James is a self-taught computer guru who made a mint when his Internet technology company went public. He's from Ponchatoula, of all places, but he spends a lot of time in the city."

"Why is he interested in orphans?" Jonni asked the question, then almost looked surprised that she'd done so.

"Good question," Daffy said. "Those journalistic instincts are still strong."

Jonni shrugged. Jonni, not Daffy, had been the editor in chief of their high school paper and an English major at Newcomb College. But once she'd gotten engaged, she'd dropped all writing pursuits, though she did help out at *The Crescent* on occasion, serving as receptionist if someone called in sick.

David finished his drink. A silver-haired gentleman passing by greeted him and the two exchanged handshakes. He smiled at the women and moved on.

"My banker," David said. "James probably gives money to the Orphan's Club because he's half orphan."

"Half?"

David shrugged. "Trying to be polite. Truth is, he's a full-fledged bastard."

Jonni looked shocked. Daffy felt only indignation at her brother-in-law's judgmental pronouncement.

"Well, I say, let him enjoy his moment in the limelight," David said, hailing a passing waiter for a refill. "The nouveaux riches never hang on to their money long."

Daffy lifted her camera. She was well over her twenty minutes, and another second of her brother-in-law's superiority complex and she just might tell him what she thought of him. She might be rich but she was proud not to be a snob. "Mind pointing him out to me?"

"No problem." He studied the room; then his glance moved to the connecting room beyond. "He's in there, with one of your former beaux."

"The dark-haired man next to Aloysius?" Daffy knew she sounded as surprised as she felt. So much for the high-water pants, tennis shoes, and pubescent pimples! "Are you sure that's Hunter James?"

David simply looked at her. Jonni accepted another glass from the waiter and said, "David's always sure."

"That's true, dear," he said, looking very pleased with her.

"I'll just take a photo and then I've got to run," Daffy said, wondering whether she should trust David. He might be playing a trick on her.

But, trick or not, she wanted a closer look at the

enigmatic stranger. Now he'd lifted Mrs. De-Longpre's gloved hand to his lips.

The elderly woman laughed, and tapped him saucily on the cheek before moving off.

"Quite the charmer," Daffy murmured, wishing Aloysius would detach himself from the man's side. Though they'd never discussed it, she and the sole heir to what was once the Carriere fortune studiously avoided each other.

Now. Walk over there, as cool as the proverbial cucumber. Flip Aloysius a smile that dares him to interfere and introduce yourself to this guy. If he really is Hunter James, you're only doing your job.

Even as her plan of action formed in her mind, Daffy was aware of the man's probing gaze. He might be standing halfway across the room, but she knew he was watching her, sensed he wanted her to know it, too. She had the strangest sensation of being catalogued from the pink polish of her toenails to the curling tendril of hair that teased her cheek.

He sensed her interest, too.

Daffy's heart beat faster.

He saw through her dress to the black satin bra and panties beneath.

He read the curiosity in her mind.

And sized her 36-C bra accurately.

The pulse in her throat fluttered.

As for himself, he gave nothing away. Oh, that he was observing her the way a man does when he spies a woman he may want to pursue was clear. But whether he would act, whether he would do more than simply study his prey, Daffy couldn't predict.

Which bugged the heck out of her.

What lay behind those dark eyes and that ready smile that he flashed just as easily at old Mrs. DeLongpre as he did at Aloysius?

She had to find out.

Her right foot moved forward. She waved off a waiter proffering a tray of salmon en croute.

Aloysius had turned the full force of a scowl on her. She moved her left foot forward, meeting his challenge. He might despise her, but he couldn't keep her from speaking to his companion.

The dark-eyed man matched her move, saying something to Aloysius as he took one step in her direction.

Daffy smiled.

The man halted, his elbow captured by Aloysius as a tiny tornado of a woman swept up from the opposite direction and launched herself at both of the men.

Not just any woman, but Tiffany Phipps. Daffy groaned inwardly, or maybe she even made a noise aloud. The man offered Tiffany a polite handshake. That wouldn't do for Tiffany. She kissed him on the cheek and Daffy could hear her gush, in a voice as loud as it always was, "I feel as if we're already the closest of friends."

Daffy stopped a waiter and snatched a crab cake canapé. Aloysius she could face down, but taking him on in tandem with Tiffany was beyond her. Not since Daffy's twelfth birthday party, when Tiffany had taken some personal sanitary items from Daffy's purse and passed them around to the giggling guests, had Daffy been able to keep her temper around Tiffany. That day she'd busted the girl's lip and both sets of parents had punished Daffy, not Tiffany. Only Daffy's best friend, Beth, hadn't laughed at her humiliation.

Dabbing her fingertips on a napkin, Daffy consoled herself. If Hunter kept company with women like Tiffany, he wasn't her type anyway. She lifted her camera, considering the irony of her thoughts. She lived in a society where many people probably saw more to condemn in Daffy than in Tiffany.

After all, what were Tiffany's faults? Selfish, spoiled, and extravagant as she was, she still performed admirable volunteer service. She was also an accomplished attorney. The same age as Daffy, she'd been divorced once and was rumored to have taken the guy, a senator wannabe from Kentucky, for quite a fortune.

But her faults, according to the standards of Daffy's world, were nothing compared to those of Daffodil Landry.

Shaking off the shadow that threatened to weigh her down, Daffy poised her shot. She edged closer. At least her editor would be pleased. Two socialites clinging to the city's latest—and sexiest—philanthropist.

Flash!

Tiffany must have sensed the camera. She snuggled up to adjust the man's bow tie.

Flash!

Flash!

Three quick snaps and Daffy turned. She walked rapidly through the crowd. She had two more events to cover.

As she descended the front stairs of the mansion, she realized with a twinge of surprise that neither of the other social galas held any interest for her. And Daffy knew the reason—the stranger with the eyes as dark as his hair would not be there.

Damn, but she was beautiful.

And more than classically so. Sure, she had the package—the sculpted body with regal bearing, flawless skin, silky blond hair, and simple clothes that whispered rather than shouted their worth. But to top it all off, the woman possessed a presence Hunter had rarely, if ever, seen.

Even while charming Mrs. DeLongpre and collecting a substantial pledge for the Orphan's Club, Hunter had checked out Daffodil Landry, the one woman in the house Aloysius begged him to avoid at all costs.

He'd watched her talking to another daffodil-haired woman, but even though Hunter could see that woman only from the back, he'd known instinctively that she'd never make the impact Daffodil Landry made.

Not on him, anyway, though the guy who joined the two women, pasting a possessive hand around her neck and shoulders, obviously thought otherwise.

Daffy moved away from the man and the woman. By this point, Hunter knew she was aware of him observing her. She soaked up the scrutiny, neither blushing, simpering, nor turning away. He had to know this woman.

"Introduce me," he said to Aloysius after Mrs. DeLongpre had left them.

"That's what I've been doing since the first guest arrived," his partner said, stubbornly refusing to acknowledge the meaning of Hunter's request.

"To *her*," Hunter said.

"Anyone but Daffy." Aloysius set his jaw.

"Whatever happened between you two must have been a doozy, but whatever it was, that's between the two of you," Hunter said, but did not inquire. He honestly didn't want to know. Certainly his own past—damn, his present—didn't bear much scrutiny.

"It's one thing when a woman dumps you," Aloysius said, obviously going to go into details anyway, "but Daffy does more than that. She looks like the spring flower you expect from a woman with a name like that, and then something happens to her and she goes off, crazy for no reason at all." Aloysius rolled his shoulders, as if shaking off an unwelcome memory. "Go after the straightforward ones."

Daffy had taken a step in his direction.

"Interesting," Hunter murmured.

"If you think so, then try getting your foot caught in a trap and chewing it off to escape."

She smiled.

He mirrored the smile and took a step in her direction.

He ought to stay away, not because of any of Aloysius's warnings, but because he should straighten out his own muddled life before embarking on a new adventure.

And Daffodil Landry, he was certain, would prove to be the greatest adventure of his life.

A hand gripped his elbow. Hunter tensed, then relaxed. Gazing at his tenacious friend, he gave him a smile, yet anyone with half an instinct for survival would have seen the danger lurking there.

"Here's Tiffany," Aloysius said in a low voice, just as a cloud of perfume and a pint-size brunette descended on them.

"Just the woman we've been looking for," Aloysius said jovially. "Tiffany Phipps, Hunter James."

Frustrated, but well schooled in his manners, Hunter extended a hand.

The green-eyed brunette ignored his hand and launched herself against him, landing a coquettish kiss on his cheek that Hunter could have done without. "I feel as if we're already the closest of friends," she said, stepping back, but not by much.

Her strong perfume invaded his nostrils just as a flash of camera light filled his vision.

He looked back toward Daffodil Landry. Tiffany reached up and played with his bow tie just as another flash of light temporarily blinded him.

He blinked several times, then checked again.

Daffodil Landry had disappeared.

3

"Don't look now," Thelma James said, "but you've got company."

Hunkered beneath the computer workstation in his mother's framing shop, concentrating on connecting the cables, Hunter did exactly as his mother suggested. His weekend trip to Ponchatoula was a quick one to allow him to hook up his mother's new computer. She had refused to let him buy her a nice new home on the "right" side of town, but at least she accepted his help in her business, a framing shop she'd worked in for years and had finally taken over after the former owner passed away.

"Well, if it isn't Emily Godchaux coming to visit."

At that annoying news, Hunter lifted his head and banged it on the edge of the desk. "Dam—"

"No, you don't, not in my shop." His mother lived by her rules—as did anyone in her orbit. Growing up, Hunter had heard a million times if he'd heard it once: "People can say anything they like about me for having a baby without benefit of a wedding ring, but they'll never be able to say one bad word about your behavior, young man."

He loved his mom. So he'd tried hard to behave. Tried. Really hard. But behaving just didn't come naturally to him.

He rose and grinned at his mother, who was leaning over her work table and holding a sample of teal matting this way and that. "Damp. It's damp under that table."

She grinned back and lifted her eyebrows as the cluster of bells on the door jangled. Eyes on the piece she was framing, Thelma said, "Morning, Emily."

"Mrs. James, good morning." Wearing a lavender linen shift and a big, floppy hat, Emily looked dressed for a garden party.

Hunter glanced down at his shorts with the bleach stains above the frayed hem and wondered what Emily was up to. At least she remembered to add the "Mrs." to his mother's name. All his school friends had called her by the honorary title, but the hateful ones had left it off on purpose. Emily, naturally, had fallen into the latter category.

Now she fluttered her lashes and said, "Oh, Hunter, you're in town!"

Her feigned surprise was so poorly done,

Hunter almost laughed. Only he didn't feel like laughing. The one time in high school he'd asked her out, she'd mocked the very idea, calling over her circle of followers to announce the insult to them, and said if he ever came near her she'd have her boyfriend, Roger, beat him up. Only now that he'd made money, Emily sang a different song.

Hunter began sorting the packing materials of the new computer. "My Jeep's parked right out front."

"Really?" She trilled an annoying note or two, then moved in for the kill. "Roger and I are having a little get-together tonight. Nothing fancy. Just the old gang. Want to come—since you're in town and all?"

"How is Roger?" That was his mother inquiring.

"Fine. Busy." Emily removed her hat, lifted her heavy hair away from her neck, and fanned it lightly. "He's always at work." Emily's full lips formed a pout and she gave Hunter an inviting look he had no trouble interpreting. "Why, you'd think he was married to that bank."

Instead of to you. Hunter caught his mother's seemingly noncommittal expression. Only the tapping of her fingertips on the matting betrayed her annoyance.

"Thanks, I'm busy," Hunter said.

"Oh, well, maybe another time." She cast a smoldering glance at him and backed out of the shop.

Hunter ripped a large piece of cardboard packing material into a more manageable size. "Wonder which one she wants more, my money or my manhood."

His mother quit tapping and smiled. "I think you know that answer. You must have been in PE with Roger."

Hunter grinned. "What a shocking thing for a mother to say to her son."

"Hmm. That reminds me of another motherly thing I have to say to you."

Thelma let go of the matting and folded her arms across the bib of the apron she always wore when framing pictures.

"Serious time," Hunter said.

She nodded. "Throwing smoke in Emily's eyes is one thing—not that you encourage that trollop. But that sweet Lucy Simone is head over heels in love with you and she deserves better than being your playmate when you have time and sitting home moping when you're busy in New Orleans."

Hunter shifted his feet. His neck prickled with warmth—something it always did when he knew he was in the wrong. He wondered fleetingly if anyone would believe that a guy who'd just made the covers of *Money* and *E-COM* could still chafe under his mother's tongue-lashing. "I never intended her to fall in love."

"Well, if that's all you can say for yourself—"

"We've dated a few times. She's nice. Sweet. Pretty." Not bad in bed, but in a functional way.

No fire within. And she never knew when he was joking and when he was serious. "She should know as well as I do that she's not the woman for me."

"No." Thelma sighed. "You'd be burned out on her in two months and light out."

Just like my father.

Hunter crossed his arms. "I never gave Lucy one reason to expect more than what exists. No promises." His voice was harsh. "I'll never run out on a commitment—and I'll never marry until I meet a woman I know I will stand by no matter what."

"And just when do you think that miracle might take place?"

At least she unfolded her arms and picked up a straight edge.

"I'll know it when I know it." A vision of the blonde in black tapped at the backs of his eyes.

Daffodil Landry.

He'd avoided pursuing her. Just over a week had passed since the fund-raiser for the Orphan's Club. He'd located her home address and her phone number. Yet he hadn't contacted her. He wasn't sure what he was waiting for, but he sensed that if he waited, the right time would show itself. Or maybe he was afraid she'd turn out to be like all the other women he'd pursued— beautiful on the surface but lacking that special quality he knew he needed for a long-term commitment. He meant what he said to his mother— he sought *the* woman capable of inspiring him to harness whatever wandering genes he'd inherited from his unknown and good-for-nothing "father."

"Humph. Humph. Humph." His mother had resorted to muttering and shaking her head.

The doorbell jangled for the second time and in walked sweet little Lucy Simone.

Trapped.

"Hi, Mrs. James."

"Hi, honey. Glass of tea?"

"That would sure be nice." Lucy smiled, revealing perfect white teeth.

Aw, hell. Thelma was capable of keeping Lucy there until Hunter addressed the subject of their relationship—or rather the lack of one. Hunter shot a glare in his mother's direction, but she'd turned around to the sun tea jar she kept filled and chilled all summer long. He knew he needed to make a clean break with Lucy, but he'd rather do it without an audience.

Lucy accepted the glass handed to her by his mother and made a beeline for the computer table, to which Hunter had retreated.

"Hunter, I didn't know you were at home." His ears pricked up. That sweetly questioning tone would turn to an all-out nag the minute Lucy had a ring slipped on her finger. He grimaced.

"Ooh, did you hurt your hand?" Lucy leaned over, reaching for his hand. The V neck of her T-shirt gave him a full view of her best assets.

He suppressed a groan and said, "I'm fine."

His mother was no doubt right—he'd led Lucy on, but those assets of hers clouded his judgment.

"Good. Do you want to go to Emily and Roger's party with me? I bumped into her and she invited me to her little get-together." Lucy sipped her tea, looking very satisfied with life.

It irritated Hunter to see how impressed Lucy was that Emily had included her. He and Lucy had been friends in school back in the days when Emily hadn't even known Lucy's name. "When was this?"

"Oh, just a few minutes ago. I was coming out of Paul's Café and she was leaving the real estate office."

He felt his reaction parade on his face as he lowered his brows. That bitch had invited Lucy, guessing she would ask Hunter to accompany her—after he'd turned Emily down. "Women," he muttered. "How about we take in a movie instead?"

Her shoulders drooped. "I've never seen their house. I heard they have a waterfall in their den."

He took her gently by the shoulders. "Lucy, she's invited you to get me there."

She jerked back, causing his hands to fall. For a second, he watched his hands in midair, not connected to her and seemingly displaced from his own body. Quite a metaphor for the state of his life.

"You've gotten a pretty big idea of yourself lately, Hunter James."

He heard his mother making that humph, humph noise of hers.

"What makes you think it's you she's after? She's got a husband, a rich one." Lucy was working herself up. "Maybe she wants to be friends with me."

"Emily's idea of friendship is a lot like a black widow's idea of love," Hunter said.

"I think we're just not good enough for you anymore. You think you've outgrown this podunk town and that's why you chase all those women in New Orleans."

Hunter shook his head, wondering how she knew anything about the women he'd gone out with—most of them at Aloysius's urging—in New Orleans. "Lucy, look at me. I'm here, on Saturday afternoon, wearing the same shorts I've worn for the last five years. This is my ancient LSU T-shirt. What's really going on?"

She sealed her lips in a mulish line. Hunter watched as her luscious breasts quivered under her cotton T-shirt and wished he'd admired them only from a distance. He'd wrestled, played tag, hell, he'd taught her how to drive and managed to stay out of her pants. What had gotten into him six months ago? Had he been lonely, maybe a little overwhelmed by the sudden fame and money, and turned to Lucy as a way of holding on to what was safe and known? If so, he deserved to be horsewhipped.

Suddenly her mouth curved into a perfect cover-girl smile. She widened her eyes and stepped forward, tracing a circle on the pocket of his shirt with one pink-tipped nail. "Take me to the party, pretty please?"

Saved by the bell. The door swung open and Lucy stepped back as Beau, her fifteen-year-old brother, dashed into the shop. He ran errands for Mrs. James and delivered the weekly entertainment tabloid *The Crescent*. Whistling, he waved one copy of the newspaper. Pointing to the stack under one skinny arm, he said, "Get your copy now! There's already a pool going over at the Pit Stop, guessing who wrote this week's letter to the Love Doc."

He winked at Hunter—man to man—and deposited his papers in the metal bin inside the shop's door.

Lucy had backed away a step from Hunter. "Wh-what letter is that?" Her voice quavered slightly.

Odd. Hunter studied her expression, which had gone so swiftly from cajoling to vaguely anxious. No, scratch the modifer. She tugged on her underlip with one forefinger and thumb.

"Loyal But Lonesome in Ponchatoula." Beau guffawed and helped himself to a glass of iced tea. "Women! Who needs 'em? Excepting you, Mrs. James," he added. "Any deliveries?"

Thelma shook her head and looked from Lucy to Hunter with a maternal intensity that made Hunter wish he could read the undertones more clearly.

Lucy started toward the stack of papers.

Hunter passed her and slid one hand on top of the stack. Whatever was in that paper was sure making Lucy nervous.

"Page eight," Beau said, swallowing a huge gulp of tea. "If I were you, Hunter, I'd go on over to the Pit Stop and lay a bet."

Hunter lifted a paper and Lucy followed. Even his mother stopped laying out the lithograph she was matting and strolled over and helped herself to a copy.

"They say at the Pit Stop that this column's almost as hot as that *Millionaire* game show was when it first came out."

"Would you hush?" Lucy glared at her brother.

Hunter examined the logo of a prescription pad in the shape of a heart that decorated the box in which the Love Doctor's column was framed. A lot too cutesy for his taste. He scanned the letter and the response quickly, noting the italicized identification of the letter's author. Sure enough—Loyal But Lonesome in Ponchatoula had sought the advice of the Love Doctor. Whoever the hell that was.

He bent his head and read the actual column. Not a word was spoken in the shop as Lucy and his mother did the same. Beau started to whistle, but evidently thought better of it when his sister leveled an even fiercer glare at him.

"I never thought they'd print it," Lucy said, dropping the paper and holding her hands to her cheeks.

"You dummy!" Beau snorted. Then he seemed

to realize what she'd actually meant. "*You* wrote that letter?"

Hunter stared from Lucy back down to the column. Her only answer to her brother's question was a sniffle as a tear trailed down her cheek.

Beau walked over, patted her on the shoulder, and said, "Well, don't tell anyone till I put in a bet over at the Pit Stop."

"Beau Simone," Thelma said, "you know better than that. That would be wrong the same way insider trading is wrong."

He shrugged and shuffled his feet. "Yes, ma'am."

Hunter heard the chattering, even had time to think it unlikely that the fifteen-year-old had any concept as to what insider trading was. But his mind focused only on the phrase that burned in his brain. Diagnosis Terminal. And the way in which the phrase was waved like a red flag—this Love Doctor had judged him terminal not just in relation to Loyal But Lonesome, but in every relationship.

He wasn't sure why he knew that; one could argue a more innocent interpretation. But Hunter never ignored his hunches.

Lucy's sniffles were now a stream of tears. Hunter dropped his paper and walked to her side. Putting an arm around her, he said, "Lucy, it's okay. There's no reason to cry. I'm not upset."

"*You're* not upset!" Lucy's voice rose to a wail. "Well, I won't be able to hold my head up in this town. I sound so pathetic."

He stroked her hair. "No, you don't. You sound—" He hesitated, caught his mother's stern glance, and said, "Sweet and loving. Which you are."

Her lashes fluttered. The tears stopped.

"We're just not meant for each other," he added, before she could get too happy.

"Hunter's too smart for you," Beau said.

"Out. Get out." Lucy pointed to the door, but her brother didn't budge.

Hunter tipped her chin up and faced her accusing gaze squarely. "Lucy, we've been friends a long time. You're sweet and I'm all rough around the edges. I'm not ready to settle down, and until I am, nothing can change that."

She smiled, and did some more of her lash-fluttering. "Okay, Hunter. I understand. But you'll be ready someday." Pulling away from him, she moved to a wall mirror and began patting her face and rearranging her hair. "I am glad you're not mad at me for writing that letter."

Beau hooted. "If you think a man is gonna stand still for being labeled Diagnosis Terminal, you've got another think coming!"

Hunter nodded. "You've got that right, Beau, but it's not Lucy I'm upset with." He snatched up the offending column. "It's this so-called expert. Who does she think she is? She doesn't know one dar—, one thing about me and yet she sits in judgment."

"How do you know she's a she?" His mother

asked the question in her sensible way, walking over to Lucy with a fresh glass of tea.

"The Love Doctor?" Hunter balled up the paper. "With a name like that, it's got to be a woman."

"Ah," was all his mother said.

"I'm going back to New Orleans and show this know-it-all a thing or two."

"You can't," Lucy said. "It's anonymous."

"What does that mean?"

"And I thought you were smarter than my sister," Beau said.

"There's no real name. It's a big deal that no one knows who writes the column. Someone even wrote a story in the *New Orleans Times* offering a reward to anyone who could reveal the identity, but no one's found out yet."

"So a lot of people read this trash." Hunter grimaced. They'd be laughing at him all over Ponchatoula, but at least in New Orleans no one would have a clue. "I guess you're a regular reader?"

Lucy moved away from the mirror. Her clear skin gave no hint that she'd been crying only minutes earlier. Her T-shirt hugged her breasts, outlining her nipples just enough to be alluring. Beneath her short shorts, her long, tanned legs called out for a man to explore their length. It was a shame, Hunter thought, that he couldn't accept the simple, good things life had to offer. Lucy was sweet, willing, and faithful. She'd gotten it right when she'd described herself as loyal.

And lonesome.

He shook his head. What was he thinking? Hitched to him, Lucy would still be lonesome. Marrying Lucy—or any woman whom he could too easily influence—would be the worst mistake of his life.

"Hunter?" Lucy was looking at him as if he were slightly delusional.

He realized he'd been staring at her breasts, and jerked his head away. He could in no way continue to lead her on. "You were saying this Love Doctor is hot?"

"All my girlfriends read it. The author's pretty funny sometimes." She sighed. "But it's not too funny when it's you and a friend she's writing about."

"You mean skewering. How much is the reward?"

"A thousand dollars."

Hunter shrugged. "Money isn't always the best means of persuasion."

"It's not?" Beau said.

"Oh, no." Hunter shook his head, real slow. "Sometimes it takes a man's tricks to catch a woman."

4

"Well, well, well." Hunter paused, one hand on the handle of the double glass doors of *The Crescent*'s mid-city offices. Just inside, perched behind a receptionist's desk, sat the blond vision who had so enticed him at the Orphan's Club fund-raiser.

After he'd dragged her identity out of the mysteriously reluctant Aloysius, he'd purposely avoided calling Daffodil Landry. He'd had to disentangle himself from Lucy, and if one good thing had come from that pain-in-the-ass Love Doctor column, it was that he'd been given an opening to clear the air with Lucy.

But he still had a bone to pick with that know-it-all columnist, which explained his trip to *The Crescent*'s offices.

And here sat Daffodil Landry.

Could the heavens have smiled more kindly on him?

Hunter had observed that heaven usually helped those who helped themselves. He'd come to the paper's offices planning to target a likely-looking employee, ply her with food and drink, and coax the answer he sought from his quarry.

What he would do when he discovered the identity of the Love Doctor, he hadn't decided. But he'd think of some fitting punishment. Diagnois Terminal, indeed! He simply hadn't met the right woman.

Or had he? After taking another long look at the blonde, who now had her head bent over the desk, Hunter smiled and pushed open the door.

She glanced up, and as her gaze focused on him, her lush lips halted in mid-curve of a welcoming smile. Fumbling with something on the desk, she looked from his face toward the door, then down at the telephone as if willing it to ring, before she met his eyes again. A slight blush tinged her cheeks.

Hunter gave her his best smile. Perhaps she was embarrassed at the direct way they'd sized up each other at the Orphan's Club fund-raiser. She needn't be, but the modesty was oddly appealing. That she remembered him, well, he'd bet his latest dot-com invention on that. Curious to see what she'd reveal, he paused.

He was glad he hadn't imagined her interest in him. She'd captured and held his attention from the first moment he'd seen her across the room that night, and if it hadn't been for Aloysius and his well-intentioned interference, Hunter was positive he and this woman would have already gotten acquainted. Intimately so.

"M-may I help you?" Her voice was softly melodic, but higher-pitched than he'd expected, not nearly as throaty as he'd heard it in his imagination. And the question, as tame as it seemed, should have carried an undertone, should have delivered a jolt to his system.

Instead, he found himself responding in an ordinary way to an ordinary question. Maybe he had been the only one affected by the not-quite meeting across the crowded room. Diagnosis Terminal? Yeah, Hunter James, hopeless romantic. Or perhaps she was merely playing it cool.

"I sure hope so," he said. "I'm thinking of placing a personal ad and I was hoping you could give me some advice." A mailbag full of letters from women was the last thing he wanted cluttering up his life, but according to the all-knowing Beau, *The Crescent* carried the hottest personals. It was as good a pretext as any for scoping out the headquarters of the Love Doctor.

The beautiful blonde folded her hands on the desk that separated her from Hunter. Funny, but up close, she just didn't carry the zing that she had across that crowded room. It was just as well he'd discovered that now, as it would save him the pursuit he'd had in mind. Still, it rankled with him. He'd experienced such a sense of magic possible between the two of them and yet here she sat, shyly assessing him, but not sending any chemical signals at all. Hunter sighed. In the light of the reception area's fluorescents, Daffodil Landry was just another 36-22-34 babe.

"Why would Hunter James want to run a personal ad?"

"So you know who I am." It wasn't a question, more a reflection. That knowledge explained her earlier interest. At least she hadn't flung herself at him the way Tiffany Phipps had—and continued to do. More women than he could count were interested in Hunter James the multimillionaire. But Hunter wanted a woman who'd love him, the bastard from Ponchatoula, for richer or for poorer—and mean it with all her heart.

"Why, yes." She smiled and went from merely beautiful to luminous. Still, she didn't affect him the way she had that night. "Doesn't everyone?"

He shrugged, an answer that could have been yes and could have been no and could have been who cares.

"I assumed"— she blushed just enough to give her pearly skin a pretty glow—"you'd be the last man in the world needing to run a personal ad. I mean, don't you have a string of women in your life?"

He leaned one arm on the front of her desk and shook his head. "It's not the string of women I care about." He fixed her with an intense look, seeking the response he wanted from her, the sensation that had been so vivid across that crowded room. "I'm looking for one *special* woman."

"That's so romantic." Her voice rose with enthusiasm, but she kept her hands primly posed, the right over the left.

Hunter stared at her hands.

He hadn't seen her hands the other night; he'd been too far away. With a sick feeling in his gut, he pictured what he'd find if he tugged her left hand out from under her right.

A wedding ring.

It was a damn good thing the electricity had vanished. That was a line he never crossed. Still, he was here—on other business—he reminded himself. Forget the extended wining and dining. He could still ask her to have coffee, pump her about the column, and get out. Fast. And he'd be willing to bet that, married or not, she'd agree to meet him for coffee. Women, he'd found, were so predictable. Especially with a guy who'd made a fortune overnight.

He produced a grin. "Yeah, that's me, Mr. Romantic, looking for one special woman who wants only one special guy." He couldn't help but stress the "only."

She nodded. "I understand exactly what you mean."

"You do?"

"Oh, yes. That's the way love should be."

This time he nodded. "So how about slipping off for a romantic cup of coffee with me?"

"Oh!" She clasped her hands tighter. "Well, I— that would be nice, but I can't leave work."

"What time do you get off?" He glanced at his

watch, the old Timex his mom had given him for winning first prize in the junior high science fair. Aloysius kept begging him to upgrade, to treat himself to a Rolex Presidential, but on some points Hunter wouldn't budge.

"Fi—uh, four."

He had a dinner date at seven with Tiffany. Unlike the watch, dates were negotiable. But truthfully, Aloysius had trapped him into this one. "Pick you up at four."

She shook her head and her blond hair glistened as it brushed against her cheeks. "I'll meet you."

God, he hated women who ran around on their men. He almost changed his mind, said forget it, and walked out the door. But it wasn't Daffodil Landry he was after—not anymore. His only quarry here was the Love Doctor. "PJ's down the street?"

"Sure. Yes. Right after four o'clock."

"Great." Hunter stepped back, then paused. "You know my name," he said, "but we haven't actually been introduced."

She blushed. That would be the third time, he decided. "I'm, um, Daffodil. Daffodil Landry."

"Nice," he said, wishing he still meant it, then turned and pushed his way out of the office and crossed the parking lot to his car. The afternoon sun had given way to a low-hanging mass of dark clouds. A big plop of rain hit his windshield as he climbed into his Blazer.

* * *

"But, Daffy, you've got to go." Jonni stared, a look of dismay on her face. "I made the date for *you*. Besides, that he came here on a day I was filling in for Yvonne means this was meant to be."

"I don't want anyone—not even you—making dates for me. I know you're trying to help by playing matchmaker, but being paired off is the last thing I want in my life."

Jonni pursed her lips. Daffy could tell her sister refused to accept that last declaration. "He's too good to pass up."

"Too good?" Daffy almost choked on a laugh. Then, as she remembered how attracted she'd been to him across even that crowded room, she quit laughing. Up close, he must be devastating. And a devastating guy was the last thing she needed. She screwed things up with every man she dated, usually on purpose. She was tired of doing that, but just not sure what it would take to change her behavior. "Well, you go have coffee with him."

"You know I can't do that," Jonni said rather wistfully.

"But you'd like to." Daffy pounced on that. "Why?"

"He's so romantic and that's such a lovely attribute in a man."

It was Daffy's turn to purse her lips. Something was going on with her sister. Her reaction went beyond mere matchmaking on her twin's behalf. Jonni's husband had to be the most unromantic man Daffy had ever met. And here was her sister sighing over the oh-so-romantic Hunter James. "I thought David didn't approve of the nouveaux riches."

Jonni, rather indignantly, said, "I don't always think exactly what David thinks."

"But you agree with him."

She flushed. "That's different. Sometimes it's just easier to agree."

And keep what you really think to yourself. Daffy finished the sentence for her silently. "Tell me to shut up if you want," she said, taking a deep breath and letting go with the question that she'd kept bottled up for years, "but just why did you marry David?"

"I love him and he keeps me balanced." Jonni said it quietly.

"Balanced? You mean under lock and key."

"If that's how you want to think of it, then, yes, he does."

Suddenly Daffy thought she understood. Reaching out a hand toward her sister, she said, "Oh, Jonni, it's because of Mother, isn't it? You're afraid if you're given too much freedom you'll stray." Funny how she'd never said those words out loud before, but now that she had, she heard them ring with truth.

"I don't think so," Jonni said slowly, "but it's not a chance I'd like to take."

It had been she who'd stumbled across their mother in bed with Aloysius's father. A tender eighteen, Jonni had tiptoed out and shared her discovery with Daffy, wanting her to make the truth go away. But Daffy had barged right in and then raced down to their father's office to blurt out what they'd discovered.

"It would be awful to hurt a man you love the way Mother did Daddy," Daffy said.

"But he forgave her and so should you," Jonni said.

Daffy didn't care for the turn of events of this conversation. "Mother always acts like I've done something wrong. Maybe she should forgive *me*."

"I'm sure she has," Jonni said. "She's just not a demonstrative person."

Jonni always saw the best in everyone. In that, she was exactly like their father, who also played the role of peacemaker. "You're a much better person than I am," Daffy said. "Perhaps I don't get along with our mother because we're too much alike."

"Sometimes it's just a matter of making a little more effort." Jonni checked her watch. "Now, what about Hunter? Are you afraid to go out with him?"

"I'm not afraid of any man," Daffy said. "I'm afraid of myself."

"Ah." Jonni leaned over and brushed a strand of hair back from her cheek. The simple gesture was full of love and concern and Daffy was shot through with a burst of gratitude for being a twin.

Jonni held out her beautifully manicured hands. "Remember when I used to chew my nails?"

Daffy nodded.

"And when you tried to help me quit, you said nothing felt as good as breaking a bad habit?"

"I do remember saying that."

Jonni regarded her hands and then held out her jacket. "Nice, hmm?"

Daffy grinned. Her sister never went straight when she could go around, but she always managed to make her point. What harm could *she* come to in a coffeehouse, anyway? "Okay, okay, I'll meet the guy. No dessert, just coffee."

Four-twenty. No Hunter.

Four-thirty. Still no Hunter.

Daffy rolled up the cuff of her sister's jacket one more turn and eyed her watch. For Jonni's sake, she'd give the guy five more minutes.

Right, she was doing this for her sister. Forget that she'd been drawn to Hunter James like a redfish with a hook in its mouth.

She opened her reporter's notebook and stared at the writing that covered the left-hand column. She owed Marguerite another Dear Love Doctor piece, but lately she'd been facing writer's block whenever it came to that deadline—rather like the block of her own love life.

The minute hand of her watch crept around.

Crept around.

The way her mother had, all the while charming her daughters and husband into not suspecting the harm she was inflicting. Both Daffy and her sister feared they were too much like their mother to have healthy, committed relationships. Jonni responded one way, Daffy another.

Daffy sighed and closed her notebook.

Four-thirty-five. Prince Charming wasn't coming and neither was Hunter James.

She stood up and turned—straight into Hunter James.

Two strong hands shot out and caught her by the shoulders. "Steady," he said. "Didn't mean to knock you over."

The pleasant warmth of his touch molded the linen jacket to her shoulders. Dark eyes, with that same all-knowing, inscrutable expression, met hers straight on. His eyelashes, she saw, were thick and almost heavy, adding to the air of distinction that had intrigued Daffy at the Orphan's Club fund-raiser. Slowly, he released his hold and stepped back, all the while studying her.

"Had you given up on me?" He smiled when he asked the question, and Daffy noticed his mouth quirked up on the left side. She hadn't been able to see that the other night.

Too charming. Best to nip this dangerous attraction in the bud. "Actually, I had." There, that was just terse enough to turn a guy off.

Instead, he grinned. "Honesty I appreciate." He pulled out two chairs. "Join me now?"

Daffy sat down.

Hunter glanced toward the coffee counter. "What's your pleasure?"

You.

"Dark roast. Black."

He nodded and walked to the counter. As he covered the length of the room with an easy stride, Daffy couldn't help but admire the picture he made. His casual slacks and polo shirt followed the sinewy lines of a body she'd love to see wearing only—

Now stop right there.

Daffy blinked and forced her gaze down to her reporter's notebook. Hunter James wanted to know how to place a personal ad. That was what he'd told Jonni. Daffy didn't believe it for a minute, but that was his story, and she would make him stick to it.

Hunter returned bearing two cups of coffee, one black, one a creamy mocha color. Sitting down, he said, "I use coffee as an excuse to get my daily dose of cream and sugar."

Daffy couldn't help but smile. "I'm afraid that would only set off my sweet tooth."

"So you're not really a coffee purist?"

"I guess not."

He was watching her almost too closely. "But you deny yourself things you like. Is this a form of self-discipline?"

"I didn't say that." She objected too quickly, because that *was* what she had said. Again he was studying her as if trying to decide some important question. "I like sweets, but I don't overdo it."

"Hmm." Hunter sipped his coffee. "What's your favorite thing you deny yourself?"

You could end up pretty high on that list. Daffy

shushed her inner voice and answered, "Anything chocolate and, around Halloween, candy corn."

"What about those little pumpkins?"

She laughed. "You like those, too?"

He nodded, grinning.

"I always liked to bite the tips off the candy corn, you know, eat each section—"

"Hey, me, too," Hunter said, stirring his coffee and fixing her with a look that would charm a bird right out of a tree.

Daffy tried to keep her resistance to him on "high." "But the stuff is deadly, you know. Once you start, it's almost impossible to stop."

His eyes had gotten almost as dark as the black coffee she still hadn't touched. "You're different at work," he said.

"What do you mean?"

"When we spoke at *The Crescent*, you were much more reserved."

"Oh. Well, that's to be expected, don't you think?"

"I'm not sure." Now he was gazing down at her hands, which she had cupped around the coffee.

"That's an unusual ring," he said.

Daffy lifted her left hand. She'd inherited the heavy gold-and-ruby band from her father's mother. "Thank you. It's a family heirloom."

He sipped his coffee.

"Well," she said after he didn't respond, "let's get started, shall we?" Daffy flipped the reporter's notebook open, found an empty page, and pulled out a pen from her purse. "So you want to run a personal ad?"

Hunter gazed at the band of rubies. Heirloom, but from her family? Or was it from a husband's family? Was she or was she not married? Damned if he'd ask outright. He hated giving away his thoughts and was known in business circles for his poker face. But this changeling woman was driving him nuts. She'd shifted from the proper person behind the desk back to the captivating vision he'd spotted at the fund-raiser.

Her satiny hair had slipped free from where she'd tucked it behind one ear. With her head bent over her notebook, her hair dipped forward. The strands grazed her cheek.

The pen tapped against the tabletop and she lifted her head. "Did you change your mind?"

He chugged another mouthful of coffee. An image of two women with similar-colored hair and identical body shapes flitted into his mind. At the fund-raiser, Daffodil Landry had stood side by side with a woman who looked a lot like her.

He almost choked on his coffee.

She was a twin, or he was a space alien.

She certainly was not the same woman who'd accepted this coffee date with him. Feeling quite cheerful, he asked the question he'd just told himself he wouldn't. "Are you married?"

A gurgle of laughter answered his query. "Why? Married people can't pen personals?"

"The question has nothing to do with the ad."

"Ah." She toyed with the pen. "Mr. James, you

said you wanted help composing an ad. I said I would assist you in that. Anything more, um, personal than that exchange of skills is not what we are here for."

Hunter leaned back in his chair. So Daffy liked to play chess. He grinned. He could find out what he needed to know in other ways. Why she was pretending and why the other woman had set the game in motion, he had no idea. But, aptly named, he relished a good hunt. "Let's write the ad."

"They use standard abbreviations for basic information. For example, S for Single, D for Divorced, P for Professional, C for Caucasian, M for Male." Glancing at him, she said, "So would you be an SCPM?"

"Accurate," Hunter said. "How about you?"

She wagged a finger at him. "This interview is about you, not me."

Sitting forward, he said, "Help me out here. What type of personal ad would you respond to?"

She stroked the tip of her nose with her index finger. Hunter studied the gesture and found himself wanting to mimic it. But it wasn't just the tip of her nose he wanted to explore. He shifted in his chair and told himself to slow down.

"Given that I've never answered one—"

He smiled and leaned closer to her. "Somehow I didn't think you had."

"And somehow I don't think you need to run an ad to find a woman."

"Ah, but we've already discussed that."

Daffy blinked and dipped her head. "Right."

That confirmed his hunch. She didn't remember asking him about why Hunter James would need to place a personal ad. She didn't remember because she wasn't the same woman.

Interesting. Very interesting. But when would she confess this detail—or would she?

5

The last time she and Jonni had swapped identities was during their senior year in high school. Daffy had played the role assigned by their senior drama producer to her more timid sister and bowed to rave applause.

That had been acting class.

This was real life.

She ought to stop the conversation right this moment and tell him it had been her twin who'd said yes to coffee, her twin who had told her Hunter's reason for placing an ad. *Mr. Romantic, looking for one special woman who wants only one special guy.*

Finally she met his expectant gaze, but rather than pulling out her driver's license and clarifying her identity, she said, "What kind of an ad would I respond to? I guess that's the question on the table."

He nodded.

Daffy surveyed the confident male dominating not just the space between them, but the entire room. She thought of his business prowess, his technical successes. More than that, she felt the heat burning in his gaze. *Just describe yourself.* "Well, I'd skip the generalities, you know— phrases like, 'SF who must love fine dining and sailing.' "

"What if I do?"

"Is that essential to you?"

He shifted even closer to her. Daffy was having trouble concentrating. She drew a circle on her notepad and added ears and a curlicue of hair to its bald head.

"No." He drained his coffee. "Are you suggesting I describe me rather than the type of woman I'm seeking?"

"Do you know what you're looking for?"

"I used to think so." He moved his hand and it was so close to Daffy's she wondered what would happen if she reached over with her pinkie and touched him. But of course she couldn't do that. This man was coming on to her. That was clear. But what was also clear was that she was not going to respond in any way. She'd had it with screwing up relationships. Until she figured out why she always messed things up and ended up hurting the other half, she was playing it safe.

Still, she couldn't resist giving him a wide-eyed

look of innocence, a four on a scale of ten when it came to seduction. "Used to?"

His hand might have made contact with the side of hers. Or she might have imagined the slight brush of a touch. "Before the Orphan's Club fund-raiser."

"Are you flirting with me, Mr. James?"

He laughed and sat back. "I never flirt."

"You do, too! I saw you with a woman old enough to be your grandmother. You had her eating out of your hand. And that's not to mention Tiffany Phipps."

"Tiffany!" Hunter checked his watch.

Daffy restrained herself from making a very unladylike face. Here she was, actually having fun with Hunter. She enjoyed the verbal jousting, and what woman could be immune to the way his gaze roamed her body? And no doubt he had a hot date with Tiffany—who would be receiving exactly the same intense, deeply searching looks and the none-too-subtle body language of an extremely virile male pursing his prey.

But instead of making his excuses and dashing off, Hunter reached for Daffy's empty cup. "May I get you a refill?"

Inexcusably smug that he was staying with her and not rushing off to an appointment with Tiffany, Daffy nodded, and he carried both cups to the counter. Instead of lusting after his body as he crossed the room, this time she put pen to paper. Thinking of what Jonni had told her, she wrote:

For Richer or Poorer, in Sickness and in Health:

*Don't answer this ad unless you know what for-
ever means.*

Slightly shaken by how spontaneously the
words had flowed, Daffy closed her notebook.

As soon as Hunter settled the coffee cups in
front of them and regained his seat, she said,
"What would you do if you got a response, and
you met and fell in love with her, but she didn't
reciprocate?"

"Oh, that wouldn't happen."

"You're awfully sure of yourself!"

He stirred his coffee and grinned. With that
dark, knowing look in his eyes, he said, "My
problem is finding the right woman to love. The
other way around"—he shrugged "—forgive me,
because I do not mean to sound cocky, but it's too
easy. So many women see only the exterior." After a sip of coffee, he said, rather dryly, "And let's
not discount the money. Add that in and they're
on me like white on rice."

"Well, well," Daffy said, studying her coffee.
What Hunter James needed was not only a lesson
in love, but a lesson in humility. "And why
wouldn't that happen?"

"Give me thirty days and I could make any
woman fall in love with me."

She almost choked on her mouthful of coffee.
Once she managed to swallow, she said, "Not me!"

"Want to bet?"

"Oh, sure," she replied, unable to refrain from a touch of sarcasm. "Like you said, what woman could resist?"

And what man could resist Daffodil Landry? Hunter shifted in his chair and attempted to appear unaffected by the blond dynamo. Did she have any idea just how sensually magnetic she was? Damn Aloysius for cornering him into this evening's foursome with him, his fiancée, and Tiffany. He'd far rather sit here with Daffy. Still, it was best to cut this meeting short. Already he'd concluded that the way to Daffy's heart lay through her mind. And paying her too much attention wouldn't get her attention.

"Meet me again to finish the ad?" He asked the question lazily, ignoring her gibe about the bet.

"You're really going to run it?"

Had he imagined the wistful touch of disappointment in her voice? "You want me to wait thirty days before I do?"

The notebook flew open. "Forget that silliness. Here's a draft." She pushed the notebook across the table.

Hunter read the lines she'd printed. Stunned, he sat back and studied her. She didn't look like the psychics who peddled their trade in the French Quarter; she looked every adorable inch like the attractive but undoubtedly spoiled Uptown young woman she was. Not a woman for a guy like Hunter James to be fooling around with. Slowly, he said, "You sure know how to get to the heart of the matter."

She shrugged. "I'm a journalist. I report what I see." She tore off the sheet of paper and handed it to him.

He took it, folded it, and tucked it into his wallet. He rose and said, "I'm an entrepreneur and I make things happen."

Leaning slightly forward, he reached out and, with the lightest of touches, smoothed the back of his thumb across the tip of her nose, exactly the spot she'd rubbed while thinking earlier. As quickly as he touched her, he dropped his hand.

She stared, apparently speechless.

Very well satisfied with her reaction, he moved a step or two toward the coffeehouse door, then turned back and called, "Oh, tell your sister hi for me."

The stunned look on her face was priceless. Hunter pushed open the door and walked out, whistling. Thirty days? No way would it take that long.

Three hours later, the only motivation he had for whistling was to hurry up the waiter so the endless dinner would come to an end.

"The city is so slow in the summer," Tiffany said. "If only the judges in federal court understood that." She turned toward Hunter for the hundredth time that evening, her cleavage doing its best to reach out and touch him. "Attorneys who only practice in state court have no idea how hard it is on the rest of us. We have to work twice as hard in the spring just so judges can take a vacation. They're cruising in the Carribbean and we're still sweating in federal court."

"But isn't the interesting stuff in federal court?" Hunter tried to avoid his firm's attorneys, but unfortunately, they had a way of tracking him down. Copyrights, patents, and contract issues were constant concerns for his burgeoning company.

Tiffany brightened. "You have such a nice way of saying things."

Aloysius beamed. "Hunter's a number one kind of guy." His fiancée smiled at her intended over her glass of wine. As much as he'd benefited from Aloysius's partnership, Hunter was damned if he could ever remember his fiancée's name. Crystal? Krissie? Hell, it might be Crysanthemum for all he knew. Of course, he had flower names on his mind, Daffodil being his favorite at the moment.

"And here are our number one entrées," Hunter said, faking a joviality he in no way felt. One thing worse than a blind date was a date with someone you already knew you had no interest in. Why Aloysius would push Tiffany on him when a woman like Daffy was available, he couldn't imagine. He pictured the mutinous glare in Daffy's eyes when he'd mentioned Tiffany. So live dangerously, he said to himself, and ask about their history.

"I ordered scallops, not mussels," Tiffany said to the waiter before he'd even settled all the plates on the table.

The waiter did his best imitation of Uriah Heep, apologizing profusely as he served the others. Hunter thought of the endless nights of his childhood during which he'd gone to sleep with nothing in his gut but a peanut butter sandwich.

Tiffany crossed her legs and one calf nudged Hunter's leg. "Really, it's so hard to find help who can get things right."

The waiter whisked away the offending mussels. Hunter considered offering to strangle Tiffany but figured he'd just end up doing life and she'd go free to torture without restraint.

Aloysius's fiancée said, "Well, training is very important. That's why I've gone into HR."

Tiffany smiled sweetly. "You mean personnel? I understand that's what people do when they don't specialize in anything else."

"Now, Tiff," Aloysius said, "HR is its own specialty. Chrissie has a certificate from Tulane."

Tiffany fluttered her lashes. "How charming. What are the salaries in HR?"

Chrissie glanced up from her amberjack to Aloysius's face. "Quite competitive."

"Oh?" Tiffany planted a hand on Hunter's arm. "Not nearly as exciting as tech companies, though."

"Or making partner in a law firm," Chrissie said. "But you haven't made partner yet, have you?"

Bravo, Hunter wanted to say. Chrissie could hold her own.

"Where is that waiter?" Tiffany added a pout to her question.

Hunter had to restrain himself from throwing down his napkin and striding out of the softly lit restaurant. Instead, he said, "So tell me, Tiff, I understand you and Daffodil Landry are friends from way back."

She had just taken a sip of wine. As he finished speaking, she choked. Aloysius leapt up, rounded the table, and pounded her on the back. Chrissie said, "My, oh, my," repeatedly.

The waiter strolled up, new entrée plate in hand, surveyed the scene, and retreated. Hunter thought he detected a satisfied smile on the poor man's face, which he didn't begrudge him at all.

When things calmed down, the waiter reappeared, settled the plate of scallops in front of Tiffany, and moved away.

"There are some things, Hunter," Tiffany said, "that a lady does not speak of."

"Nor a gentleman," Aloysius added.

"Meaning neither one of you will tell me why Daffodil Landry is not a person I should get to know?"

Aloysius and Tiffany exchanged looks across the table. In candlelight or fluorescent, it would have been hard to miss.

"Well, I for one would like to know what the big secret is," Chrissie put in. "And I'm your fiancée, Aloysius, so I think I have a right to know."

"Now you've done it," Tiffany said. She suddenly seemed more interested in her scallops than in Hunter, for which he uttered a silent prayer of thanks.

"Look, Hunter, I guess you have a right to know," Aloysius said, leaving his steak untouched. "Daffy's mother and my father had an affair. It was quite the scandal of the season. And for whatever reason, Daffy and I turned to each other. For comfort, I thought," he added with more than a touch of bitterness. "We were even engaged—"

Chrissie gasped. "You never told me that."

"Well, I'm sorry. It's true, but it's meaningless. Tiffany's brother, Eric, was going to be best man in my wedding, and the night before the rehearsal dinner, she and Eric, well, I don't think I need to say more."

Chrissie patted her face with her napkin.

Tiffany scarfed down the scallops.

Hunter chewed his own steak, considering how much pain Daffy must have been in to turn around and punish the man's son. Or had that been her motive?

"So you can see why she's not exactly our favorite person," Aloysius said.

Hunter nodded.

Tiffany put down her fork. "Forget about her," she said. "She's nothing but trouble. What you need is a woman in your life who understands how to deal with success."

Chrissie hadn't touched her dinner. "Aloysius, I need to speak with you. In private."

Looking like he was about to be led to the tumbril en route to La Guillotine, Aloysius nodded, and followed Chrissie toward the foyer of the restaurant.

"Now, that's a perfectly matched couple," Tiffany said.

"Why do you say that?" Hunter sliced a bite of steak.

"She asks, and he responds."

"Pussy-whipped," Hunter said around a mouthful of steak.

"What was that?"

"Never mind," Hunter said.

Daffy nibbled on the end of her Mont Blanc as she stared at her blank computer screen. She composed her column on the computer, but sometimes the old-fashioned comfort of a pen between her lips provided just the inspiration she needed. She reread the letter she was answering and wondered what got into guys' heads sometimes.

Dear Love Doctor,

I sure am hoping you have the Rx for my relationship. I've done everything I can think of to win my lady's love. I take her to dinner, send her flowers. I wash and wax her car and fill it with gas every week. I'm even nice to her dog and believe me, if you'd ever met that little rat, you'd be impressed by that statement. Yet she still won't say she'll marry me. She says she loves me but she's not sure we're right for each other. What else can I do?

Signed,
Perplexed in Plaquemines Parish

And I bet you call her every day. No, ten times a day, Daffy amended. And in the two days since she'd agreed—just to please her sister—to have coffee with Hunter James, he hadn't called her once.

Leaving aside her fountain pen, Daffy let her fingers hop across the keyboard.

Dear Perplexed,

What a pushover you are! You want to get a woman's attention? Try ignoring her!

Yeah, but only after you've tantalized her. That thought rang so true that Daffy typed it in next. Then she added:

I'll probably get skewered for this statement, but women like masterful men. Wimps are yesterday's news.

Masterful—like the dark-eyed satyr who'd told her with a straight face that, given thirty days, he could make any woman fall in love with him.

What you lack is confidence. If you want something badly enough, you have to be prepared to

*walk away from the table. There's your Rx. Try
that. Write back and let me know your wedding
date.*

Two days, and all she'd thought about was
Hunter James—followed by all the reasons she
had no business thinking about him. Of course he
hadn't meant to follow up on that outrageous
boast. He'd said it to get her goat and she'd
obliged him by rising to the occasion.

Her phone buzzed and Daffy glared at it. She
hated to be interrupted when writing her Love
Doctor column, an unreasonable reaction, as the
receptionist certainly had no idea that was what
Daffodil Landry, socialite, was busy doing.

It was Jonni.

Jonni, who never called Daffy at work and
lately hadn't phoned her much at home, either.

"Sis, what's up?" The words of her column
danced on the monitor and Daffy deleted an extra
space as she waited for her twin to answer. Daffy
had dutifully—and not too truthfully—reported
the other day that she'd had coffee with Hunter
and that had been that.

"Oh, nothing. I was just wondering if you had
seen Hunter James again."

Daffy gripped the phone. She wanted to tell her
sister to quit matchmaking, but restrained herself.
"No. Any reason I should have?"

"Well, the loveliest bouquet of flowers just arrived—from him."

Daffy bolted upright, fueled by a spurt of jealousy she could scarcely credit. She tried to be cool, though. "Really?" Did Hunter have the two of them confused? "How thoughtful of him."

"I don't think he was thinking of me," Jonni said rather pointedly.

"No?" She was itching to ask what message the card contained, but not even to her twin could she reveal that. She had her pride.

"The card says: thanks for agreeing to have coffee."

"He does have us confused!" Daffy blurted out her response before she could bite her tongue.

"Oh, Daffy, of course he doesn't. You're supposed to be a wordsmith. He said 'agreeing to have coffee.' That's his way of saying he knows I accepted on your behalf, and that he's grateful."

"You think so?" Boy, did she sound pathetic.

"Definitely."

"You're a good sister," Daffy said. "And I guess you can explain why I haven't heard from him."

"Maybe you should write to that Love Doctor."

That stilled her tongue. Daffy had kept her identity secret even from her sister. Her own words mocked her from the computer screen. *Try ignoring her!* "Maybe I will," Daffy said. "Lord knows my love life, or lack thereof, could use some help."

"Don't be afraid to accept it once it comes to you," Jonni said. "Would you like me to send this card to you?"

"That's not necessary," she said, wishing she'd screamed out *yes*!

"It might be better if I did. I wouldn't want David to think another man was sending me flowers for romantic reasons."

"Ah," Daffy said. "Put the card in the mail to me at home." She'd slip it under her pillow and dream about what might have been.

6

Hunter hadn't gotten where he was in life by lying around dreaming.

He plotted. He planned. He executed.

Standing in his office high in the sky in downtown New Orleans, gazing out across the spectacular view of the winding Mississippi River, he checked his faithful Timex. Ten more ticks and his phone should ring.

Given the exodus of oil companies from the city, Aloysius had rented their plush offices at a steal. Normally, Hunter fully appreciated the sights afforded by the floor-to-ceiling windows of the forty-second floor. Today, though, visions of Daffy Landry filled his mind.

The leather couch across the expanse of muted ivory carpeting beckoned to him. What he wouldn't give to have Daffy on that couch with him!

Again he glanced at his watch. He allowed himself a slight smile, picturing her beneath him on the sofa, her silky hair fanning out as she reached up to him even as he leaned to kiss her lips.

From the first moment he'd seen her, he'd been intrigued by her. Face it, Hunter, you wanted her. It wasn't curiosity. It was male need, possibly even pure and simple lust.

And the more his friends warned him away from Daffodil Landry, the more determined he grew to win her.

When he'd been eight, he'd fought battles with his fists. In high school, he'd learned to conquer with his charm. In college and since then, he'd surged ahead, relying on his brains and then on his instincts for creating software products just enough ahead of their time to corner the market.

No matter the weapons used, a swift and successful strike demanded precision.

His phone rang.

He answered, listened to the messenger's report, smiled, and hung up. After counting to twenty-five, he lifted the phone and punched in the number of *The Crescent*.

A receptionist with a Brooklyn twang answered and said, "*The Crescent*-holderminute," all in one breath. Must be Daffy's sister's day off. Thank goodness she'd been there the other day. Hunter wasn't sure why, but he suspected Daffy never would have agreed to meet him. Not for coffee, not for tea. There'd been chemistry between them, undeniably, but she'd also been on her guard.

Just about now, though, according to his brilliantly conceived plan, those defenses should be weakening. Women couldn't resist thoughtful men who listened—really listened—to the little things they said about themselves.

He didn't like to get too far ahead of himself, but he was pretty sure he wouldn't need thirty days to win Daffy. She'd been hot enough to melt the carpeting at the Orphan's Club fund-raiser—and that from clear across the room.

Hunter began to whistle, for once not minding having been put on hold.

Across town, Daffy hugged her arms to her chest and gazed raptly at the package she'd just opened. "What a sweetie," she murmured, lifting the PJ's coffee tumbler filled with candy corn. "He actually listened to what I said—and remembered!"

Jonni could keep her flowers. This candy corn was more special than any floral offering Daffy had ever received—and she'd received more than an FTD florist restocking from a wholesale horticulturist.

Her intercom buzzed and she ignored it. Reaching for the lid of the tumbler, she popped it off and scooped out one lone candy corn. Smiling, she lifted it toward her lips, eyeing the white tip and picturing Hunter sitting so close beside her at PJ's only two days earlier. And she'd worried she'd never hear from him again!

Twice more the intercom buzzed. Maybe it was Marguerite on the rampage. Daffy grabbed her phone.

The temporary receptionist came on the line. "I'd take this call if I were you."

Wondering if she was capable of attracting a gorgeous, desirable, wonderful man without seeking to turn around and destroy him like the black widow she feared she was, Daffy said, "Oh, and why is that?"

"Sexy, doll. Just give him a listen."

And with that, the receptionist rang off. Daffy started to follow suit when the weirdest idea popped into her mind. Could it be Hunter? If so, why now, right at this moment when she was sucking on a delicious piece of candy corn and thinking he walked on water? Now, could that be a coincidence?

"Daffy Landry," she said, her voice in its most clipped reportorial style.

"Hunter James," came his voice, slow and silky and ready to spend the rest of the day caressing her.

Daffy gripped the phone. Silly images like those had to be banished from her mind. Hunter James was far too sure of himself.

Someone had to teach him a lesson.

And it looked like it was going to be Daffodil Landry who wrote the syllabus.

She let silence speak for her, sitting back down and circling her ankle to form the first ten letters of the alphabet. All the while, she held that one silly piece of candy corn in her right hand. After she'd completed a J with a flourish of toes, she said, "And what can *The Crescent* do for you today?"

His answer was a long time coming. Finally he said, "Just thought I'd follow up on our conversation of the other day."

"Mmm," Daffy murmured. Conversation! He wanted her to throw herself at his feet, like a dog groveling over a barbecue-flavored dog bone. He'd calculated his gift, right down to the timing of the delivery! Tickling the sweet tip of the candy corn with her tongue, she said, "You still want to run that ad with us?"

"Ad?"

She smiled. He'd forgotten all about his personal ad. Clearly that had been a pretext to procure a coffee date with her. Silly man. Hunter James wasn't the kind of guy a girl needed an excuse to go out with. Not that she'd let him in on that secret right now. "You remember—the ad that will send the woman of your dreams straight to your door?"

"Right."

Daffy smothered a grin. Hunter had out-clevered himself. He'd obviously known the exact moment the package would be delivered. He'd called expecting her to fling herself, via the telephone, into his arms. "I'm tied up till five today, but if you'd like, I can send an assistant over to help you. I have an intern from Tulane who's very good." That ought to whet his appetite. He'd be expecting a sorority chick and who would appear but Greg, who led the front line in rushing for the Tulane Green Wave. "Where's your office located?"

"Downtown, but never mind the intern. Pick you up at five?"

He recovered fairly quickly, she'd give him that.

"No can do," she said, managing to sound wistfully disappointed. "I'm busy." Yeah, busy opening a can of cat food for Mae West.

"Well," Hunter said, dragging out the word, "have a nice day."

And he hung up.

Daffy glared at the receiver of her telephone. "Have a nice day?" She slammed it down on the cradle. From the next cubicle over, she heard an amused "Temper, temper."

Her glance fell on the engagement calendar open on her desk. The month of April was chock-full of assignments, parties she had to attend to photograph the beautiful, the socially responsible, and the upwardly bound of New Orleans. She turned a page; May looked pretty much the same, only not yet as full.

Hunter had proclaimed he could make any woman fall for him in thirty days. Daffy nibbled the tip off the piece of candy corn she still held in her hand, then added the orange midsection. She'd met him on Tuesday at PJ's. That was three days ago. Finishing off the yellow top of the corn, she reached for a red marker. Beginning with Tuesday, she numbered the days one through thirty, which brought her to the third week in May.

"Okay, Hunter" she murmured, "show me your best stuff." Thirty days—well, less than that now—wasn't much of a siege. The candy corn had been a clever opening gambit, but he'd overdone it with the phone call. She nibbled another piece of candy and smiled as she thought about him remembering what she'd said and going to all the bother to find the candy and put it in the coffee mug. Hunter was not only sexy, he was romantic, too. Any woman who didn't fall for him would be nuts.

She sighed and circled the thirtieth day. She wasn't going to lose a bet as simple as this one. It was day thirty-one that worried her.

In his office high above the city, Hunter slowly let go of the phone. He could have sworn he'd detected the aroma of that candy corn. His secretary had informed him that she'd gone to a lot of trouble to locate the traditional Halloween fare at a time when the stores were full of chocolate Easter bunnies and fluffy marshmallow chicks. As motherly as she was, she'd be disappointed to learn her efforts had been somewhat torpedoed.

He grinned, rather reluctantly. This round went to Daffy. Any other woman would have done exactly as he had predicted.

But then, it wasn't any other woman he wanted.

* * *

Four o'clock found him lounging against a planter box outside the rear walkway of *The Crescent*'s offices. Locating Daffy's car had been simpler than he could have hoped. The personalized plates on the BMW convertible said it all: DAFFY.

"Which is what you are, standing around in a parking lot," he said out loud. Never in his life had he pursued a woman in quite this way. The way women were always after him, he'd never had to exert himself. Even when he'd been the poor kid in town growing up without a father, he'd had girlfriends. Oh, not the snooty rich ones like Emily Godchaux, but plenty of others.

Admiring Daffy's car, Hunter considered a concept he'd studiously avoided. Without a doubt, Daffy fell into the rich-girl category. Anyone in Aloysius's childhood circle qualified. But was she snooty? Would she look twice at a guy like Hunter had he not ridden the high tech-and-IPO money wave into the big time?

Hell, would she look twice at him today? With his plan in mind, he'd changed into his gym clothes at the office. Aloysius had insisted on introducing him to membership in the New Orleans Athletic Club and they often worked out after work. Aloysius sported designer outfits; Hunter stuck to his habits of years past. He glanced down at his gray sweat shorts and T-shirt. Well, at least they were clean. He'd stuffed his feet into an ancient pair of flip-flops he kept for some unclear reason in the back of his Jeep.

Being rich took a lot of getting used to.

He heard the rustle of footsteps approaching and swung his gaze toward the back door. Four-fifteen. He grinned. Wouldn't Daffy be surprised to see him!

Not wanting to frighten or startle her, he'd positioned himself in full view of the back door, smack in the middle of the path to her car. He might be lying in wait, but skulking and lurking were not his style.

Daffy, however, appeared lost in thought and completely unaware that he stood in full view of her. She carried a purse over one shoulder, a camera bag over the other, and in one hand she cradled the PJ's tumbler.

"Having a nice day?" Hunter never used that cornball expression, but since he'd been hornswoggled by her cool nonchalance on the phone earlier and the inane sentiment had popped out of his mouth, he might as well use it again. "Turn a weakness into a strength" was one of his favorite mottoes.

She stopped in her tracks, then shifted into reverse a step or so. Her sunglasses hid her expression from him, but he'd be willing to bet he'd achieved his mission of taking her by surprise.

Thinking of taking her led his mind to places it was better off not traveling to—at least not yet. Her simple cotton dress, the same color as his mother's favorite deep pink roses, clung softly to the curves of her body. The neckline was cut in a U deep enough to beckon Hunter to look more closely, which, of course, he did. Her camera bag had tugged the dress slightly off one shoulder and Hunter admired the slope of her neck and shoulder. The hemline skipped above her knees by several inches, inviting the eye to travel upward, which, of course, he accepted. He thought he spied a hint of an outline of a bikini pantie but decided no feminine daytime attire could be quite so scanty.

Daffy clutched the coffeehouse tumbler. He was doing it again, that trick he had of looking at her as if he could see through her dress. Why, if she asked him, he could probably tell her that she was wearing a thong the color of crushed raspberries.

Not, of course, that she was going to ask him any such thing. "I'm certainly having an interesting day," she said at last. "Are you headed to the gym?"

He plucked at his gray cotton T-shirt. Daffy's mouth watered at the way the fabric clung to his broad chest. The shorts reminded her of her junior high journalism teacher's favorite expression when asked how long a story should be: long enough to cover the subject, but short enough to be interesting. Hunter's legs shouted strength. They were tanned, like he'd been lounging poolside, and had just enough hair to give them that manly cast Daffy loved.

"Jazzfest," he said.

"Now?"

"No time like the present."

She started forward. "Don't let me hold you up. They close the Fair Grounds at seven." She paused. "Did you know that?"

"Yep."

He hadn't budged. She'd have to brush by him to get to her car. Daffy hesitated.

"Go with me?"

She should have kept walking. "I'm pretty busy," she said, though reluctantly. The idea of doing something so carefree as going to Jazzfest for the last two hours of the day appealed strongly to her. Surprisingly, she'd never done that before. She visited the annual confab of music, food booths, and crafts every few years but had never gone so late in the day, probably feeling she wouldn't get her money's worth for the price of admission.

Though with Hunter at her side, who cared about throwing away twenty dollars?

"So you mentioned."

Daffy glared at him, thankful for her dark glasses. He wasn't going to make this easy. She'd trumped him earlier, but at the moment, she didn't feel like resisting him. Making a motion with the tumbler, she said, "Thanks for the candy."

He smiled. "You're welcome. By the way, I know how to own up to a mistake when I make one. It was presumptuous of me to call you this morning."

Daffy laughed. "You're one smooth operator, I

must say. Okay, I'll go to Jazzfest with you, but I'll have to change clothes."

"Shall I drive you to your place?"

"That'll take too much time. I'll just follow your lead." She reached out and touched the soft cotton of his T-shirt right over his heart. His gaze flickered and then held, his eyes darkening. Two could play at pursuit. Slowly, she withdrew her hand. "I always keep a gym bag in my car. Give me five minutes."

Letting go of the breath he'd been holding, Hunter nodded. He reached into the pocket of his T-shirt and pulled out his own sunglasses. He should have been wearing them all along. He strongly suspected Daffy saw right through him. She whisked over to her car, dumped her things, and sped past him, disappearing into the offices of the paper.

The paper ... Hunter frowned. He'd been so distracted by Daffy that he'd almost forgotten the original reason he'd visited this building. He'd been in search of the Love Doctor's identity. Funny, but those stinging words didn't rankle quite so much now that Daffy Landry had entered his life.

Still, he might as well kill two birds with one stone. Jeez, but he was full of platitudes today. Well, why not? The sky was a bright blue, a breeze kept the eighty-degree temperature in check, and Daffy Landry had agreed to go to Jazzfest with him.

What more could a man ask for?

Daffy reappeared and Hunter knew instantly the answer to his own question.

Daffy's gym clothes bore absolutely no resemblance to Hunter's loose-fitting shorts and ages-old T-shirt. For one thing, the skimpy, body-molding crop top was made of Lycra, or did Saran Wrap now come in designer colors? A bright slash of hot pink across the black background highlighted her breasts. Not that Daffy's breasts needed the extra exclamation of color to call attention to them.

Hunter swallowed. The shorts were of the same fabric and stopped mid-thigh. Thank goodness she'd tied some sort of wrap around her waist or Hunter might have started salivating right then and there. He must have been staring at it, because Daffy gave him a half smile and said, "I know it's not cool enough for a wrap, but the sun's still strong enough that it'll come in handy to protect my shoulders."

Right. "Your shoulders," Hunter said. "They are almost bare."

She nodded and smiled sunnily this time. "I'm ready if you are."

He was ready, all right, but thoughts of Jazzfest were fast slipping from his mind.

"Do you have a car or did you walk over?"

Her sensible question cut short his visions of sweeping her into his Jeep and driving straight to his place. Good thing. He was still camping out with Aloysius at his aunt's tony Garden District house, and the last spot on earth he wanted to take Daffy was anywhere within vision radius of his business partner.

"Car." He pushed off the planter box, where he'd taken up residence, and pointed toward his four-wheel drive. "Over here."

Daffy fell into step beside him and Hunter enjoyed several sidelong glances at the hot-pink stripe. "Nice gym clothes," he said.

"Thanks. Yours, too."

"These old things?" Hunter was actually surprised.

"I have no idea how old they are, but they do show your body to advantage."

Hunter opened the passenger door. "Remind me never to throw them away," he said, helping her step up to the seat.

Mistake.

He only touched her arm, right above the wrist.

She settled into the seat, a calm expression on her face. Hunter felt as if he'd been singed by a hot plate, like the one his mother cooked on when their stove broke and the landlord refused to replace it.

How could she remain so oblivious?

One touch made him crave another.

"Comfortable?" He asked the question as he stood beside the open passenger door.

"Quite, thanks," she said, her lips beginning to curve upwards.

"I'm making a fool of myself, is that it?" Hunter knew the answer but asked anyway.

Daffy smiled.

Then, given how coolly she was acting, she did the most surprising thing.

She leaned over and fluttered a kiss across his lips.

7

Daffy opened her eyes wide. Had she really done that? Kissed Hunter James!

She ran her tongue lightly over her lower lip. He'd backed away a step, which was just as well, because at the merest taste of him, she was sorely tempted to be the fool. "Well, you did tell me to have a nice day," she said, giving him an impish smile. She had to be careful or she'd betray just how much he affected her. "And now that I'm in a festive spirit, let's go party."

Without another word, he walked around the car and slid in behind the wheel. Casting her a sideways glance, he said, "When is the last time you went to Jazzfest?"

So he was going to play it cool. Daffy half turned in the seat and tucked one bare leg under her. She wasn't sure, but she thought he

shifted a bit behind the wheel. Good. She was going to give Mr. Irresistible a run for his money. He
might have forgotten or even been joking about
his thirty-day challenge, but she sure hadn't.
'Course, the only problem was that with every
additional second she spent around him, she
knew he hadn't boasted idly.

Darn him.

At last she said, "Oh, it's been a few years. How
about you?"

He stopped at a light. "Never miss it. At least
not since I discovered it five years ago." He
flipped on the radio, tuning it to WWOZ, the local
jazz station that broadcast live from the Fair
Grounds. Marcia Ball's vibrant voice belted out.

"You must be a real jazz fan." Funny, but she
would have picked him for a rock kind of guy.

"I guess you'd say I'm a fan of the total experience." The light changed; they surged forward
and in one smooth move, he now rested his arm
on the back of her seat.

Suddenly the Jeep seemed too small. Even
though he wasn't touching her shoulder, she
could feel him on her skin. Right now, music and
crafts weren't the total experience Daffy was con-
templating. She hadn't had sex since she had sabotaged her blossoming relationship with Jonni's
last candidate for husband of the month, a new
doctor in town.

Daffy sighed. That was months ago.

"Penny for your thoughts," Hunter said, and

this time he did brush his fingertips ever so lightly across her bare shoulder.

Sex. She almost said it. Instead, she swallowed the word in a mixture of cough and laugh and said, "Do you usually go this late in the day?"

He'd moved his hand to the headrest of her seat. Grinning what she could only describe as a wicked grin, he said, "It depends what time my date gets off work."

"I really was leaving at five," she said, feeling a need to defend her actions.

"An assignment came in?"

"I'm too honest," Daffy said. "No assignment. I thought you might show up, so I decided to out-smart you."

"We sure are two people set on outsmarting one another," Hunter said softly. "What do you think would happen if we declared a truce on that point?"

Sex. Most definitely. Daffy glanced out the window, anywhere but at Hunter. Sex would be okay. Was she kidding? It would be great. And sex wouldn't mean she'd lost the thirty-day bet. Turning back to him, she said, "Friends? We'd be friends?"

Friends? Hunter studied her profile. "Friends" wasn't the word he was thinking of, but it would sure do for starters. He moved his hand off the back of Daffy's seat and extended it to shake hands. She accepted his hand, they touched for the briefest—and most electric—of moments, and

Hunter had to hide a smile. She wanted him as much as he wanted her. Placing both hands on the wheel, he began to whistle.

He negotiated the thick traffic in silence until he'd snagged a parking spot just vacated by a station wagon full of singing, sunburned, and no doubt slightly beer-logged college-age kids. Ah, yes, the total experience of Jazzfest.

Hunter leaned across Daffy, careful not to give in to the temptation to brush her knees as he opened the glove box. He came up with the tube he was seeking, pulled it out, and said, "Sunscreen?"

"Great," Daffy answered. "But you don't look like a man who carries sunblock around."

"I'm naturally dark," he said. Like his father, according to his mother. Not that now was the time to be thinking of his worthless old man. Not on a beautiful day like today, a day full of promise. "But this stuff comes in handy on fishing trips."

Daffy shuddered. "You mean you actually stick worms on hooks?"

Hunter unscrewed the cap off the sunscreen. "I have, but now I mostly go out in the Gulf for deep-sea fishing. Scoot around and I'll do your back."

Scooping her hair to one side, Daffy gave him a long, scorching look before turning sideways. Her top was cut lower in the front than the back, but he still found an enticing expanse of perfect flesh beckoning to him. He squeezed out a drop of lotion and began on her left side, circling lower across her shoulders and then slowly onto the tops of her arms. He couldn't swear to it, but he thought he heard her sigh softly.

Good. As for himself, he was getting harder than the gearshift on his Jeep. The blues group on the radio crooned on and this time he definitely heard Daffy sigh. He'd better get out fast or they wouldn't make it inside the gates of the Fair Grounds.

Daffy had to be thinking the same thoughts. She shifted around. She too was breathing faster than usual. But instead of reaching for the door handle and doing the sensible thing of getting beyond his reach, she held out her hand and said, "Thanks. I'll do my front."

Hunter nodded and handed over the sunscreen. He swallowed hard as she dabbed a spot of lotion above her right breast. The tight-fitting exercise top already did enough to call his heated attention to her full breasts, but when she started stroking the rounded line over the right one and moved in a sensuous path to her cleavage, he had to stare. No pretending to look elsewhere.

"Are you trying to drive me nuts?" Hunter couldn't stop from grinding out the question.

Tipping down her sunglasses to reveal blue eyes now darkened almost to the color of midnight, she said in a voice of all innocence, "Friends don't let friends get sunburned." Then she plucked her hand from between her breasts, leaned forward, and dabbed a bit of sunscreen on his nose and forehead.

"Ready," she said, opening her door and slipping out.

He followed, grumbling under his breath. He was the pursuer here, dammit. If anyone was going to drive the other one crazy with desire, it was supposed to be him doing it to her. Hell, if he didn't cool down fast, he'd be doing something as stupid as writing to that useless Love Doctor. Which reminded him—he ought to go ahead and ask Daffy for any clues she might give him.

Rounding the car, he smiled down at Daffy. No point in letting her see just how much she could ruffle him. She smiled back, rather impishly. Still looking down, he easily saw the reason.

His shorts did nothing to hide the effect Daffy had on him.

"Let's go," he said, beginning to walk rapidly up the block.

She kept up with him, chatting away about how long it had been since she'd been to Jazzfest. The streets around the Fair Grounds were full of their own mini-festivities, with kids hawking bottles of water and beer sold from Coleman coolers, and old men offering their front lawns as parking lots. Always a way to earn a buck. Hunter smiled up at the sun, thankful to be out enjoying the day rather than working for survival.

He bought their tickets at the gate, handed Daffy's to her, and gazed around at the crowds still pouring in and at the early visitors, many now heading homeward.

Looking down, he gave her hand the briefest of squeezes and said, "Don't get lost, okay?"

She nodded. "What's your favorite stage?"

They continued toward the interior of the Fair Grounds, an immense expanse of trampled brown grasses and dusty walkways surrounded by food booths offering local favorites and stages pouring out everything from jazz to blues to zydeco to rock to rap to gospel. Hunter looked around and said, "Now, that's a hard choice to make. Maybe the zydeco. What about you?"

"Blues. With good blues, I can hear the singer's soul."

"You surprise me, Daffodil Landry." He stopped abruptly, in order to miss a herd of kids dashing across the pathway. She bumped against his side. Hunter dropped her hand and put his arms on her shoulders. "Okay?"

"Yes. I don't know why my comment should surprise you. Uptown girls have soul, too."

"Ah, yes, Uptown girls." Hunter once again heard that interior voice warning him away. His friends he could easily ignore, but his own sonar of danger was another factor altogether. "Maybe you're an exception. You and your sister seem pretty down-to-earth."

Daffy kicked one toe into the dusty ground and shrugged. She could have assured Hunter that being born with a silver, socially correct spoon in one's mouth wasn't the key to happiness. But the last thing she wanted to do today was get into a philosophical conversation that would end up with her losing out on a great time with Hunter James. "Want to see just how down-to-earth I am? Let's go second line in the Gospel Tent." Daffy loved the New Orleans tradition of spontaneously parading to music.

Hunter leafed through the schedule of events that had come with the tickets. "They're on a break for another fifteen minutes. How about a little two-stepping in the meantime?"

"Okay." Zydeco wasn't her strong suit, but today she'd try anything, especially when Hunter captured her hand. They strolled off toward the Fais Do-Do stage. Between the still strong late-afternoon sun and the sizzling warmth generated by Hunter's touch, Daffy reveled in her pleasantly overheated state. Skirting around one of the craft marketplaces, listening to Hunter humming what sounded like "When the Saints Come Marching In," Daffy decided life couldn't get much better.

Until after seven o'clock, when the Fair Grounds closed. Then, ah, then things would get even hotter. She held Hunter's hand just a little more tightly and smiled up at him. The sounds of a zydeco band were growing louder.

"Daffy, hey!"

At the sound of her name being called, Daffy halted, as did Hunter. Looking around, Daffy spotted two couples, both of whom she'd grown up with. It was a fact of life that a New Orleanian could never go to Jazzfest without running into at least a few friends and acquaintances. But just once, Daffy wished they'd outrun the statistical chances.

"Friends of yours?" Hunter was checking out the foursome descending on them.

Daffy nodded and exchanged greetings with the two men and women, whom she introduced as MeToo, SuSu, Bienville, and R. J.

R. J. shook hands with Hunter, and Daffy could have kicked him because of the sympathetic way he was looking at her date. He probably wanted to pull Hunter aside and warn him to have nothing to do with her. Daffy smiled her most brilliant smile and, knowing what the response would be, she said, "We're just going to try a little two-step. Want to come along?" MeToo hated anything Cajun and would refuse the invitation.

"Slumming, Daff?" Bienville asked the question as he wrapped an arm around MeToo's shoulders.

"Just taking in the Jazzfest experience," Hunter said.

SuSu shook a spot of dust off her pink linen blouse. "It's always so dusty out here. I don't know why I come."

"Because I asked you to," R. J. said. "So, Hunter, are you the one and the same Hunter James whose company controls the gateway to the Internet?"

"I'm not sure I'd state the case that broadly," Hunter said.

Daffy perked up. Was Hunter that famous? To

R. J., whom she'd dated and dumped three years ago, after which he'd rebounded and married SuSu, she said, "Hunter is the soul of modesty."

Hunter grinned. "I wouldn't go that far, Daffy. It's pretty much true that the routing software we developed is essential to any ISP protocol."

R. J. whistled. "I'm glad I bought that stock, even if I did miss out on the IPO."

Hunter nodded. "It's holding its own, even during the market shakedowns."

"Anyone want another beer?" MeToo tapped her foot on the ground. "I'm thirsty."

Bienville, who'd been silently standing by, said, "I'll get you one."

"I'm afraid too much business talk is boring," Hunter said. "And that zydeco is calling. Nice to meet you." He held out his hand and Daffy slipped hers back into it.

And just like that, they escaped the foursome and threaded their way into the dancing crowd.

Masterful, Daffy thought, enjoying Hunter's guiding touch as he led her into the vigorous Cajun waltz. Let him boast; he deserved to.

Hunter let the music wash away his irritation. The woman in pink reminded him strongly of Emily, hanging on to her man while making eyes at other guys. And the one named R. J. had looked at him with such a mixture of sympathy and jealousy that Hunter could draw only one conclusion: he, too, was another one of Daffy's jilts. Jeez, how many did she have?

Glancing down at her, dancing easily and

freely in his arms, he could honestly say he didn't care if they numbered in the hundreds—as long as they were all in her past. Oh, it drove him ballistic to think of her with another guy, a funny thought for him to be having. He was involved in a simple chase-and-catch, nothing more. He'd enjoy the next few weeks and move on with his life, to his next flirtation, until he met the woman who would rule his heart forever and ever.

And the chances of that woman being Daffodil Landry were slim to none. Fidelity—mutual fidelity—was a given in his expectations. And from what he'd heard, there wasn't much chance of that gift coming from Daffy.

Her skin gleamed and her breasts rounded up even more fully from her brief top as they dipped and swayed and circled the dusty field of dancing couples. Let the future take care of itself. Today he'd live for the moment.

The band stopped and Hunter and Daffy joined all the other dancers in applause.

Flushed and happy-looking, she said, "That was marvelous. I had no idea I could even follow the Cajun two-step!"

He brushed a lock of hair from her cheek. "You follow beautifully," he murmured. She was standing against him, tight and close, packed in by the crowd. Their legs were practically entwined and a lightning strike of heat coursed through him. Placing his hands lightly on her shoulders, he made no effort to hide the effect she had on him.

Daffy tipped her face up to his. "You lead beautifully," she replied.

The band struck a note and Hunter heard the crowd start to shift into dance mode as the two guys playing the spoons hammered on their metal-washboard breastplates.

But Hunter wasn't moving, not except to lower his hands to Daffy's waist.

She wriggled against him and all he could do was thank the stars they were in full public view or he would have taken her then and there.

With a soft sigh, she parted her lips and Hunter forced himself to pull back, to fight the temptation to taste that beautiful, inviting mouth. Too much too fast was not the right recipe for success with Daffodil Landry. "Ready for the Gospel Tent?"

Daffy rocked back. "Gospel Tent?" Her voice was dazed from desire.

Hunter grinned. She was his for the taking. "Sure, let's go get some of that old-time religion." Some vocal amens might be just what he needed to cool his own hard-on.

His hands back on her shoulders, he guided her from the mass of dancers. They were halfway to the Gospel Tent before she seemed to come back to earth.

"You should probably be labeled with a warning notice," Daffy said.

That made him smile. "And what would the label say?"

"Danger. Do not touch."

"And if you were labeled, what would yours say?"

Immediately, she answered, "Danger. Explosive."

He laughed, but then realized that with all the warnings he'd been given, laughing was the last thing he should be doing. Running in the opposite direction from Daffy was no doubt the recommended option.

"Ooh, Hunter!"

He stopped. He'd know that female voice anywhere.

"Friends of yours?" Daffy said, a wicked smile on her face as she repeated his own words to him.

Emily, with Roger in tow, descended in a flurry of cheek kisses that put Tiffany Phipps quite in the shade. Hunter performed the introductions, hiding his reluctance behind the company manners his mother had drummed into him. Emily was one woman he refused to call friend. Roger he actually felt sorry for.

"You were naughty to skip my party," Emily said.

Daffy picked up quickly on Hunter's tension. She also noted the woman's wedding ring—a carat at least. She had no business gunning for Hunter.

Turning to Daffy, Emily said, "Hunter, Roger, and I go way back. Only now that he's rich and famous, he doesn't have time for us folks back home." She pouted in what was supposed to be a becoming fashion, Daffy supposed, and lay a possessive hand on Hunter's forearm. Daffy was pleased to see Hunter shift his arm free.

"Where's home?" Daffy asked the question, realizing she'd never asked Hunter. Well, it wasn't as if she'd spent much time with him. Yet.

"Ponchatoula," Hunter answered before Emily could. Daffy noticed he didn't apologize for missing her party.

"And fancy running into you way down here in the city at Jazzfest," Emily cooed. Roger nodded, more bored than threatened. "I know," Emily continued, "now that we've bumped into each other, let's make up for that missed party. We're heading over to the Acura stage."

"That's going to be a great performance," Daffy said, almost surprising herself by how swiftly she thought up the lie, "but we're going to have to miss it. I'm on my way to visit my aunt in the hospital and we were just heading to the exit."

"Your poor, dear aunt will be wondering what happened to you," Hunter said.

"Oh. Well." Emily appeared stymied; then her sharp gaze sharpened even more. "But, Hunter, surely you can join us later. We'll be at the House of Blues, at the private party Aaron Neville is throwing."

What a name-dropper. Daffy could have rolled over her playing that game but decided not to lower herself. She also could have told Emily that Aaron Neville would be nowhere near that party but his record label had thought it prudent to toss a bash for his fans flocking to Jazzfest. Smiling sweetly, she tapped her watch and glanced up at Hunter.

"Sorry, Emily," he said, "but I already have plans. Emily, Roger, see you next time. Mustn't keep Daffy's aunt waiting."

And with that, he guided the two of them clear of the pesky Emily.

As soon as they were out of earshot, Hunter said, "You don't really have a sick aunt, do you?"

She shook her head. "And do you really have plans for later?"

Hunter looked at her, that slow, head-to-toe scrutiny that laid her open to him—body and soul. Daffy tried to quell a quivering tremble of desire that coursed through her. She touched her upper lip with the tip of her tongue, yearning to feel his mouth on hers.

He leaned toward her, his body shadowing hers. "Oh, do I have plans," he murmured.

8

Daffy had to bite her tongue to keep from asking, "With me or with someone else?" Instead, she answered, "That's nice," leading the way to the edge of the standing-room-only Gospel Tent. "I'd hate to think of you all alone on a Friday night."

"I have problems," Hunter said, "but that's seldom one of them." He grinned and then positioned himself behind her.

The music surged around them, led by a black choir with a male lead singer who mopped his face even as his voice reached the heights and far corners of the tent with a power Daffy had seldom heard. She swayed and clapped along with the others in the crowded tent, surprisingly content.

A group of joyous celebrants had formed a second line and was parading up and down the aisles of the tent, waving everything from gaily decorated umbrellas to hankies to something Daffy would have sworn was a Pampers. Hunter's body brushed against her as she moved with the music. Amen. Amen. She wanted him. Careful, Daff, she tried to say, but she didn't feel one bit like exercising caution.

She'd wrecked enough hearts and lives without damaging another. But he's tough and he's out to get what he can, she argued back. Like that makes anything you do okay?

The leader of the band was working up the responsive crowd. "Say ye-ah!" he cried.

"Ye-ah!"

"Say ye-aaaahhh!"

"Oh, ye-eah," Hunter said, his voice speaking only to her sounding oddly quiet in the tent full of thunderous music. "You know something?"

"What?" Daffy wet her lips and waited for his answer. She sure knew how on fire she was for him.

"Time to go."

Any other trip to Jazzfest and Daffy would have protested. They hadn't yet sipped a strawberry lemonade or savored a crawfish pie. Tonight, though, she was ready to leave.

The crowd had surged to its feet, responding to the gospel rhythms. The second line had grown, with more people joining in than were left standing in many of the rows of seats. Oh, ye-ah! Daffy slipped out of the tent with Hunter.

By the time Hunter took the turn that led to the

parking lot at her office, Daffy was beginning to wonder if she was imagining Hunter's heated interest. Was it only her own desires creating the need she'd felt in his casual touches, his searching, searing glances? That would certainly explain his pulling up beside the only car left in the lot at *The Crescent*.

"Yours?" He turned toward her, his right arm on the back of her seat, close enough for her to sense his heat, yet not near enough to answer her tingling need to be touched by him.

Daffy nodded. She couldn't make herself reach for the door handle. Why hadn't they gone to his place? Or hers?

He brushed a strand of hair from her cheek. "Okay if I follow you to your place?"

She was so relieved she almost yelled. Instead, she nodded, shyly enough, and said, "If we get separated, my address is 6302 Perrier."

"Uh—"

"I forgot. You're not from here. Perrier runs parallel to St. Charles on the riverside. My house is on the last block before Audubon Park."

He grinned. "I do know what riverside means."

She smiled in return and before she could say "Thanks" or "I had a great time" or anything else equally predictable, he was out of his seat and around the car, opening the door for her. He stood back and watched as she climbed into her BMW, then hopped back into his Jeep.

No kiss. No touch. Daffy gunned her engine and headed for the street. Was he trying to drive her nuts? If so, he was certainly succeeding!

Heading toward her Uptown home, she lectured herself on behavior, morals, and propriety. Hunter was behaving like a perfect gentleman; she on the other hand, closely resembled a cat in heat. Take a chill pill, she advised herself, and determined then and there, at the red light at Louisiana, not to have sex with him on the first real date, no matter how much he entreated her. Denial whetted one's appetite, a lesson he'd been trying out on her all afternoon and evening.

Oh, ye-ah, did it ever!

Hunter followed Daffy in her dash out of the lot. She drove the way she approached life—like Don Quixote tilting at windmills. Boy, did she have style, he thought. And unlike those friends of hers, Daffy was Uptown but somehow grounded to the real world in a manner he hadn't expected, given her background. Aloysius, in between warning Hunter away from Daffy, had given him a clear enough picture of her privileged upbringing. She'd been a maid in several Carnival courts—the ones that counted in the pecking order of New Orleans' society, according to Aloysius—though never Queen of Carnival. After what he'd learned about Daffy's mother, Hunter wasn't too surprised about that. Surely people who flaunted society's rules couldn't carry the scepter.

Daffy's background was a world away from his own childhood and adolescence. But some elements were universal. He grimaced as he thought of Emily and Roger and the social order of the much smaller town he'd called home. There were the haves and the have-nots and ne'er the twain should cross paths.

He stopped at the light at Louisiana and admired the view he had of the back of Daffy's head. He couldn't see much as his Jeep rode higher than her BMW, but he could have sworn she tossed her head in a most determined fashion. Grinning, Hunter moved forward with the green light and wondered just how she'd take his next move in this chess game of attraction the two of them were playing.

Sixty-three-oh-two Perrier was blessed by the presence of a driveway, a luxury often missing in New Orleans's neighborhoods. Hunter pulled in behind Daffy and climbed out of the car, moving in tandem with her. He could almost feel her body brushing against his as he turned and closed his car door at the same moment she closed hers. Yet they stood a car length apart. Puzzled at the intensity of his feelings, Hunter paused for a long moment before he walked toward her and crossed the short sidewalk leading to her front porch.

She waited, unruffled, calm, completely in control. Or was she just really good at pretending? Hunter let his arm brush against hers as they climbed the steps to her porch, but refrained from taking her hand again. He wanted her on edge— hanging over the edge, gasping with need—before he made his move. After that miscalculation with the candy corn, he wasn't risking a second misstep in the same day.

"Tonight was fun," Daffy said, stopping beside one of two oversized rocking chairs near the front door.

She had her key in her hand, but she hadn't reached for the door. Suddenly Hunter got the oddest feeling that she wasn't going to ask him in. After all the signals she'd given off, why put him off now? Why, when he wanted her to ask him in so he could be the one to stride away?

Moving closer, he said, his voice huskier than before, "Tonight isn't over yet."

She was standing so near to him he could feel her breath moving in and out. "No?" As she asked the question, she lifted one hand to his shirtfront.

Dammit, now she could feel just how fast his own heart was beating. He clasped one hand over hers and tipped her chin gently upward. Smiling into her eyes, he said, "Thanks for my best trip to Jazzfest ever."

"But we were hardly there." She curled her fingers a bit more and he could have sworn his heart speeded up just from that gentle gesture. "And we didn't eat. Eating is a big part of Jazzfest."

Hunter cupped a hand behind her head. "Food isn't everything," he said, forcing himself to wait when all he wanted to do was to take her mouth like a starving man—the way he'd been dying to taste her lips all day.

He stroked the back of her head with his thumb. Her eyes had grown even larger; her lips had parted, inviting his touch. "Company is much more important," he said, shifting so only a whisper could pass between their bodies.

She moved in response and he almost swore as a jolt of desire tore through his groin. She wasn't exactly rubbing against him. He couldn't describe Daffy that way. But the merest of pressures of her shorts-clad legs against his had set the blood rushing.

To everywhere except his brain.

Which probably explained why, when she rustled the keys she held in her hand, he nodded and, bodies almost locked together, they moved toward the front door.

Go in and you're doomed.

The voice came from out of nowhere, overpowering any other thought, even his blatant horniness. Spend the night with Daffy and he'd be just like all the other guys she'd used and discarded. *Who cares?* cried his baser instincts.

Hunter stopped her hand in his before she could stick her key into the lock. "Allow me?"

Surprise clear in her expression, Daffy said, "Sure. That's a lovely old-fashioned gesture, but one I appreciate."

He nodded. If she only knew. He slipped the key into the lock, then turned back to face Daffy. Oh, she was hot for him. Her chest rose and fell rapidly and the tight-fitting Lycra of her top did a great job of highlighting the puckered state of her generous nipples. He bit back a groan and leaned forward. Cupping her head again, he held her gaze, then lowered his mouth to hers.

As kisses went, it was brief. Modest, almost. More of an appetizer than a first course.

But it shook Hunter to the core. Her lips had opened, had invited him in. The breathy moan she uttered as he lifted his mouth from hers almost undid him. He loved women who made noise during sex. But more than that, his own reaction to her touch shocked him, as not only desire but an unexpected wave of tender protectiveness hit him.

If he hadn't been planning to leave her there on the porch, he might have turned tail and run anyway. Hunter wasn't ready to be rocked by any woman.

"Wow," Daffy murmured. "This is going to be a beautiful evening."

"Has been." Hunter said, stepping backward one very long pace. "I actually do have to be somewhere else. Go on inside so I know you're safe."

"Excuse me?" She sounded stunned.

Well, he understood that reaction. But now that he'd maneuvered the situation to achieve exactly that response, he sure wished he could just bundle her into his arms, kick the door open, and march inside to her bedroom.

"Gotta go," he said.

She rallied, somewhat slowly. "You did say that. Earlier you said that to your friends from Ponchatoula."

He nodded. "Yep."

She smiled and lifted one hand in a wave. "Don't let me make you late," she said, sounding almost cheerful as she stepped into the entryway of her house.

"Right," Hunter muttered, bounding down the steps, his movements awkward due to the inevitable reaction she aroused in his body. How did she do it to him?

Daffy leaned against the interior of her front door and closed her eyes. Pressing her knees together, she cursed herself for her flush of desire. The touch of his hand on hers had already caused her to thaw even while she tried to fool herself she was only playing at his game of attract and pounce. But that kiss! That kiss not only had melted her thin veil of self-control but had puddled her insides.

She stood there longing for him, yet knowing she'd done the right thing, despite her frustration. Even her panties were damp, and he'd kissed her only once. Lightly she banged her head against her own front door.

She forced her head from the door and straightened up. The evening was yet young. She'd think of some new way to outwit Hunter at his game of driving her crazy.

Oddly enough, she heard an echoing knock to that which she'd made with her head.

Daffy stared at the door. Could it be? Had he been unable to resist and turned right back around?

A smile formed on her face, widening as she considered what she'd say when she opened the door to Hunter.

Make him beg.

Tell him you've got another date.

Don't even answer the door.

The knock sounded again, this time a bit louder. It would be just like Hunter to demand admittance.

Her hand on the doorknob, Daffy remembered her common sense. Never open the door to a stranger. She leaned toward the peephole to verify it was indeed Hunter.

Not Hunter.

Jonni.

Daffy opened the door, happy as always to see her twin. And if Hunter did come back, Jonni would keep her from making a fool of herself over the man. "Hi, sis, this is a nice surprise." It was unusual for Jonni to stop by on a Friday evening.

"I'm sorry to barge in on you like this," Jonni said, following her to the back parlor, Daffy's favorite and most soothing room.

Jonni dropped into an overstuffed chair and said somewhat softly, "I am glad to find you at home."

Home and not in bed with Hunter. Perhaps things worked for the best, Daffy thought wryly. "Me, too. Is something wrong?"

Jonni smiled wanly and said, "I'm not sure anything's wrong, but David's working late and the au pair is with Erika and I was just feeling, oh, you know, lonesome."

"Lonesome?" In the chair next to Jonni's, Daffy kicked off her shoes and tucked her feet under her. Getting a straight story out of Jonni could be tough under the most ordinary of circumstances. Tonight was clearly going to be even more difficult. As close as the two of them were in many ways, each guarded her own privacy in a peculiar but set fashion. For instance, they rarely talked about Jonni's choice of husband. And Jonni's matchmaking was done so subtly—until Hunter.

Hunter she'd shoved right at her. And at the same time they had discussed David. Maybe they were not only growing up but also growing even closer.

Jonni had started playing with her watchband.

Knowing there was more to come of this story, Daffy said gently, "Shall we have some tea while we talk?"

"Yes. No." Jonni sat up straighter and said, "David said he was working late tonight."

Daffy stayed where she was. The tea could wait. She checked the clock on the mantel. Almost eight, which made sense because Jazzfest closed at seven and she and Hunter had slipped out before closing.

"How late?" Many of the lawyers Daffy knew frequently worked till seven or eight or even later. David was no exception as far as she knew.

"How late isn't the point. I called his office to ask him a question. I don't even know what it was now. Probably something like would he rather have asparagus or broccoli for dinner." At that she started crying softly.

Daffy wondered why her sister would even call with that kind of question. She sighed, and reflected that if her life ever took a turn in that direction, she'd run as far as she could the other way. Clearly it was going to take Jonni a long time to get to the point of her crisis. "Sweetie," she said, "do you think David is cheating on you?"

Jonni stared at her in horror. "I did not say that!" She edged back in her chair, as if trying to distance herself from the very idea.

Oops. Daffy knew better than to rush her sister, but she so much preferred getting to the point. "I'm sorry, Jonni."

"Anyway, I called the office and one of the other attorneys answered, which is pretty unusual, but he said that David wasn't there. And when I asked if he was in a meeting or at a deposition, the attorney said he and some of the paralegals had taken off a few hours earlier and gone to Jazzfest." Jonni's voice broke on the last word.

Well, well, well. At least she hadn't run into him. Daffy considered the facts, rather than jumping to conclusions. She was always ready to condemn Jonni's arrogant husband, but in this case, she ought to attempt to be fair. But she smelled a rat.

"I'm sure it was just a spur-of-the-moment

thing," Jonni said. "Someone said you want to go, and he said why not, and pushed the papers and books away for a few hours."

Daffy stared at her sister, knowing her expression was as incredulous as if she'd spotted a cockroach on Jonni's nose. "There's thinking the best of people, Jonni, but there's also facing the facts."

"Well, you don't know the facts and neither do I."

Daffy blinked at the stern note in her twin's voice. Her sister had to suspect her husband, or why else would she have come seeking comfort?

"His going off for a few hours doesn't have to hold the makings of a marital crisis. But he didn't call and tell me, and it's not just that he went with some other people from his office, most of whom I'm sure are female. We're hosting a party for the whole firm tomorrow night and how am I supposed to act, wondering if some of them know something I don't?"

Daffy sighed and wished she knew how to answer her sister. Jonni definitely suspected David of cheating on her but couldn't bring herself to say or even think the words. She had to respect that tenderness and definitely tiptoe around the crux of the matter.

"This is very hard for me to talk about, but things aren't quite the way they usually are between us." Jonni sniffled and dabbed at her eyes with an embroidered handkerchief. Glancing up for a moment, then averting her eyes, she said, "We don't make love as much as we used to."

Daffy didn't know how to respond. How often did a married couple with a toddler underfoot have sex?

"It's been almost two weeks, and now, if what that other attorney said is true, he's gone to Jazzfest without me." Her tears had stopped flowing, and suddenly Jonni sounded fiercely determined. "I don't know what I've done wrong, but I'm going to fix it."

Jonni's assumption of responsibility pushed one button too many. Daffy leapt up and said, "I'll go make that tea."

Walking rapidly from the room, Daffy vowed to discover the truth. Her sister might be willing to hide her head in the sand, but if David were cheating on Jonni, she'd make him sorry he'd ever looked twice at any woman other than her kindhearted, far-too-generous twin.

For starters, she'd get Jonni to invite her to tomorrow night's party. That would also make her legitimately unavailable should the devastatingly sexy Hunter James call to ask her out.

9

Hunter fingered the fine wool fabric of one of the rows of dark suits hanging in the closet of the room he occupied in Aloysius's aunt's house. He hadn't yet had time to find a suitable house, but under his partner's tutelage, he'd found the time to order seven suits.

One for each day of the week, he'd explained to the tailor down on Canal Street. Aloysius had urged him to order at least a dozen, but Hunter wasn't so caught in the grip of sudden-wealth syndrome that he could expend his money quite so extravagantly. Besides, he wasn't all that comfortable in a suit. Give him jeans and a polo shirt any day.

That thought prompted him to toss one of his favorite pairs of faded jeans into the carry-on bag atop his bed. This trip to Vegas was a quick one.

Keynote speaker of the semiannual TekWare convention. Aloysius would be wanting to drag him around the golf course, a torture Hunter had no intention of inflicting on himself. He had to hand it to his partner; if not for Aloysius's initial start-up capital, Hunter would probably be sitting in a cubicle working as a grunt for some other software genius.

But Aloysius had seen the potential in Hunter's designs. And even though they had nothing in common and had circled around each other as suspiciously as a pedigreed poodle and a street mutt on their first encounter, the two of them had become like brothers. A little lopsided at times, their relationship, but all in all, it worked out surprisingly well.

Except for the times Aloysius tried to brush the country dust off Hunter and pass him off as one of his own kind. Hunter always bucked when it came to that. He was proud to be nouveau riche and too smart to pretend he was anything but.

Thinking of pretending brought Daffy squarely to mind. He hadn't intended not to tell her he was going out of town. Yet he hadn't meant to let the information slip.

So what in the hell had he intended?

Thinking of his high state of arousal when he'd stumbled away from her front porch only last night, Hunter knew exactly what he'd wanted—yet he had followed through with his plan. He'd resisted her charms.

Fat good that it did him.

He was set to leave for Las Vegas, to be gone for more than forty-eight hours.

Would Daffodil Landry still be salivating for him when he returned?

Part of him wanted to say yes, of course. Look how hot she'd been after only a few days.

Yet Daffy wasn't just any woman.

She was an equal at the game of seduction.

Hunter frowned and stared at the phone beside his bed. He should call her. Dangle the possibility of a date.

Dangle—hell, ask her to go to Vegas.

He wasn't sure where that thought had come from. But as Hunter folded a second polo and added a second suit—for what reason he knew not, except that it was so richly tailored, and as a youngster he'd never known anyone with two such exceptional suits to his name—he seriously considered the idea.

She'd think it sporting of him. Daring. Sexy.

Insane.

They hadn't even had sex and he was considering asking her to go to Vegas with him?

Hunter stroked the silky wool of the fabric. Why not? To take by surprise and stealth was the plan most favored by strategic generals; guys trying to snag a date should follow that very format.

A smile forming on his face, he reached for the phone. Wouldn't Daffy be surprised?

His fingers outstretched, he pictured Daffy in the limo next to him, arriving at Caesar's Palace in royal style from the airport. As keynote speaker for TekWare, Hunter would be accorded every luxury. He pictured a suite at Caesar's, decadent beyond his wildest dreams. Oh, yes, he should invite Daffy.

He curled his hand around the phone.

It rang.

"May I speak to Hunter James, please?"

Hunter wrinkled his forehead. Funny how Daffy's sister sounded so much like her yet carried such a different energy. "Speaking."

Jonni identified herself, apologized for bothering him—was she bothering him? But of course she was; he was such a busy man. She'd gotten the number from Aloysius; she hoped that was okay.

Hunter held the receiver slightly away from his ear and waited for Daffy's sister to tell him why she was calling him on a Saturday morning. Finally she did.

"It's a cocktail party, mainly lawyers from my husband's firm, but I've asked Daffy to help me out and she said she would. And I was thinking, well, hoping, actually, that you might want to attend also. Though I do apologize for the short notice."

More matchmaking? Hunter smiled, liking that possibility. He didn't know what he'd done to win her favor, but he appreciated her assistance. "When is the party?"

"At seven."

"The date?"

"Um, tonight."

Tonight at seven, Hunter had planned to be rolling dice at a hot craps table. *Had* planned. Past tense.

"Sure," Hunter said. "Happy to help out. Just give me the address, or do you want me to pick Daffy up at her place?"

A silence followed, probably the first breath Jonni had taken during the conversation. So Daffy didn't know the ever-resourceful Jonni was inviting him.

"We're on Octavia, just off St. Charles. It might be best . . ."

"Don't worry, I'll just appear on your doorstep, so woeful to find myself surrounded by nothing but lawyers that Daffy will no doubt have pity on me and take me under her wing."

Jonni laughed and gave him the street address. He memorized it as she launched into a thank-you for the beautiful bouquet he'd sent, and then he managed a fairly quick good-bye, and hung up.

Then he punched in the number of his travel agent.

She was more than happy to switch his full-fare, first-class ticket—courtesy of TekWare—to the red-eye flight. And two seats—not one? But of course.

To pay for the second seat, Hunter rattled off his American Express number.

Money might not buy happiness, Hunter reflected, but it sure could purchase opportunity.

* * *

Her sister sure knew how to throw a party. But then, so did Daffy. It was a skill both of them had learned at their mother's knees. Her mother was much better at teaching flower arranging and napkin folding than she was at expressing affection.

Daffy ducked behind a bushy palm on her sister's rear patio. She'd just spotted one of David's partners she'd made the mistake of dating two too many times.

Suppressing a delicate shudder, Daffy sipped her mineral water topped with a twist of lime and surveyed the gaily chatting couples and trios dotting the terrazzo-floored area between the back of the house and the pool.

It was funny how she could tell which ones were lawyers and which ones were lawyers' wives. The female attorneys looked like men and weighed about twice as much as the butterfly ladies hovering on the arms of their husbands.

Studying the contrasting female styles, Daffy felt a bit like an alien. She didn't fit in with either type, so what did that say about her? Well, tonight was about helping her sister, not about worrying over her own stalemated life.

Familiar with all the movers and shakers of the city, Daffy picked out the firm's three senior partners. At most events of this nature, she'd have a camera in hand, ready to capture the smiles manufactured for the paper. Two of the partners served on some of the most prestigious boards and fund-raisers in the city. The other had a thing for animals and was well known in SPCA circles. Daffy rather preferred the animal lover to the others and attempted to give him more photo coverage whenever possible.

Tonight, however, she carried no protective gear. She was present clearly as a socialite, the sadly single sister-in-law of the firm's junior partner.

As such, she had to be prepared for approaches she'd rather not experience.

She should have brought a date, Daffy reflected as she scowled into her drink in hopes of deflecting a man descending on her.

"Daffodil, how lovely to see you," said the man.

"Thank you," she said, quite unable to remember his name.

"Carroll," he said, "Carroll Dunbar."

"Yes," Daffy said, "I know." Well, perhaps lying at cocktail parties was only a venial sin.

"It's been ages since I've seen you. Where have you been keeping yourself?"

"Working?"

He laughed and leaned too close. Arching his brows, he said, "A lady as pretty as you shouldn't be working herself to the bone."

She smiled. Even an idiot could have seen she was not amused. "I guess it's a good thing I'm not skin and bones, then," she said. "Excuse me, Darroll, I have to help my sister."

"Carroll," he said, sounding far more indignant than Daffy thought he had a right to sound. "That's Carroll."

Daffy swept off, feeling strangely alone in the sea of people.

When she'd asked her sister if David had told her he'd gone to Jazzfest, Jonni had answered in a more roundabout fashion than usual, admitting that he'd said he'd stopped for a beer on the way home.

And no, she hadn't asked him outright. She didn't want to be a nag.

There were at least five women at the party not clinging to someone's arm. She spotted David, drink in hand, speaking earnestly to a clone in a dark suit. At least he wasn't flirting with anyone in his own home.

Oh, yes, they all looked like lawyers and talked so importantly.

Everyone except her.

"Hello, there." A man's rich voice called to her from almost within her mind. It couldn't really be . . .

Hunter.

Hunter? Here? Impossible!

Daffy refused to move with any speed. Negligently, she allowed her neck to swivel oh-so-slowly around and her body to follow. "What a surprise," she said, almost drawling her words, trying to absorb the fact that the only man she wanted to talk to was standing right there on Jonni's terrace. Her sister must have loved those flowers!

Hunter smiled, his eyes bright and yet at the same moment as dark as midnight. "You are a beautiful spot in a jungle of darkness," he said, bending over her hand and capturing it in his. His eyes roving her body, he said, "Now, that's what I call a *dress*."

"You don't think it's too much?" As soon as she said the words, Daffy wanted to bite her lips. She needed Hunter's approval as much as she needed Carroll's attentions. "For a dull and prosaic evening, that is." She added the modifier, hoping to take away from her comment.

Still holding the hand he'd claimed, he rocked back on his heels. Daffy began to burn from above her knees where the form-fitting red cock-tail sheath stopped, up past her belly button, and across her cleavage—much of which the dress exposed to view.

"Beautiful," he said. "Please don't ever dress like everybody else."

She smiled, despite herself. "What brings you here?"

"You," he said, far too promptly for her self-control.

"Don't you mean Jonni?" Daffy couldn't resist teasing him just a bit. "She's the woman over there who looks a lot like me and thinks she can—"

She stopped, this time actually biting her lip. She'd been about to say—*who thinks she can find me the perfect man*. Those were words this egotist did not need to hear.

"Help make you happy?" Hunter murmured the words, awfully close to her right ear. His breath stirred her hair and Daffy wished the rest of the guests far, far away. Then, slowly, she remembered her mission this night was to help her sister, not to lose herself completely the first moment Hunter threw out one of his all-too-hard-to-resist lures.

"I think Jonni just wanted a bit of moral support tonight," Daffy said, quickly adding, "You know, a few guests who have nothing to do with law."

She didn't want to hint at anything else. Jonni had taken her sister into her confidence and it wasn't like Daffy to violate that. But she'd love to know Hunter's take on the scenario. She'd be willing to bet he could tell by looking whether or not a man was walking over the double yellow line.

Hunter grinned. "Well, that's me. The only thing I have to do with lawyers is to pay their bills. And boy, can they bill." He gazed around the room. "Do they ever quit working?"

Daffy shook her head. "I think it's a point of pride with them."

Hunter grimaced. "And to think I've been told I'm a workaholic."

"By whom?"

"Aloy—" Hunter stopped in mid-word.

"That's okay," Daffy said, easing another glass of mineral water off a tray proffered by a circulating waiter. "You can say Aloysius to my face. I won't go ballistic."

"That's good to know."

"I think, now that Aloysius has found the love of his life, he'll be able to put the past behind him." She sighed softly. "We would have made a terrible couple, you know."

"Why is that?" Hunter's voice was low and he was looking at her far too intently for her comfort level.

"Maybe we should circulate," Daffy said.

Hunter put his arm out, blocking her from the rest of the crowd. "Sure. As soon as we play twenty-one."

She stuck her tongue out. "You're awfully bossy."

He answered in kind. "You bring it out in me. What's wrong with Aloysius and you?"

Daffy was surprised he'd asked the question that way. For a man supposedly pursuing *her*, why try to couple her with another guy? She furrowed her brow. Was this some sort of Hunter reverse reasoning? Shooting a glance at him from under her lashes, she said, very sweetly, "He puts ketchup on his eggs."

"That's disgusting!" Hunter made a face, then laughed.

Daffy grinned at him. She'd gotten his mind off her real answer and he realized that. She appreciated a man with wit and perception. Softly, she said, "Aloysius wants the perfect dress-up doll of a wife. And that I will never be."

Hunter toyed with the stem of the glass he'd been holding. "I see."

Daffy waited, but he said no more. In a way,

that pleased her. Hunter and Aloysius might be business partners, but Daffy sensed they had nothing in common when it came to choosing the perfect partner. Aloysius wanted a Mrs. Junior Leaguer Stepford Wife.

But what did Hunter want?

"Would you like to go out after this is over?"

"Hmm?" Daffy was startled out of her reverie by his question, pleasantly so.

"You know, go somewhere else, as in you and me, out and about?"

He'd leaned forward as he asked the question and Daffy swore not two inches separated his face from hers. What was she thinking? She'd spent all her time dwelling on Hunter and not once scoping out the women at the party who might be dwelling too much on Jonni's husband. She muffled a breathy sigh of anticipation, and said, "What did you have in mind?"

"I was thinking of trying Vegas."

Vegas. For someone who covered the social scene, keeping on top of all the nighttime hot spots and new restaurants was second nature to her. But the name didn't ring a bell. "Is that new?"

He grinned. "Compared to New Orleans, I guess it is."

Daffy drew back. "Vegas? As in Las Vegas?"

He nodded. "As in Nevada. Tonight. The red-eye." He tapped his breast pocket. "First class. Only the best."

Daffy started to laugh. "You can't be serious."

"I can't?" He touched her then, the lightest of strokes on her bare upper arm. If he'd suckled her puckered-up nipple, she wouldn't have reacted more strongly. Desire built in her like a wave about to smack the beach, and Daffy said, somewhat breathlessly, "How could I just up and go to Vegas? With you?"

He cupped his chin in his hand and said slowly, "On an airplane?"

"Be serious."

"Oh, I am. And don't worry. We have time before the flight to swing by your place for you to pack."

"You think of everything, don't you?" She was torn between admiration and amazement.

He took her in his arms, his hands on her shoulders, his body closing on hers. "I promise you won't regret it."

Daffy swallowed. She wanted him. Tonight. Last night. Now. No, she wouldn't regret that part. But would she regret this feeling that threatened to take over her reasoning self and push her into his arms? Slowly, she realized they were dancing and he wasn't holding her shoulders but had slipped his arms around her, and they were moving cheek to cheek, as the three-piece string trio Jonni had hired slipped into "Crazy."

She snuggled against him. Dancing didn't mean she was going to Vegas with him. But it did mean she didn't have to talk while her brain whirled through the possibilities.

So much for dancing. She had barely made two

circles around the small dance floor set aside on the rear patio when she felt a tap on her shoulder. Unwilling to let go of Hunter, Daffy pretended to ignore the interruption. Then she realized Hunter had stopped moving.

It was Jonni, standing next to her husband.

"Hey, sis," Daffy said, looking from her twin to her brother-in-law. On the surface, things looked just like always. David dominated; Jonni stood by. But something about the overly bright sparkle in Jonni's eyes hinted to Daffy that all was not as it appeared.

"We wanted to meet the famous Hunter James," David said, practically looking down his nose as he said the words.

Jonni extended a hand and said, "Thanks so much for escorting Daffy."

Daffy bristled. She wasn't some object of pity who had to have an escort arranged for her. She was a hot property—unfortunately, so hot that none of the guys who moved in her circle knew how to handle her. But she quickly picked up on Jonni's statement. Jonni didn't want her husband to know that she'd already met Hunter.

"You're welcome, Mrs. DeVries. Your party is lovely. And, Mr. DeVries, it's nice to meet you. I've heard a lot about you."

"Have you?" David preened, and Daffy was willing to bet he wanted to ask for details.

"My lawyers do a lot of business with your firm." Hunter rattled off the name of another one of the city's old-line law firms. Daffy restrained herself from making a sour face; of course, Hunter, with Aloysius as his partner, would have retained the Carriere family firm.

"We'll leave you two to talk business," Jonni said lightly, drawing Daffy by the hand to the side of the cluster of dancing couples.

"Well?"

Daffy smiled. "He's great."

Jonni sighed. "Oh, Daffy, of course he is. I told you that the other day." Jonni clasped one hand with the other. The magnificent diamond bracelet on her wrist glittered as it caught the light. David had given it to her as an engagement present. "I'm sorry I bothered you with my moodiness last night, but I'm glad you could come to our party. I hope you're not peeved with me for inviting Hunter, too."

Daffy patted her sister's hand. "This is one matchmaking effort I actually appreciate," she said, her gaze resting on Hunter. He smiled at her across the several yards that separated them.

David, however, did not glance their way. Daffy noted his attention seemed pinned on a couple seated on a bench beside the pool. Even as she observed this fact, the man rose from the bench and drifted off. David excused himself from Hunter and headed for the bench. She'd been having such a good time flirting—because surely that was all she'd been doing—with Hunter that she hadn't been investigating the other women at the party.

Hunter headed toward her and when he reached them, Daffy took his hand and placed it in Jonni's. "Dance with the hostess," she said. "There's someone I need to see."

10

Careful to keep out of her brother-in-law's range of vision, Daffy circled toward the bench near the pool. It would be nothing. Her sister's husband was the most rule-oriented man she knew. As guided as he was by convention, he surely wouldn't stray outside his marriage.

Or would he?

Stationed behind a convenient bush, Daffy overheard David say, "Wednesday at two. Nothing will keep me away."

The slender young woman—younger and even slimmer than Jonni—grasped David's hand, then quickly let it go. "I don't know how to thank you," she said.

David rose. With a brief smile, he said, "Words aren't necessary."

Yeah, right, Daffy thought. There were other

ways to spell thank you. As quickly as he'd appeared beside the woman, David moved off. Daffy waited a beat, then edged around the bush. With a friendly smile, she pointed to the space next to the woman and said, "Do you mind if I join you? My feet are killing me!"

The woman nodded but didn't glance up. She was maybe twenty-six, Daffy decided. Simple black dress, no jewelry to speak of, no wedding band. Her blond hair was fashioned into a loose French knot, recalling sharply to Daffy's mind the image of her twin on her wedding day. But after the baby, Jonni had cut her hair. Well, at least David was running true to type. Then she reminded herself not to jump to conclusions.

"I'm Daffy," she said. "I don't believe we've met."

"N-no, I don't think so." Casting a shy glance upward, the woman said, "My name's Nina."

Nina. Daffy filed that away. "Have you worked at the firm long?"

"I'm an intern." Nina straightened and spoke with a bit more confidence. "I'm learning to be a paralegal."

Daffy nodded, indicating she was impressed. An intern. It was just like David to find a young, impressionable woman to mold in his image. He'd been doing that to Jonni since the day they'd met. "So who's your supervisor?"

"David DeVries. He's terrific." Nina couldn't hide the glow in her eyes. For the first time, Daffy began to worry. "I've only been there six weeks and already I've learned more than I did in school. Dav—I mean Mr. DeVries—says paralegal school can't teach the real world. But I'm going to finish anyway, because I'm almost done. Where do you work?"

"Different floor from Mr. DeVries," Daffy ad-libbed. "That's probably why we've never met. So how much longer is your internship?" Translation: when will you be out of my sister's life?

"Only three more weeks," Nina said, her sigh speaking volumes. "But I might have a chance of being hired there when I finish. Mr. DeVries said he'd put in a good word for me with the personnel director."

I just bet he will, too. Daffy forced another friendly smile and said, "It's a great place to work." She leaned closer and, every inch the conspirator, said, "Especially if you like to have a good time." Daffy threw in a wink and then gazed around the patio. "There are some sexy guys at this firm."

Nina blushed and said, "I'm not exactly in the market right now."

"No?"

"I'm actually just going through a divorce."

Daffy didn't like that bit of news at all. "I bet Mr. DeVries has been very supportive."

"He's been super. It must be nice to be married to a man like that." Nina's tone was wistful.

"Ask my sister," Daffy said, sharpening her claws. "She's his wife."

"Oh!" Nina's eyes widened and she clapped a

hand over her mouth. "I didn't mean anything by my comments."

"Of course not," Daffy said, all sweetness. "You were complimenting your boss. Anyone could tell that."

Nina stood up, tugging at the form-fitting skirt of her black dress. She didn't have a spare ounce of flesh on her hips. Give her five years, Daffy thought, then rose. "Good luck with your divorce," she said.

"Thank you," Nina replied.

Daffy moved off. For now, she'd say nothing to Jonni. On Wednesday, she'd follow David to his two o'clock assignation with Nina.

"Hey," Hunter said, his voice low and confident, and also concerned. "Want to tell me what's wrong?"

"Am I that transparent?" Daffy said the words lightly, but as she prided herself on her ability to maintain a poker face, she was surprised Hunter could tell that yes, she was upset.

Hunter flicked a stray hair back from her cheek. "Probably not to anyone else."

"There you go again, overestimating yourself." But she smiled as she teased him.

Putting an arm lightly around her shoulders, he drew her back toward the pool, then past the length of it, to a bench exactly like the one she'd occupied with Nina, only this bench was set at the very back of Jonni's spacious yard. The sounds of the trio found them there, but more gently, joining in an evening chorus with the springtime cicadas and a few birds that had stayed up past their bedtime.

"I haven't known you very long, have I?" Hunter said the words almost as if he were thinking aloud.

"No." Daffy settled beside him, arm brushing arm, thigh skimming thigh.

"So why is it I can read such a range of emotions on your face?"

"If I had to guess," Daffy said, "I'd say you're smarter than the average bear."

Hunter grinned. One of the things he'd noticed about Daffy was how she was able to be serious and yet humorous, all wrapped up in one bright and beautiful package. "I'm smart enough to know a fantastic woman when I meet her." Turning, he tipped her chin up so that he could, even in the dimly lit yard, devour her with his eyes. "I want you to come to Vegas with me, but first I'd like to help with whatever's wrong."

She lowered her lashes. Geez, even those were beautiful, thick, and heavy, like only cover-girl models were supposed to possess. Reluctantly, he let go and dropped his hand. Daffy wasn't a fence to be rushed.

"Isn't Vegas a bit of a jump for a first date?"

"Fourth."

She opened her eyes wide. "How do you calculate that?"

He ticked off on his fingers. "Coffee. Jazzfest. This party. Not to mention we first met at the Orphan's Club fund-raiser."

"Those weren't dates." She tossed her head back as she spoke. One skinny strap of her cocktail dress slipped over her shoulder blade. Hunter eyed it, biding his time. Soon, with any luck, he'd be easing the other strap off her other shoulder. He could picture her, half naked beneath him—

"Well?" She interrupted his mental image.

"Whatever you say," Hunter said, quite uncharacteristically for him. "Then let's make this our first date. I promise you'll never forget this weekend. We'll leave tonight and be back by Monday morning."

Daffy pursed her lips. He could tell she was tempted.

"No pressure," he said softly.

"What do you mean?"

"You say the word and I'll get separate rooms. We'll dance, we'll stay out all night, we'll gamble, see some shows. Have fun getting to know each other." So help him, Hunter slipped one hand behind his back and crossed his fingers.

Daffy grinned and leaned around him before he knew what she was doing. Tapping on his crossed fingers, she said, "You are hard to resist."

He placed a kiss on the top of her head. "I hope so. Now, do you want to tell me why you're sad?"

"Not sad exactly," Daffy said. She cupped her chin in her hand. "It's complicated and involves my sister, and I can't share her secrets, but I'm left wondering what the meaning of loyalty is and whether fidelity exists. I mean, is it an impossible thing to maintain happy and satisfied monogamy?"

"I hope not," Hunter said, his own intensity surprising him. For a guy who'd been quite the playboy, he still held out the ideal. He just hadn't figured out how to attain it.

Daffy nodded. "Me, too," she said, and the wistful note in her voice tugged at Hunter's gut. After all the horror stories he'd heard about her from Aloysius, it seemed incongruous that she was searching for the same ideal that he sought. But perhaps she'd put all that craziness behind her.

"Anyway," Daffy said, much more briskly, "this is a party, not a wake. If we're doing this crazy thing, what time do we leave?"

"If?" Hunter let the query hang in the air. Behind them, a bird trilled.

He didn't want her hesitant; he wanted her wholeheartedly with him.

Daffy watched him watching her, rather like an attentive cat beneath its favorite bird's nest. Was it safe to say yes to Hunter James?

Safe for whom? Daffy was the one who always hurt the guy. What would happen if this man got under her skin and then turned the tables on her?

So stay home and be safe. Stay home and write another column of advice to lovers, she mocked herself. Write about what you're afraid to experience. Fix everyone else's love life and leave your own in limbo.

She gazed across the pool. Jonni stood side by

side with David. Nina and a man Daffy didn't recognize stood next to them. The four were chatting amiably. Let go, she told herself. Don't use your worries about your sister's life as an excuse to avoid living your own.

Turning to Hunter, she held out her hand. "Count me in," she said.

He grinned like a guy who'd just won the Powerball.

Daffy rose. "Just remember, my going on this wild date with you in no way indicates you've won your bet."

"Oh, that!" Hunter stood with a lazy grace and, smiling down at her, said, "Forgive me that boast?"

"After the month has passed." Daffy wasn't letting down her guard—not all the way. Hunter was pure charm, but she needed to protect her interests here. He was used to wooing and winning any woman he wanted. No doubt all she represented was one more notch on his belt.

"And what a month it will be," he murmured.

"I need to talk to my sister before I can leave," Daffy said.

"Shall I make myself scarce?"

"Yes. No." Oddly enough, he made her feel safe, standing close and warm beside her.

"Dare I ask if that's your final answer?"

Daffy groaned. "Not that worn-out line!" She held out her hand and he accepted it. She clasped it gratefully. Two calluses on his palm rubbed against her skin. A guy's hand. Daffy liked that.

They threaded their way back into the midst of the party. Nina, Daffy noted, remained talking with Jonni and David, but the other man had moved off. Perfect. Picking up her stride, she practically swooped down on the threesome, Hunter in tow.

One test of David's innocence wouldn't hurt.

"Sis," she said gaily, "I've been looking for you. And David, too, of course." Then she paused and said to Nina, "Didn't we just meet by the pool?"

Nina nodded. Daffy could have sworn David glanced sharply at the sweet-faced intern.

"Hunter and I are going out on the town," Daffy continued. "Yesterday we went to Jazzfest together. Skipped out on a Friday afternoon. Can you imagine?" Jonni was looking at her as if she'd gone nuts. Daffy knew she was rattling on like one of those airheads Hunter detested, but she had her purpose.

Hunter tightened his grasp on her hand and smiled down at her. Catching on somehow, he said, "Best time to go is when almost everyone else is at work."

"David wouldn't know about that, would you?" Daffy watched carefully. If he had gone yesterday, now would be the perfect time to fess up. All he had to say was, actually, I got a hair up my butt and did the same thing yesterday.

Nina parted her lips. Before she could speak, David said, "Well, that's very well for you freewheeling types but us hardworking lawyers have to bill, bill, bill."

Nina had cast her eyes toward the floor. Daffy's heart sank. Well, she wasn't going to ruin her sister's evening. She'd do some more investigating on her own, then report. But if the skunk was cheating on Jonni, she'd find a way to make him pay.

Jonni was smiling now, happy with her husband's response, believing David over whoever had answered the phone at the office the evening before. Daffy said, much more slowly and in her own normal voice, "I'll call you Monday, Jonni. Thanks for inviting us."

Her sister gave her a hug, and then bestowed one on Hunter, too. "You two have fun," she said, slipping her hand around David's elbow.

Daffy was pleased to hear Nina joining in with her own good-byes. Good-bye and good riddance, Daffy added.

By the time their plane landed in Las Vegas, Daffy felt very much like Cinderella at her own private ball. Only it was way past midnight and there was no clock poised to strike the hour.

A waiting limousine driver collected them and shepherded them through the gleaming airport's maze of casino displays, slot machines, and advertisements for the hottest shows on the Strip. To her surprise, Daffy had fallen asleep early during the flight and Hunter said he'd done the same.

"Which is a good thing," he said, handing her into the sleek car and sliding in next to her, "because it's a shame to waste time sleeping in Vegas."

Then he smiled and pointed to a bottle of champagne in an ice bucket. "Toast to our fourth date?"

Alive with anticipation, Daffy nodded. The limo moved smoothly into traffic as Hunter popped the cork and filled the two waiting glasses. She almost pinched herself to make sure she wasn't dreaming. What a dream date!

She accepted a glass from Hunter. His knee brushed hers as he settled the bottle back into the ice bucket, then turned to face her. The dim interior of the plush car, lit only by discreetly placed lights along the carpeted floor, added to the intimacy of the moment.

Hunter watched her watching him. He lifted his glass to hers and murmured, "Thanks for coming with me."

"Thanks for asking me," she replied, meaning it. "Though I thought you were kidding when you first mentioned it."

He smiled. "Naturally. But there are some things I never joke about."

"Oh?"

He nodded. "To the serious things in life: you and me."

Daffy clinked her glass against his, but his comment made her nervous. "I thought we were here to have fun," she said, trying for a light note before sipping her champagne.

"Fun is also one of the things I never joke about." Hunter sat back against the cushions, one arm draped along the back of the seat above Daffy's shoulders. Again he did that not-quite-touching trick that drove her wild with anticipation for the moment he would touch her.

She tipped her head slightly and teased his hand with her hair.

"So when's the last time you were in Vegas?" Hunter asked, toying with the tips of her hair.

"Well . . ." Daffy took another sip. For someone as sophisticated as she was, she hated to admit there was a destination she'd never visited.

"Don't tell me you've never been to Vegas!" Hunter looked shocked.

"Okay."

"I thought everyone had been here at one time or another." He took a drink and studied her like a scientist who'd just discovered a new species.

"Not me."

"I bet you travel a lot, though."

"Oh, yes. I love seeing new places, new countries, new people." Here was sure territory. Daffy had spent her junior year abroad in Paris, and every year in high school, her parents had taken her and Jonni to some foreign locale for summer vacation. "What's your favorite country?"

"America," Hunter answered promptly.

Suddenly Daffy realized she'd stepped into

conversational quicksand. Not everyone had grown up the way she had. "You don't travel much?"

He shook his head. "Not in the past, but now things are different."

"You mean because of the success of your company?"

Hunter shifted forward. Tipping his glass toward Daffy, he let his voice drift lower. He'd had enough of chitchat and he didn't want any more reminders of the differences between his past and the pampered youth of the elegant and desirable woman sitting beside him in this limousine, sent courtesy of TekWare. "I mean," he said, letting his fingers explore the soft skin at her nape, "now that I've met the dream travel companion, I think I'll be seeing a lot more of the world."

Her lips had parted slightly and her eyes were even larger and darker and more alluring than usual. God, he wanted her. But could he win her over? For all the signs of desire she exhibited, she played a rather devious game of kiss and catch. Should he kiss her? He could almost taste her lips. Nah. One thing he'd bet more than a C-note on was that Daffodil Landry needed to be worked way up and over before she let go of her mind so that the passion pooled within her could come rushing out.

Hunter sat back against the cushions. "For starters," he said, pointing out the window of the limo, "let me show you Las Vegas."

Daffy seemed to wriggle and suppress a sigh before she answered with, "Great. What's first on the agenda?"

Hunter hid his grin by once again glancing out the window. The lights of the Strip were beaming full force on them as the car traveled toward the boulevard of neon, cash, credit, and dreams come true and dreams gone bust. He had to hand it to Daffy. She recovered quickly. She could go from panting to sounding all business in the blink of an eye. He'd never met a woman who could parry his thrusts quite so well.

That phrase grabbed his mind and he pictured her beneath him, passionate, driving him wilder than wild, sucking him in, deeper, deeper, deeper . . .

"Hunter?"

"What?"

"So what's our first stop?" She was running her tongue over the lip of the champagne glass and Hunter had the silliest sensation that she had read his mind.

"Dance?" They were stopped at the light by Mandalay Bay, site of a hot dance club. "At one A.M., this place is just starting to rock."

"I'm up for anything," Daffy said, brushing his thigh with her hand as she leaned over to glance out the window.

Hunter bit back a groan. Daffy had set off a whole new slow burn in him with that touch. To be too needy would be a strategic error. The last thing he wanted to do was take her to bed too soon.

Dancing would be good. Maybe it would burn off some of the fire threatening to make him forget all about taking it slow with Daffodil Landry.

11

Dancing achieved exactly the opposite effect. By the time Hunter made it to the suite reserved by TekWare at Caesar's Palace, he felt like a high school dweeb on his first date.

Daffy moved with the speed of sound waves carried over space and time. Her body flowed and levitated and wound around him, teasing him with every caressing movement. Her dress slipped off one shoulder and he soaked up the sight of the sexiest bare shoulder he'd ever seen until he wanted to stop the music and pull the other skimpy strap off and take her there on the floor under the throbbing lights and heat with the marimba band pounding in a crescendo that matched and beat and carried till their climax overtook all other sensations.

Get a grip, James, he ordered himself as he

opened the door to their suite. You're Mr. Cool, just out for a good time. That doesn't mean you have to lose your mind over the babe. He handed her the second key and pushed open the door. "After you, my dear," he said.

Her eyes widened and she slipped past him, her body brushing the front of his. As with their dancing, the touch appeared to serve as a hint of things to come. But was it an invitation, or was Daffy playing her own game of Bet You Can't Catch Me? TekWare had reserved a two-bedroom suite for its keynote speaker, and Hunter had made sure Daffy knew she had her own room if she wanted it.

As if he didn't expect to have sex. Well, a guy didn't need a bedroom for that.

Daffy paused inside the door and glanced back at him. "Coming?"

Oh, yeah. He nodded and stepped into the foyer. "Nice digs," he said.

"Nice?" Daffy danced forward into the large sitting room. "It's lovely. And so spacious." She cocked her head and glanced around, probably counting the doors that led discreetly from the center room. One to the right, one to the left, plus the door to the mini-bath off the foyer.

"I'm glad you like it." And he was. For someone who was used to the best from birth, and the world traveler that she was, Daffy might easily have sniffed at the nouveau-Vegas accommodations. Hunter didn't know much about furniture, but he doubted that the overstuffed sofas and side chairs and marble-topped tables and crystal lamps dated back much earlier than Y2K.

"And look at the view!" Daffy knew she was chattering, but she couldn't stop the flow of words. She wanted to ask what came next, but she was both too nervous and too savvy to utter those words. So she kept up the river of talk, one part of her wishing he would take her in his arms and dam the flow with his mouth.

His mouth. Those full, warm lips that curved upward, welcoming everything the world had to offer. Her own mouth watered as she watched him move toward her, slide one arm around her shoulders, and guide them across the room to the floor-to-ceiling windows.

"Do the lights stay on all night?" All too aware of his arm around her, Daffy pointed at the neon rainbow arching across what should have been nighttime darkness.

Hunter shifted his left arm enough to reveal his wristwatch. More than the incredibly late hour of 4:15 A.M., what stood out was the simplicity of the watch. Maybe he'd worn it before, but she hadn't noticed. It looked like an ancient Timex.

"Since it's after four," Hunter said, "I guess you might say they stay on all night." He must have seen her staring at his watch, because he added, "What? You expected something a bit more upscale?"

Embarrassed, Daffy shook her head, then admitted, "Well, yes."

He laughed and pulled her closer. "That's one of the things I like about you. You're so honest."

All of a sudden they weren't side by side, but rather face-to-face, hip to hip. His hands traced circles on her shoulders and, scarcely breathing, Daffy tilted her head to meet his kiss.

Cupping the back of her head, he gazed into her eyes until she thought she'd drown in the depths of his midnight eyes. He traced the line of her mouth with the back of his thumb and said, "I haven't always been rich, Daffy, but I have always known what I like in a woman."

Her heart skipped and she knew her lips parted of their own accord. She forgot she'd vowed to toy with him, to tease him, to drive him wild as he plotted to prove he could win her heart within the month. A slow curl of heat low in her body sparked and her legs quivered in anticipation.

The kiss was everything she knew it would be. Gentle, assessing, tasting. When she moaned with desire, he responded by exploring her mouth even more thoroughly. Clearly he was far too masterful a lover to cede to her own desperate need and speed the quenching of the sexual flames he ignited in her.

"We have all night long," he murmured after she lifted her hands to the back of his neck and tried to return his kiss with the heat she could no longer control.

Now his hands were on the sides of her face, drawing her to him as he tasted her mouth. Daffy knew she moaned, but she had moved past caring about her pride. He was driving her beyond sanity.

He knew it, too. He chuckled softly, then suddenly switched tempo and took her mouth and her tongue with all the force she'd been craving. She gasped and answered him in kind, dragging her fingers through his hair as her tongue mated and danced with his.

They fell onto the closest sofa, Hunter on top of her but somehow managing not to crush her. Not that she would have noticed. Her entire world had become the touch and feel and heat of their bodies. He was taking all of her mouth, his kisses seeking, knowing, possessive.

And suddenly he stopped. Daffy gasped for air, one fingertip to her swollen lips. Her panties were damp through. Her lipstick and mascara streaked Hunter's collar.

And then he smiled, his look every inch the predator who has claimed his prey. "You are incredible," he said in a low, roughened voice. He was straddling her on the sofa, one knee between her dress, which Daffy realized had scooted up around her hips, revealing a lacy garter and the tops of her stockings.

She didn't trust her voice. She nodded, licked her lips, and said, "You, too." What she wanted to say was, "Don't stop!"

Did she?

Hunter lowered his head toward her, but this

time he only skimmed a touch of his mouth over hers before he took the side of her neck in a possessive kiss.

Daffy cried out.

He stopped at once. "Too rough?"

"Oh, no. Too good." Then she blushed.

"No such thing," Hunter said, placing a kiss on her right shoulder, then one on her left. Half sitting, he shrugged out of his jacket and tossed it onto the floor. He reached backward and slipped free the one heel Daffy still wore, then kicked his own shoes off.

All the while she lay there watching him, her breasts rising and falling with shallow pants, her nipples puckering and straining to break through the silky fabric, proclaiming just how much she wanted this man.

"Now," Hunter said, easing down beside her, "we can make some progress."

As close as he lay, Daffy could tell from his heated erection that more progress wasn't what was called for. They needed release; they needed satisfaction. Adopting a slightly naughty smile, she folded her hand around his manhood and said, "I adore progress."

Hunter growled and moved against her hand. "Hey, who's in charge here?"

She grinned. "We haven't known each other all that long, but somehow I think the answer has to be 'Both of us.' "

He laughed and before Daffy knew that he'd moved, he buried the sound against her breasts.

Her dress wasn't much more than a slip with straps and even through the fabric, her nipples danced against his touch, leaping in response.

He shifted and her hand dropped from his body. Fine, Daffy thought dreamily, for now I'll just let him have his way with me.

His face buried in her breasts, Hunter said a prayer of thanks as Daffy's warm fingers slipped free of his overheated erection. So much for being in control—her touch had almost pushed him over the edge. And there was too much pleasure he wanted to experience—and to share with Daffy—before he lost his grip on things.

Easing upward, he soaked in the sight of Daffy lost to the ecstasy he was creating in her. Her eyes were half closed, her head thrown back on the couch cushions in a way that had her hair spread out like a golden halo. He shook his head slightly as that thought chased across his mind. Silly, Hunter. She was no angel—just one hot babe, ripe for the plucking.

The top of her dress had fallen halfway off. He worked it lower, revealing even more of her lush breasts mounding above a scrap of lace she called a bra.

He made a noise low in his throat. He had to have this woman.

She wriggled beneath him, lifting her hips and nudging his groin as she moved. Hunter captured her wrists and pushed them over her head. Her eyes opened fully and her mouth rounded in a delectable "O" of surprise.

"You're mine," he said, "all mine."

Daffy ran her tongue over her lower lip, no doubt still tasting him. He accepted the invitation to remind her again of his lips and, still holding her hands captive, plundered her mouth. She answered him as savagely as he claimed her, and Hunter knew he was the one who'd become a prisoner.

He broke free of the kiss and lowered his mouth to her breasts. Working first one nipple, then the other, he reveled in the way she arched her back and whimpered for him to take pity on her and give her the satisfaction she craved. Oh, she didn't actually say those words, but he heard the request in the breathy moans that escaped her lips and the way her hips kept rising to meet his, in the way she'd thrown her head even farther back to offer her breasts completely to his demanding touch.

Unable to hold off, Hunter reached for his belt buckle with his free hand.

He had it halfway loosened when Daffy whispered, "Please, hurry, Hunter. I can't wait anymore."

Hunter smiled. Stilling his hand and forcing himself to count silently to ten, he said, "Not even just a little bit more?"

"No!" Then she laughed, but the sound was more ragged desire than humor.

Hunter let go of his belt buckle and trailed his hand along the inside of one thigh. She quivered at his touch and he wondered whether he could hold out himself. The idea of Daffodil Landry begging him to impale himself in her pleased him to no end, but this was a dangerous game he was playing. His own control might not outlast the sweet torture with which he wanted to torment her.

His fingers reached the top of her stocking. "I didn't know women wore these anymore," he murmured, fingering the garter where it engaged the top of her hose.

"Undo it and I won't be wearing it either," Daffy said, then blushed. "Now that's ladylike reticence, isn't it?"

Again he smiled. He realized he'd smiled more since they'd arrived in Vegas than he could remember doing of late. "Most ladylike," he said, leaving the stocking in place and easing aside the scrap of satin that she called a pantie.

Daffy gasped and rocked against him. He'd loosened his hold on her hands and she bolted up to catch him by the shoulders. "Hunter!"

"Yes, Daffy?" Even as he eased one finger inside her, he lowered her back to the cushions, this time keeping a firmer grip on her wrists with his other hand. She was his, but she needed to be at his mercy. He didn't know how he knew that, but somehow he did. Daffodil Landry was a woman used to being in charge, and taking that command away from her would only heighten her passion.

She was wet. She practically sucked his finger inward. Hunter withdrew his finger just to watch the look of need on her face, then slowly claimed her again, opening and teasing her with his exploration while he leaned forward and kissed the back of her arm raised above her head.

She moaned and her breath came more quickly. He tasted the lobe of her ear and circled her clit with his finger. He flicked his tongue inside her ear even as he palmed her. Oh, yeah, she was his.

Daffy couldn't remember when she'd last taken a breath. Hunter had consumed her body and her passion-drugged senses now ruled her mind. She rocked against his hand as he palmed her, one finger leading her to climax like a conductor's baton urging on an orchestra.

She strained to reach for his belt, free him from his zipper, and encase him in her panting warmth. But any movement on her part was met with another kiss—this time on her wrists, then on her palms, then skipping up her arm to the rounded top of her shoulder.

"You're mine," he whispered. "Let me guide your pleasure."

Her answer was another breathy moan as her climax built. Through her hazy vision, she noted his satisfied expression. Too, too late, she realized he had triumphed. But as his clever finger found the center of her desire and another wave of pleasure uncurled within her, Daffy forgot all about not letting Hunter win a victory over her.

She arched against his hand. He covered her mouth with his. Between kisses, he led her upward, his words wrapping around her while his body claimed possession of her. "Give it to me, Daffy," he said. "Let me take you where you want to go."

A pounding began, louder even than the blood beating in her ears as it matched the rhythm pulsing within her feminine core. She was sensation, she was sex itself, she was putty under Hunter's touch. Daffy cried out as she pulsed against Hunter's hand. He let go of her wrists and she clasped him around the neck, shuddering and laughing from the joyous sensations he'd created.

"That's my girl," Hunter said, holding her close.

She wrapped her legs around him and tugged at his belt buckle. "You're not even naked and look what you did to me."

He grinned. "Just wait for Act Two."

The pounding grew louder.

Someone was at their door.

One hand on his zipper, Hunter called out, "Go away!"

Instead of obeying, the intruder wanna be grew even more obnoxious. Through the hazy afterglow of her orgasm, Daffy heard Hunter's name called out, in a none-too-sober male voice raised high enough to wake the dead.

"Let me in, Hunter. Brought you a present!"

"Shit!"

Daffy almost echoed Hunter's expletive as the man yelled again, and this time she recognized the voice. Aloysius's.

Hunter smoothed his thumb over her cheek.

"Let me get rid of him," he said, easing his body off her. "Then we can get back to the business of pleasure."

Daffy nodded. Without Hunter's touch, she felt incredibly abandoned. Vulnerable, too. As Hunter straightened his clothing—an impossible task, given his arousal—she glanced at her disheveled dress, her legs spread wide, her breasts open to Hunter's hungry gaze.

Shyness battled with satiation. She should blush, but with the languid warmth he'd released in her, she could scarcely move to cover herself.

"Don't budge," Hunter said in a commanding voice, kneeling beside her. "Please?"

She smiled and nodded, touched by the raw edge of desire in his entreaty. She had the mighty Hunter James eating out of her hand.

He headed toward the door, calling, "Pipe down. I'm coming."

Daffy smiled at his word choice. Absent the pesky Aloysius, his words would be true. What an amazing lover. Daffy took in again her dress hiked above her garters, her panties pushed aside to reveal her damp and still gently throbbing inner lips. She rubbed her thighs together. No wonder he'd bragged—

Bragged. Daffy sat up and listened to the voices drifting in from the doorway. The men appeared to be arguing, a condition natural to both of them.

The word "bragged" buzzed in her mind and Daffy frowned. He'd opened her as easily as the full afternoon sun spread the petals of her favorite pink roses. Why, she'd been ready to rip his pants off him and beg him to bury his shaft deep inside her. No holding back for Daffodil Landry tonight.

What had happened to her resolve not to become involved with another man until she'd figured out why she always sabotaged her relationships? And become involved with Hunter she knew she would. The two of them had answered needs and desires in the other in a way Daffy had never experienced. She had felt it and would bet her fortune he had, too.

"That resolve went right out the window," she muttered, pulling her dress back over her breasts and tugging the skirt down over her thighs.

Perhaps Aloysius had done her a favor with his untimely interruption.

Rather than disappearing, Aloysius's voice grew louder. Suddenly Daffy realized he was making his way into the suite. Thank goodness she'd rearranged her clothing! She wished she could leap under the sofa, but there was not enough room to hide.

Hunter was grabbing at his business partner's arm. He glanced over and Daffy met his gaze. When he saw she'd redressed herself, he let go of Aloysius.

Daffy stared at the man she'd once been engaged to marry. He was as suavely dressed as always, and only the tiny skewing of his bow tie and a hint of sway in his walk revealed his inebriation. But Daffy knew better than to assume that meant Aloysius wasn't pretty far gone. He could be functioning one moment and passed out the next. He strolled into the room and looked around. He hadn't quite focused, for which Daffy could only be thankful.

But it wasn't so much the tipsy Aloysius who held her attention, but the two females who accompanied him, walking behind him like backup singers in a bad stage production.

The two strolled arm in arm, dressed in matching black leather strapless mini-dresses. Knee boots with spike heels sheathed their legs. One was a redhead, the other a blonde, but those colors weren't created by Mother Nature. Daffy stared, her mouth actually falling open. The women had to be . . . hookers.

"What's the matter, chickie, you've never met a working woman before?" The redhead spoke, delivering a broad wink to Hunter as she did. Letting go of her compatriot, she sashayed over to Aloysius and rode up and down the front of his body in a move designed to titillate, and no doubt to increase her tip.

Aloysius cupped her rear and ground against her. The other woman, apparently not to be undone, advanced on Hunter.

Daffy leapt up from the sofa and placed herself between Hunter and the blonde.

"A three-way costs extra," the blonde said somewhat apologetically, her eyes roving Daffy's body in a way that made the back of Daffy's neck prickle.

"Aloysius!" Hunter's voice got through.

"Yes?"

"Get rid of them."

"But I told you I brought you a present." He pouted and pulled the redhead off him.

"Thanks, but I'm doing okay all on my own."

Aloysius suddenly seemed to realize another woman stood beside Hunter. He blinked and leaned forward, and then an expression of horror hit his face. "Oh, no, you didn't bring *her* to Las Vegas!"

"Hello, Aloysius," Daffy said. "I gather Chrissie didn't make the trip with you?"

"Chrissie?" Aloysius puckered his brow. The redhead put her hand on his crotch.

"Your fiancée." Daffy smiled sweetly at the redhead as she said the word, but apparently the woman didn't register the term or it made no difference to her.

"It's just a job," the blonde said in a low voice. "We get a lot of engaged guys. You know, last fling and all that."

"No, I didn't know." Daffy realized she shouldn't cast stones at Aloysius; goodness only knew she'd treated him terribly. But the image of him with two prostitutes was more than she could stand. "Aloysius, you love Chrissie."

"Oh, yes, I love Chrissie." Slowly, Aloysius turned his head and stared at the redhead. "But you're not Chrissie."

The blonde had wandered over to the mini-bar. She helped herself to a bottle of champagne, working the cork free with an explosive bang just as Aloysius swayed and crumpled toward the floor.

Hunter leapt and caught him before he hit the carpet. Dragging him to the sofa opposite the one where Daffy and he had lain together, Hunter deposited him, none too gently. "Okay, girls, the party's over."

The blonde waved her champagne bottle. "I thought it was just getting started."

The redhead shrugged. "He passed out before he paid. You going to cover him?"

"You think I'm some country boy who doesn't know how things work in the big, bad city?" Hunter put an arm around the redhead and another around the blonde. "I'm sure my pal paid in advance, with his credit card. And now that you've got a couple hours free, you can go earn double. There's a big convention in town, or hadn't you heard? Bunch of computer geeks, probably can't get a girl without paying."

The redhead perked up. "Great. Where do you think most of them are staying?"

Daffy wasn't sure she heard him right, but she thought Hunter said as he hustled them out the door, "Motel Six."

Something told her there was a story behind that answer, but it was a story she'd discover another night. Aloysius began to snore and Hunter, returning to the sitting room, chucked a pillow at him.

The idea of Chrissie home alone while Aloysius

partied in Vegas burned in Daffy's mind. Add to that her ex-fiancée slumbering on the sofa and the hauntings of her own past mistakes and her fears of what she still remained capable of, and Daffy knew she was destined to sleep alone that night.

Hunter looked every inch as sexy as he had before the untimely interruption, but she knew she wasn't up for Act Two.

"Like you told them," Daffy said, smothering a yawn and feeling slightly guilty, considering the pleasure he'd given her, but knowing now wasn't the right time for more intimacy, "the party's over."

12

The party's over.

Even though her hair was still tousled and her lips deliciously puffy from their wild kisses, Daffy had edged away from him. Aloysius snored away on the sofa that stood between the two of them, and she kept her gaze carefully averted from that sight.

He didn't blame her one bit. He moved a step or two closer to her, turning so their backs were to the occupied couch. "I wish I could have shielded you from that scene," he said softly.

A glimmer of light returned to her eyes. "Thanks," she said, "but I'm a big girl."

He put an arm around her and hugged her. "Maybe, but I'm bigger and I should have slammed the door in his face."

"Why didn't you?" She sounded merely curious, not at all judgmental.

"Do you have any idea what terrible snoops the members of the press are?"

"I have a pretty good idea." She grinned at him.

Hunter laughed. "Guess I walked into that one. You don't seem like the reporters who call themselves journalists and don't know the difference between a story fit for *The National Enquirer* and one for the Money section."

"And if someone had discovered Aloysius drunk and with two prostitutes outside your hotel room door, it could have affected your company?"

Hunter shrugged. "It's not something I want to risk. We're in pretty sensitive talks right now with another business run by some fairly conservative types."

"Then why . . ." Her voice trailed off and she blushed.

"Why invite you to Las Vegas with me?" Hunter pulled her closer and kissed the top of her head. "Temporary sanity?"

"Don't you mean insanity?" She curled against his chest and murmured the question somewhere below his chin.

"You are a world away from my loony partner dancing around with two ladies of the night, and I hope you know it."

"I hope I am," she said even more softly.

Daffy was falling asleep standing up in his embrace. Small wonder. They'd been up most of the night and Hunter had to deliver a speech in less than three hours.

It took more resolve than Hunter thought he possessed, but he said, "I think it's bedtime and I mean time for sleep."

She tucked her face more snugly against his chest. "Whatever you say."

He wished he had a tape recorder for that comment. Smiling, he led her to the smaller bedroom, where he'd had the limo driver have her bag delivered. The "master bedroom" of the suite was one he was saving to introduce to Daffy later—when they were both wide awake and able to appreciate its sensual amenities.

From the chaise where he'd seated her, Daffy watched Hunter move about the bedroom. The bed had been turned back earlier by the hotel staff, but he plumped the pillows and turned off all the lights but one bedside lamp.

She hadn't intended to relax into his arms. Not after Aloysius's arrival had so abruptly reminded her of the dangers of trusting another and the difficult task of becoming a person worthy of trust. But Hunter had been so sweet. If he'd tried to resume where they'd left off, she would have retreated into the room and slammed the door.

But Hunter was a master of strategy.

"There," he said with a note of satisfaction in his voice, "everything's ready. If you'd like to come with me to the convention, I'll set the alarm."

He looked at her with expectant eyes, almost

like a little boy waiting to hear if he would really get a puppy for Christmas.

Darn it, but he was hard to resist.

"Of course I'm going to the convention," Daffy said, rising from the chaise. "I may have to take a nap later, but I wouldn't miss your speech for the world."

"Thank you," Hunter said. "And thanks for coming to Vegas with me."

He paused in front of her, so close she felt more than saw his chest rise and fall. His eyes were dark and wide and he watched her like a hungry hawk. Despite his restraint, he definitely wanted to take up where they'd left off.

Daffy felt her exhaustion fade as her pulse picked up its pace. She was one second away from pulling him down to the bed with her when she noticed the dark shadows under his eyes. He must be worn out—and he had to deliver a keynote address in less than three hours.

"Thanks for asking me," she said softly. Then she kissed him lightly on the mouth and said, "Now go get some sleep."

He backed out of the room, his gaze never leaving her face. Daffy wondered what effort it cost him to exit the room, cross the suite, and go to sleep alone. She, after all, had found explosive release from the sexual volcano the two of them had created.

Hunter had not.

But in the immortal words of Margaret Mitchell's Scarlett, "Tomorrow is another day."

As she slipped into bed, Daffy couldn't help but smile as she anticipated the unfinished business that remained between her and Hunter.

Backing out of that room cost Hunter about all the self-control he possessed. He pulled shut the door blocking Daffy from him with a gentle click.

The kick he delivered to the sofa where Aloysius slumbered was anything but gentle.

And the dope didn't even skip a beat of his raspy snoring.

"So much for the upper class," Hunter muttered and took himself off to a bed that was far too big and empty for one person.

Morning found him much less grumpy. He jumped up in plenty of time to roust Aloysius and pack him off to his own room for a reviving shower. The bum didn't even remember he'd blundered in with a hooker on each arm.

Hunter raced back to the suite, practically colliding with a silver-haired room-service waiter knocking on the door.

The door swung open. Daffy, dressed in a pale yellow sheath and looking fresher than her floral namesake, waved the waiter in.

Hunter clapped a hand over his stubbly chin. He was a weed next to a flower.

"Good morning," she said, way too cheerful for someone who'd caught only twenty winks. "I ordered a light breakfast."

"Great," Hunter muttered. He should have thought of that himself. Before his first cup of coffee, though, his brain didn't function on all cylinders.

The waiter busied himself at one of the tables in the sitting room.

Hunter stood rooted in the doorway.

Daffy took a step nearer. Concern in her voice, she said, "I hope you don't mind."

He must have been scowling without realizing it. "Of course not. You were an angel to think of it. It's just . . ."

"Just what?"

One hand still on his chin, Hunter drank in the sight of Daffodil Landry. Her hair gleamed; her eyes were bright, with not a hint of the long night behind them, her makeup was so minimal he couldn't say for sure she had any on, but somehow he knew she did. The dress hinted at her luscious figure without flaunting it and flowed to just above her knees. Hunter finished his appreciative inspection, down to her feet—which were, he noted with a smile—bare.

"Hunter, what is it?" Patience was definitely not in Daffy's repertoire.

In a voice low enough to shield their conversation from the waiter, Hunter dropped his hand from his own wreck of a face and said, "Are you always this beautiful first thing in the morning?"

She blushed lightly, which charmed him. "I suppose I should say yes, but then"—Daffy winked—"you might find out otherwise."

The idea of spending enough nights together in order to conduct a scientifically sound sampling appealed to Hunter. Too bad they were flying back to New Orleans later that evening for a meeting he had to attend first thing the next morning.

The waiter cleared his throat loudly enough to prevent Hunter from checking to see if Daffy tasted as good as she looked.

She turned around and took the room-service check to sign. Hunter watched for a long moment; then, as his mind moved from sex to money, he said, "Hey, I'll take care of that."

But, of course, he didn't have any bills on him for a tip. He wore only the pair of shorts and T-shirt he'd thrown on before getting rid of Aloysius.

Daffy had the tip in hand. "That's okay," she said. "I've got it."

The grandfatherly waiter glanced from one to the other and smiled. "You two remind me of me and the missus when we were first married. I wish you a happy life together."

Hunter swept Daffy to his side and said, "Thank you, sir."

The waiter left and Daffy danced out of his embrace.

"Really, Hunter!"

He was all innocence. After all, he had far too much to do with his life right now to worry about finding the woman he'd spend the rest of it with. Ask anyone who knew him and they'd tell you that Hunter trolled for women the way some men trolled for fish. Just look how that obnoxious Love Doctor had described him: Terminal Diagnosis. "He was such a sweet guy, I couldn't bear to disillusion him."

"Oh." She sounded almost disappointed.

And watching her sidle toward the coffeepot, Hunter felt a certain hollowness himself. Had it actually felt good to pretend, if only for a moment, that Daffy was his bride?

He shook his head, warding off such a thought. "I'd better grab a shower," he said.

"Sure. Want a cup of coffee to take in with you?"

That brightened him up. He'd half expected Daffy to want them to sit properly at the table, but Hunter rarely sat down to his breakfast. She poured a cup.

"Cream? Sugar?"

He wondered if she was in the Junior League, or a member of that fancy club on St. Charles Avenue where the ladies had to wear white gloves. She looked the role as she presided over the table, and Hunter realized it was just as well he wasn't dreaming of Daffy as his ever-after. They were worlds apart.

"Sugar." He moved to take the cup from her and added, "Please." There, never let it be said Thelma hadn't taught him manners.

Their fingers brushed as the cup moved from her hand to his. She didn't look nearly as cheerful as when he'd first walked back in. But the clock was ticking and Hunter had to arrive at the convention on time. "Don't think too hard," he said softly, and was glad when she smiled in response.

Daffy was impressed with the speedy way Hunter got ready for his appearance at the convention—and with the results. With his dark good looks, height, and magnetic smile, he stood out in any room of people; the Orphan's Club fund-raiser was a testimonial to that fact. Standing next to her in the elevator, close enough to make her think of nothing but how he'd made her feel last night, Hunter was enough to stop Daffy's breath.

And when they arrived at the Convention Center, pennants flying from the limousine, and a bevy of dark-suited men and women flocked to Hunter's side, Daffy realized that by far she was not the only person susceptible to his charms.

But she was the only woman stepping from the car and standing by his side. Curious eyes surveyed her; envious ones, too. Some of the men ogled.

Shielding her with an arm held lightly against the middle of her back, Hunter guided her through the throng, introducing her to Melanie, a round, brown woman who appeared to be in charge of details, as "his friend from New Orleans."

The woman nodded, shook her hand, and kept them moving at a brisk pace into a large hall. She hustled Hunter backstage, then guided Daffy to a seat in the press section in the front of the hall and told her Hunter would collect her there after his speech. Before leaving her side, Melanie said, "I'm very pleased to meet a woman Hunter introduces as his friend."

"Why, thank you," Daffy said, actually relieved Hunter hadn't put a more romantic slant to her presence. She might be a social columnist, but she didn't want to find herself linked in the press with a man she knew in her heart was only playing a game of "Can the cat catch the mouse?" with her.

Melanie regarded her in silence, then said just loud enough for Daffy to hear her over the noisy rumble of the crowd, "I guess you don't know that he's never done that before."

What did he usually do? Squire prostitutes, à la Aloysius, around computer conventions? Introduce his babes as his bedmates? Daffy smiled, somewhat perfunctorily.

Melanie sighed and patted her arm. "It's good to see Hunter bite the dust," she said. Then, before Daffy could react, she disappeared into the throng.

The man in the next seat turned to her. "New in the press box?"

She shook her head. She wasn't about to tell this guy she was in Vegas having a fling with the keynote speaker. "I'm with *The Crescent*."

He regarded her with cynical eyes. "Brewster. *TechTown Times*. You just don't look like one of the regulars."

Daffy glanced down the several rows reserved for the press. Those who covered technology appeared to be a breed of their own. No wonder her editor had sent someone else to interview Hunter James in New Orleans. Her custom-made linen dress and jacket—in a color her cousin, one of New Orleans's own couturier designers, called lemon glacé—had nothing in common with the khakis and sport shirts the mostly male corps wore. The few women present had more in common with the guys' wardrobe than with Daffy's attire.

Daffy opened her Dior purse and pulled out a pen and the small spiral-bound notebook she carried out of habit. "I make it a practice not to look—or write—like the crowd," she said sweetly.

He turned to the man on his other side, but not before he had muttered under his breath what sounded a lot like "witch." Daffy kept her smile on her face. The guy was a lousy reporter or he would have sniffed out the sure story staring him in the face.

Because she didn't look or act like a journalist. And sitting there in the sea of people waiting for the man knocking on the microphone to settle the crowd and introduce Hunter James, Daffy couldn't help but ask herself why she had settled for dabbling at her profession.

Social columnist defined dabbling. Oh, she enjoyed knowing just about anybody who was anybody in her beloved city. And the Dear Love

Doctor column—what was that but an attempt to avoid the issues of her own life by concentrating her energies on helping other people solve their problems?

She stared at the blank page of the notebook lying open in her palm. What had happened to her loftier ambitions? What had happened to her dreams of writing for magazines? What had happened to that neglected novel that consisted of half a chapter and a drawer full of scribbled notes?

The man at the podium began speaking and Daffy jerked her attention from her own soul-searching to the stage. He must have already started to introduce Hunter, because Daffy caught on quickly to a rags-to-riches theme in his words.

Hunter was an odd combination of free-market entrepreneur and philanthropist, it seemed. Daffy followed enough of the bio to give her the clear impression that almost any company running software that effectively accessed the Internet relied on a key product designed by Hunter and produced by Hunter's company.

She might not understand the technology, but she admired the business savvy. No wonder her brother-in-law had bought the stock.

Applause ricocheted around the hall as Hunter approached the podium. Daffy clasped her hands together and gazed up at this tall, dark-haired, serious-eyed master of all he surveyed. Had she really lain, half naked and open and throbbing with need and desire, beneath this giant of a man? And only last night?

Her body warmed as the flood of sensations answered her question. She hadn't dreamed it—oh, no, every touch, every kiss, every rocketing eruption of desire had been real.

The guy next to her leaned over and interrupted her reverie. "Hey, James has quite the rep as a ladies' man." He winked, but it came off as more of a leer. "Maybe you could get an interview—up close and personal."

Daffy stared him down, then turned her attention back to Hunter onstage.

"The Next Wave," Hunter was saying, "is the title of this talk. This is where I'm supposed to gaze into the future and report what it is I see as the next breakthrough in technology." He took a sip of water and as he swallowed, Daffy felt the memory of his mouth on hers.

"I remember a children's book called *You Will Go to the Moon*." He smiled. "And the Dick Tracy cartoon with his two-way radio wristwatch. And I remember car phones that had to be carted around in a wheelbarrow, they were so big and clunky. Now we carry our access to the world in our palms."

He had the audience. Daffy glanced around. The reporters were scribbling; the earlier roar of the voices in the hall had dimmed to a hush. Where was he going? Daffy wondered along with the rest of them what new product, what innovation he would announce and then make it essential for the rest of the world to purchase.

"Those of us in this room take these tools for granted. Gone is our sense of marvel. And maybe that's a good thing. After all, we don't stand around staring at our BMWs and Porsches drawling, 'Golly, whatever happened to those Conestoga wagons?'"

Laughter rippled across the room. Hunter had a loose, comfortable, engaging style. He was every bit as good behind a microphone as he was . . .

What, Daffy? Finish the sentence, she teased herself; finish it honestly. Say he's every bit as good as he is in bed. The convention hall grew even warmer. Daffy fanned herself with her small notebook.

"But not everyone drives a Porsche. Believe it or not, not everyone carries a cell phone."

Someone's phone rang just as he said this. He smiled, then became more serious. "And even more unbelievable in this country of affluence, not every household is stocked with a computer, or on-line access, or the training to put today's technology to work or to play."

Hunter cited statistics on the number of schools in inner cities and poor rural areas without access to the on-line world. He cited the numbers of unemployed who possessed none of the skills necessary to get a job in a world run by computers.

Daffy sat up straighter. She sensed him honing in on his goal.

"There's been a lot of ink spilled over my rags-to-riches story. And that's okay by me—as long as the customers keep coming and we keep increasing those riches!" He laughed along with the audience. Daffy watched as many of its members exchanged knowing looks and nods. They'd grown rich on their tech stocks and their IPOs and they were hungry to see what Hunter would feed them next.

"Well, here's a headline for you. It's easier to be rich than it is to be poor." Hunter paused as the crowd reacted with nervous humor, then, in all seriousness, said, "But to forget what it feels like to go to bed hungry or not have a new bike when every other kid on the block does—that's something I swore never to do.

"Some of you are probably asking, 'What's your point, James? What's The Next Wave you're holding out to us?'"

He paused again and looked out over the sea of people. With his searching gaze, Daffy felt as if his eyes never left her face, yet she sensed every other member of the audience must have felt the same.

"The Next Wave," Hunter said, "is the name of a new foundation I am setting up. Its purpose—to ensure that all citizens of this country have access to the education and training necessary to compete in a technology-driven workplace."

A slow scatter of applause began, and started

to build. Daffy was part of it, but Hunter held up his hand. "Today, I'm launching this foundation with a personal donation of one million dollars."

Daffy stared, her heart in her throat. He was giving away one million dollars. Because he cared—about his country, his community, and the boys and girls who lived the life of deprivation he'd obviously led. He was no playboy, no heartless gadabout with never a care in his head.

Hunter was far more saint than sinner.

The applause had grown to a roar and threatened to bring down the banners hanging along the stage. After it quieted, Hunter grinned, then said, "And I am challenging each and every one of you to pledge one percent of your company's net profit—and one percent of your personal income—to join me in fueling this effort."

Over the reaction of the attendees, Hunter said, "United we stand and divided—economically—we will fall."

This time when his gaze sought the faces and found her own, Daffy knew he had eyes only for her. The crowd continued to applaud and Daffy lifted one hand to her lips and blew him a kiss.

She didn't know what the rest of the press corps would make of that gesture and she didn't care. Daffy was proud to be called a friend by Hunter James.

13

It was after noon before Hunter and Daffy made their escape from the Convention Center. There had been the cavalcade of the press Q & A, the crush of well-wishers, along with the predictable naysayers. There had been a brief tour of the floor of the Convention Center, a maze of booths and demonstration areas thronged by men and women in suits and dotted with women in high heels and bunny outfits passing out literature.

Eager to have Daffy all to himself, Hunter had cut that part as short as he could. He'd not been blind to the speculative looks cast at Daffy, whom he kept close by his side. Fortunately, Aloysius was busy overseeing their own spacious booth's operation—more of a suite, given his partner's penchant for the luxuries of life—and Hunter had managed to keep him out of Daffy's line of sight.

She'd given him a hug as soon as he'd re-claimed her from the press section. A hug and a kiss on the cheek and a whispered "I think you're wonderful."

Her praise meant more to him than all the ac-claim of his fellow entrepreneurs—something that scared him just a tad. Why did what Daffy thought matter so much? He barely knew the woman.

But when he handed her into the limousine waiting for them amidst a sea of rumbling charter buses and the blaring horns of taxicabs, Hunter knew that wasn't true. He might not have been acquainted very long with her in real time, but the two of them had connected in a way that made Greenwich Mean Time irrelevant.

"Wow," Daffy said. "This is a crazy place."

"Second largest convention held in Las Vegas," Hunter said.

"What's the largest?" She looked up at him, ob-viously confident that he would know the answer.

Hunter settled against the cushions of the limo and smiled at Daffy, relaxing at last. "Historically, CES, which is a show similar to this one, but for the consumer electronics industry."

"More booths?" Daffy wrinkled her nose. "More bunnies?"

He grinned. "Granted, these shows are still geared to guys."

"Geeky ones, you mean," Daffy said. "That re-minds me of a confession I should probably keep

to myself, but when I first went to the Orphan's
Club . . ."

Hunter capped her words with a kiss. God, but
she tasted good. Against her mouth, he murmured, "I know what you're going to say and I
just want to remind you that geeks come in all
shapes and sizes and flavors."

He took her mouth then, pulling her to him,
half onto his lap. She gasped and he felt her
breath enter his own lips and steal down his
throat. He groaned and his body leapt in response
as she matched his hungry kiss thrust by greedy
thrust.

He'd told the driver to head to an out-of-the-
way restaurant known mainly to locals. Mistake.
The one place the two of them needed to go was
straight back to their hotel.

Daffy had her hand on his groin and if she
moved another inch he knew he'd just have the
driver pull over then and there. The dark glass
separating the back of the car from the front provided complete privacy. Hunter didn't know
why, because as a rule he took his action where he
found it, but slowly, he pulled his mouth from
Daffy's. She gazed up at him, blinking slightly, as
dazed as he was by their passion.

He brushed her hair back from her cheeks, and
whispered, "Not here. Not like this. I want our
first time to be"—he placed a kiss just above the
quivering pulse in her neck and sucked gently—
"special."

She was his, ripe for the taking, and he was pulling back. What had she done to his mind?

What she'd done to his body was evident. He could barely sit still, he was so aroused. And after last night's buildup with no release, he was ready to burst.

Daffy touched her tongue to her lip and he said in a voice rough with need, "Do that and I might change my mind and take you right here in the car."

She smiled and took his hand. She kissed the back of it, then rearranged her dress. Her breasts rose and fell with the quickened rhythm of her breathing. Hunter stared, unable to drag his gaze away.

With a slight grin, she said, "Keep doing that and you might get into trouble sooner than you think."

He laughed. "Maybe we should talk about food. Hungry?"

Daffy nodded. She glanced out the window. "Look at that water park! It's humongous!"

A good dousing in cold water was exactly what Hunter needed. Either that or Daffy wild and winsome beneath his hard and driving body. "I've never been to this one."

"You like them?"

He nodded. "I've gone to the one outside Baton Rouge a lot."

"I did that once," Daffy said. "My sister was chaperoning a party of kids and she asked me to help. It was fun, but almost everyone is there with children."

"Yeah. When I realized that, I started taking kids from the Orphan's Club. And somehow I enjoyed it even more."

Daffy leaned over and kissed him. "You're the most thoughtful man I know." She smoothed her skirt. "Too bad we're not dressed for it or we could go today."

"You'd really like to go?" Hunter was pleased. He'd enjoy watching her lose herself in the abandonment of splashing slides and swooping body falls down torrents of rushing water.

She nodded, then said, "If we had the right clothes."

Hunter winked, pressed the intercom button, and asked the driver to pull over at the first multipurpose store he saw. "I didn't give away *all* my money today."

And before Daffy could say "water spout," they'd gone into a souvenir store that also carried, in addition to a plethora of miniature slot machines, overly large, fuzzy dice, and authentic Western Indian souvenirs imported from China, a selection of swimwear, beach towels, sunscreen, and flip-flops.

Hunter headed straight for a carousel displaying the skimpiest bikinis Daffy had ever seen outside of a Victoria's Secret catalogue.

"Let me pick?" he asked, a teasing look in his eyes.

"As long as I hold veto power," she answered.

He held up a scrap of a thong, then shook his head. "Very sexy but can't be comfortable."

Daffy laughed. "Only good for a photo shoot."

"Or a bedroom," he murmured, then selected a backless item with a plunging neckline that could only be called a one-piece by virtue of not having the belly button cut out.

Daffy started to shake her head, but before she could ask how she was supposed to keep such a suit on her body, Hunter returned it in exchange for a rather modest turquoise bikini that might actually cover half of her breasts. "Better," he said.

"Really?" Daffy couldn't hide her surprise.

"Don't want every guy in the water park slobbering over you, do we?"

Oddly flattered by his possessive comment, Daffy accepted the suit, checked that it was her size, as she had thought, and then said, "Now let me pick for you."

"None of those Speedo rubber suits," Hunter protested, even as she lifted a form-fitting ounce of fabric from the men's rack.

Daffy let her gaze travel from Hunter's face ever so slowly down his body, studying it the way she'd watched him study her. When she settled on his evident arousal, she said, "Well, I can see those might be uncomfortably . . . tight."

Hunter choked. "Quite the minx, aren't you?" But he smiled and Daffy wondered for a fleeting second why it was they were on their way to the water park when she wanted to back him into a corner of the shop and make voracious love to him.

Then she remembered she'd asked to visit the park. She sighed and selected a serviceable pair of navy blue swim trunks. She didn't want to spend the afternoon fighting off all the young babes they were sure to encounter.

"Just what I would have picked," Hunter said, accepting the trunks from her and guiding them to the stacks of beach towels and other water-play paraphernalia.

Piled high with their purchases, they stood in line behind a customer purchasing a disposable camera. He seemed to be having trouble with the foreign exchange rate, and while he and the clerk negotiated the terms, Daffy glanced around.

A small TV blared behind the counter. What looked like a local newsbreak came on, and suddenly she saw Hunter's image.

She tugged on his sleeve and pointed toward the screen.

The customer before them finished and they moved forward. The man behind the counter snapped his gum, stared hard at Hunter, then began to ring up their purchases.

"You two having fun in town?"

"Oh, yes," Daffy said.

"First time?"

"How did you know?" Daffy glanced around, wondering if she wore a sign. Why, she'd traveled Europe, Asia, and Australia and always fit in easily.

The man shrugged. "After a while, you can just tell." He totaled the merchandise and announced the amount, holding his hand out to Hunter. "Now, you, you sure look familiar. Can't say why, though."

The news brief ended and a commercial blared its way onto the screen.

The man swiped Hunter's card, returned it to him without glancing at the signature, and finished the transaction.

Daffy kept her reaction bottled up until the two of them had left the shop. They climbed into the waiting limousine and then she said, "You're famous. That man actually recognized you!"

Hunter shrugged. "No big deal."

"But . . ." Daffy trailed off. He was right; it wasn't any big deal. Daffy had photographed everyone who was anyone in New Orleans's social circles and many of those people fell into the category of famous or at least semi-famous. But somehow, sitting here in a chauffeured limousine next to a man who had just that morning announced the formation of a foundation to save the technologically underprivileged of America, she felt herself in the presence of fame.

And fortune.

One couldn't discount the effect that could have on a person.

"Would you prefer if I were plain Mr. James from Ponchatoula who worked in the strawberry fields and came home every night bellowing for his supper?"

"On, no, definitely not." Daffy made a face. "I'm not much of a cook, I'm afraid."

"Seriously, Daffy, I'm no different now than I was ten years ago—not the inner core of a person that I am. And that's what matters—who you are inside."

Daffy nodded. Clearly Hunter had some deep feelings on this subject, which she respected.

Then, as if he didn't want to pursue such a heavy topic on such a beautiful day, Hunter leaned over, kissed her cheek, and said, "Let's change."

"Here? I mean, in the car?" She knew she sounded shocked, but she was. What about the driver? Lord only knew she was no prude, but she had her boundaries of behavior.

"He can't see a thing," Hunter said, kicking off his shoes. He rustled the sack and pulled out the swim trunks.

"But I can." As soon as she finished the sentence, Daffy dissolved in a blush of confusion.

Hunter smiled. He loved hearing her objections. He'd been half afraid she was as wild a hoyden as Aloysius claimed. But she was far more inclined to behave with propriety than with abandon. Though, he thought hungrily, there'd been nothing restrained at all in the way the two of them had tangled on the sofa the night before. His body hardened yet again at the memory. Holding the swim trunks over his thighs, he said, "Okay. I'll close my eyes if you close yours."

She seemed to consider his proposal as if looking for possible objections or traps, but after a long moment, she nodded. "Okay. You first."

She placed her hands over her eyes. Hunter saw the upward curve to her mouth. It was, he realized with a start, fun to have fun. He'd been working so hard he'd almost forgotten what fun felt like. And most of the women he dated were more into glamour and being seen at all the right places.

Exactly what he'd expected of Daffy. Hunter tugged off his shoes, stripped his tie free, and pulled his shirt from his pants.

Daffy scooted closer, and dropped her hands from her face to his chest.

"I thought we said no peeking," Hunter said, not objecting at all.

"Oh, I still have my eyes closed."

Her hands roamed his chest until they finally settled on one of the middle buttons of his shirt. Her face muffled against his throat, she sucked on the skin there while she slowly unfastened the button.

Hunter caught his breath and, then, as she moved to the next button, let it slowly out. She would be the death of him. Hungrily, he bent his head to seek her lips, but she put one finger against his chin and tipped him back against the seat. "Not now," she said. "We're undressing."

"You sure know how to torture a guy."

Daffy, her eyes still closed, murmured something that sounded like, "Why, thank you, sir." She had two more buttons loosened and quit working on the rest to lap at one nipple.

"Oh, no, you don't." Hunter caught her head gently and said, "Any more and we'll never make it to the water park. So sit back like a good girl and let me change my clothes all by myself."

Daffy grinned and lay back against the cushions of the limo. She loved getting him going. But she also didn't think she could hold out much longer herself. For two cents she'd vote to call off the water play and hightail it to the hotel. But Hunter wanted to go; she'd seen it in his face. And as much as she wanted to abandon herself to the wild, tumultuous sex she knew the two of them were building to, she also wanted to make him happy.

And that was a rare state of affairs for Daffodil Landry. Had she ever really cared about any of the other men who had passed through her life? Oh, she'd enjoyed their company, their conversation, and their bodies, but had any one of them ever reached through and touched her somewhere deep inside in a way that made her say she wanted to make him happy?

She sighed softly.

"Almost done," Hunter said.

Would those same words describe the two of them sooner rather than later? Lord, she hoped not. Daffy scrunched her eyes closed even more tightly and to herself whispered, "Please don't let me screw this one up."

"Your turn, my little tease."

Daffy let her eyelids flutter open.

It was a darn good thing he hadn't purchased

the scrap of a Speedo. As it was, Daffy couldn't take her eyes off his almost-nude body. Where had she gotten the idea that all computer geniuses were skinny dudes with no chest hair and not even a shadow of muscle definition?

She reached out and traced a finger along the waistband of his trunks, roaming his perfectly formed chest up to his pecs. "Nice," she said, not wanting to give him too big a head.

He grinned. "Thank you, ma'am." Handing her the sack of purchases, he said, "Your turn."

Daffy shrugged out of her jacket, slipped off her pumps, and then halted. Hunter was sitting there watching her every move. She cast him a puzzled glance, and he said, "Well, you can't blame me for trying."

She smiled and he closed his eyes.

"Let me know if you need any help," he said, stretching out in a way that showed his long, lean, tanned legs to advantage.

Turnabout was certainly fair play with the two of them, and as Daffy began removing the rest of her clothing, she expected at any moment to feel Hunter's hands caressing her body. She'd half turned in the seat to provide a touch more privacy, which was probably silly considering what the two of them had already shared, but it seemed the appropriate thing to do.

After wriggling out of her stockings and panties, she donned the bikini bottom, then pulled her dress up over her head. Unable to stand the anticipation of him touching her, she turned to find him still stretched out in the seat, his hands now behind his head.

She studied him for a second, then scooted so her back was to him and swapped her bra for the bikini top. Her nipples had moved beyond desire to frustration and were so puckered they pushed upward through the fabric of the bikini top in an embarrassingly obvious fashion. The bikini top fastened with a tie and she reached around to make a bow, certain then that Hunter would cheat and take the fabric in his hands. And then his hands would be on her body and the top discarded on the seat, forgotten.

Daffy shook her head. What was wrong with her? She'd asked him to give her privacy and he was according her proper respect by fulfilling her wishes.

And in doing so, he was driving her over the edge.

"All done," she said, turning around.

"Great." Hunter remained stretched out, but even though the rest of his body didn't move, his eyes moved over her breasts and bare belly and in and around her thighs. "Great," he repeated.

Daffy was tingling, she was so on edge. The limo stopped and the driver's voice came over the intercom. "We're at the water park, sir."

"Go around the block again," Hunter said, much to Daffy's surprise.

14

Of course he had peeked. Good thing he had tucked his hands behind his head or he would have been all over Daffy. Even the sight of her silky back whetted Hunter's appetite, but add to that the curve of her breast and the slow, sexy way Daffy had slipped her dress over her head. She'd moved enticingly, almost as if she'd known he was watching.

Almost as if she expected him to make a move on her.

Hunter patted the seat right beside him. She slid closer, and the wide-eyed look she gave him did him in. He'd intended to hold this discussion without letting his body get involved, but damned if he could resist.

He pulled her into his arms.

She snuggled against him, her bikini top not

quite staying with her body with every little move she made. Good selection of swimwear, he thought, but oddly enough, his mind wasn't so much on her incredible body but on his own emotional reaction to holding her close.

Funny, yet it seemed to him that she belonged there in his embrace, tucked against his chest as if she'd always been a part of him.

He hardly knew this woman. And what he did know should scare the hell out of him.

"There's a conversation I want to have," he said, tucking a strand of hair behind her cheek.

"Yes?"

He could tell by her surprised reaction and the curious way she was regarding him that a conversation was the last thing she'd expected. No doubt she was waiting for him to push aside that scrap of fabric which separated his mouth from her breasts and suckle her until she screamed and demanded release from the fires the two of them had been stoking in each other. God only knew he wanted exactly that for himself!

But he wanted something more important than just sex. And that he did bothered him, even though Hunter wasn't a guy to ignore his instincts. He'd done okay by following them.

"It's not like me to bring this up out of context," he said slowly, "but you and I both know that one of these days, maybe even when we finally make it back to our hotel, nothing is going to keep us apart."

Daffy blushed slightly. Hunter held her more tightly, pleased by her reaction.

He was aptly named; he enjoyed the pursuit of the opposite sex and he appreciated the way Daffy played to that and yet didn't overtake the lead. On his first—and only—date with Tiffany Phipps, she'd been reaching for his zipper at the same moment she'd been unlocking her front door. He still couldn't believe he hadn't let her supply the oral pleasure she'd offered, but his heart hadn't been in it. Tiffany reminded him too strongly of Emily, and Hunter would be willing to bet Emily had abandoned her willingness to perform oral sex the moment she'd tossed her bridal bouquet.

Besides, after one glimpse of Daffy, he hadn't wanted anyone else.

He stirred. Was that true? Daffy was watching him so intently Hunter was afraid for a moment that he'd spoken out loud. Wasn't he just trying to prove the boast he'd made that day in the coffeehouse—to show her he could make any woman fall for him?

"You're very serious," she murmured.

"Birth control is a serious topic."

"And a most important one." She paused for only a moment, then added, "I take it that is our topic?"

He had to hand it to her; she'd answered as smoothly as if he'd observed that the sun was shining. Maybe he could have waited; he certainly hadn't stopped to discuss it prior to tugging her down on the couch with him last night. Daffy might be the one woman with the power and the passion to cause Hunter to forget the cardinal rule by which he lived.

He nodded.

Daffy drew back a bit from the shelter of Hunter's arms, not because she wanted him to let go of her, but to give herself a better view of his face. Yes, it was as serious as his tone of voice.

Good.

"Do you know you're the first man I've ever gone out with who introduced this topic . . . um, ahead of the moment?"

"Really?"

She held up one hand and prepared to tick off on her fingers the men who'd followed the other route.

Hunter closed his hands over hers. "Let's skip the details."

Ooh, he sounded a little bit jealous. No, more than a little bit. Daffy smiled inwardly. "Anyway, I've been on the pill for years, but thanks for bringing up the subject. And despite my reputation, I lead a fairly dull life."

"Meaning?" He'd managed to tuck her back against his side and was gently stroking her neck with the pad of his thumb.

She made a face. "Meaning I'm no Typhoid Mary."

He laughed. "But we'll play it safe, okay?"

"Sure." Daffy sighed.

"What's wrong?"

"Nothing."

"Uh-oh," Hunter said. "In my experience, when a woman says nothing is wrong, that means I'm supposed to figure out what *is* wrong."

She laughed softly. "Did you know you're smarter than the average guy?"

He nodded. "So what's wrong?"

"I was remembering the day my mother delivered Jonni and me to her doctor's office and had him explain the facts of life to us. We were sixteen and already knew more than the doctor even hinted at. What did surprise us both was that our mother had him put us on the pill, and boy, was that premature!"

"Really?" Since he sounded sincerely interested, Daffy continued with the story. She enjoyed talking to Hunter almost as much as she enjoyed making out with him. A good combination. No, better than good. Perfect.

"We were pretty sheltered." She shrugged, remembering the irony. "All-girl school. After school, we had soccer or swim team, then homework. Jonni and I spent more time with our noses to the grindstone than we did on dates."

"I find that very hard to believe," he murmured, still circling his thumb lightly over her neck.

She flipped him a grin. "Well, if I'd known *you* in high school . . ."

"I daresay you wouldn't have looked at me

twice," he said, sounding much less contented than only a moment before. His thumb stilled and Daffy knew there was a story behind his reaction, one he might share with her someday, as she might eventually share the story of her mother's betrayal.

She touched his cheek. "Then you don't know me very well."

"So when did you . . ." Hunter's voice trailed off, but Daffy knew exactly what he was asking.

"So you really want to know when I misplaced my virginity?"

"Yeah." He tightened his hold on her and Daffy realized he didn't really want the answer. Every guy wanted to believe he was the first, last, and only, even when the evidence waved itself like a flag in front of his face.

"I went a little nuts the summer after my freshman year in college," Daffy said, trying for a light tone. She hated remembering the pain and loss of that horrible year. "What about you?"

"I guess you'd call me precocious."

Daffy smiled. "That means your answer is, way younger than me. Let me guess. You were fifteen and she was a cheerleader."

"Fourteen and she was that year's senior class valedictorian."

"You amaze me." Daffy laughed and sat upright. That was when she realized her breasts were practically parading bare for Hunter's appreciative gaze. In a belated attempt at modesty, she rearranged the bikini top.

"I liked it better the other way," Hunter said.

Before she could reply, the intercom buzzed and the driver's voice came through. "We're back at the water park again, sir."

Hunter glanced from the round speaker above the mini-bar back to Daffy. "I almost hate to leave the car."

She nodded. "It feels like a cocoon, doesn't it?" she added, hugging her arms around her knees.

He smiled, then his lips broadened into a mischievous grin. "But I would like to see that bikini soaking wet on you."

Daffy responded by ogling his groin and Hunter winked at her and clicked on the intercom. "Drop us at the front gate." Then he caught her hands and said, "I have a feeling we've only scratched the surface of several themes during this discussion. Until later?"

Daffy nodded, touched by his insight and his desire to communicate with her. Hunter James, she reflected, really could make any woman fall for him, even if he wasn't trying.

The driver opened the door and Daffy followed Hunter from the car. She couldn't help but notice the limousine chauffeur staring at the two of them. And she couldn't help but blush.

As soon as they were beyond the man's earshot, Daffy said, "Hunter, I could swear that man thinks we were having sex the entire time!"

He grinned. "I knew I liked that driver."

About two hours later, Hunter took back his words. He and Daffy had just navigated the highest, longest, most daring slide in the park and were laughing and dashing droplets from their eyes.

Daffy looked like a twelve-year-old, well, make that a sixteen-year-old, he corrected himself as he admired her body sculpted by her wet bikini. He held out a hand to her and together they splashed through the knee-deep water toward the edge of the pool.

"Do it again?" Hunter asked, pleased that she was having such a good time. Who would have thought it? Daffy had washed away a lifetime of Hunter's stereotypes of upper-crust rich girls.

Daffy stopped in her tracks, one foot in the water, the other on the edge of the pool. She tugged at his hand. Looking down, Hunter saw that her sunny expression had been chased away.

"What's *he* doing here?" She directed her gaze across the paving stones that led to one of several gazebos offering shelter from the desert sun.

Lounging in a chaise, as out of place poolside in his dark business suit as a penguin at a Sunday barbecue, sat Aloysius.

"Good question." Hunter helped Daffy from the pool. Still holding her hand, he said, "Want to pretend we didn't see him?"

She giggled. Then, as her mirth subsided, she replied, "That would serve him right, but surely he wouldn't be here if there weren't some sort of emergency."

Thinking of last night's untoward interruption,

Hunter wasn't convinced he agreed with Daffy. "With Aloysius, one never knows. Look, I'll go see what's up."

Daffy didn't let go of his hand. "I'll come, too. He doesn't scare me."

"Are you sure?"

She tossed her head and water droplets scattered. Hunter wished he could lick off the drops that landed on her cleavage. Damn Aloysius for interrupting them again!

"Just because he and I don't speak is no reason for me not to stand by your side."

Hunter nodded. They were halfway to Aloysius by that point anyway, and he knew better than to argue with Daffy. Once her mind was made up, that was it. It hadn't taken him long to understand that about her.

To his surprise, Daffy greeted Aloysius quite sweetly. His partner, eyes hidden behind dark glasses, ignored Daffy. Instead, he rose and said, "Hunter, I need to talk to you."

"Sure. First, though, tell me how you found us."

"Easy enough. I paged your limo driver."

Hunter glanced at Daffy. Suddenly she didn't look quite as calm and collected. He had a fair idea she was picturing the driver filling Aloysius in on his own imaginary version of the prolonged drive from the Convention Center to the water park, a drive that should have taken far less time than it had.

Aloysius wagged his brows above his impenetrably dark glasses, pretty much confirming Hunter's guess. "Well, what is it? The NuTech deal?"

Aloysius shook his head. "Need to discuss this in private."

"I'll take a stroll," Daffy said. She smiled and this time Hunter saw straight through the saccharine to the starch beneath. "A very short stroll."

As soon as she was out of earshot, Aloysius grabbed his arm and pulled the two of them down to facing chairs. "What's *she* doing with *you*?"

"Swimming. Why are *you* here?"

"Hunter, you're my business partner. I've got a lot invested in you. The moment Melanie described the woman you were with this morning, my heart stopped beating. She was going on and on about how enchanted you were and how you'd never introduced any woman as your friend. Hunter, she was practically planning the press release for your wedding!"

Surprisingly, Hunter found himself grinning like a goofy kid. "Really? She said all that?"

Aloysius reached over and shook his arm. "Snap out of it!"

Hunter closed his hand around Aloysius's much skinnier arm and lifted it off his. "Is this what you came here to tell me?"

"I knew you'd get upset." He shook his head. "That's why I went to the trouble to track you down, so you'd understand the urgency."

Hunter stared at his partner, at a man he called friend. "There's something else going on here, something deeper I don't understand. Want to tell me what it is?"

"Daffy's a flirt," Aloysius said bitterly. "She'll entrance you, then tease you, then the next thing you know, you'll promise her anything. That body—" He broke off. "She can drive a man wild, but that's all she does."

"What do you mean?" Hunter hated listening to Aloysius talk about Daffy. His brain was forced to acknowledge the two of them had been engaged, but when he thought of Aloysius touching her, making love to her—no, that was more than he'd let into his mind. Daffy was his.

"Have you had sex with her yet?"

Hunter hesitated.

Aloysius slapped his hands together. "I knew it! Same old MO. All tease and no please."

"Are you telling me you and Daffy were engaged and never did it?" Hunter couldn't believe it, but he was damn glad to hear it.

Aloysius shook his head. "You're beginning to get the picture. And I'll wager you a thousand bucks you don't get any, either."

"Can't take that bet." Hunter knew he'd win it, but he wasn't making her the subject of a bet like that. Another woman maybe, but he respected Daffy too much to do that to her.

Besides, if she found out, he'd never hear the end of it.

"You know, Aloysius, I just don't get it. You race out here to tell me she won't put out. Doesn't compute."

"For someone as smart as you are, you sure are dense. Don't forget what she did to me the night before our wedding."

"Ah." That was the heart of the matter. Daffy had refused to have sex with her fiancé, then screwed his best man.

"You just won't listen." Aloysius rose. "I know what you're thinking. 'She did it to him, but I'm different.' You're a man. And that's all it takes to make her go weird. One day that woman will break your heart, and I hope I'm friend enough not to say I told you so."

He was certainly sincere, and right about what Hunter was thinking. She'd never do that to him. He couldn't say why, but he knew it in his gut. He saw her approaching and waved her over.

Aloysius stared at her, his jaw working.

Daffy glanced from one to the other. "So, everything settled?"

No one answered.

"Maybe it's time we cleared the air, Aloysius," Daffy said.

He laughed.

"Why don't I apologize?"

"That would be a good starting point," Aloysius said, his mouth twisting in a bitter smile. "Wreck a man's life, then say oh, by the way, sorry."

"You know very well I didn't wreck your life."

"No, you saved me from a fate worse than death—marriage to you."

Hunter watched the two of them spar. Better to

have it out than let the anger stay bottled up inside. At last he understood the depth of Aloysius's ego-wounds. It wasn't so much that Daffy had screwed his best man that made him so furious, it was that she hadn't let *him* do it.

"Marriage, and divorce." Daffy jabbed a finger at him. "If I were married to you and found you with a hooker on either arm, that would be the end."

"Hookers? What are you talking about? You're the one who sleeps with anything that crawls."

Clearly wrong on that point, Hunter thought, keeping score. She'd exempted Aloysius from that list. Remembering her comment about not being a Typhoid Mary, Hunter wondered just how she managed to maintain a reputation for sexual wildness when the evidence seemed to point to the opposite.

"You don't remember last night, do you?"

Aloysius looked over at Hunter. "What's she talking about?"

"You came to our suite last night with one hooker for you and, most generously, you brought one for me."

"I did that?" Aloysius slumped onto the chaise. "I wouldn't do that to Chrissie."

"Apparently you weren't thinking much about your fiancée last night," Daffy said.

Aloysius held his chin in his hands. "Are you going to tell Chrissie?"

Daffy tapped her foot on the paved surface. "Let me think. Am I going to tell Chrissie?"

Hunter grinned. She had him now. He waited for her to strike home.

"Are you going to forgive me for what I did to you?"

Aloysius jutted his jaw, stubborn as ever.

"Please?"

He rose slowly. "I guess a person can make a mistake." He extended a hand to Daffy and the two of them shook.

Then he grinned. "I never wanted to marry you anyway."

"Then why did you propose?"

He dropped her hand. "I think you were the one who actually proposed."

"I did not!"

Hunter held up his hands. "Hey, you two, you called a truce, so let's stop there." No doubt Aloysius had offered the peace branch only to prevent Chrissie from finding out about his errant behavior, but Hunter would rather have his partner on at least speaking terms with his girlfriend.

Girlfriend?

Daffy wasn't his girlfriend. She was his date, a companion for a romp to Las Vegas. No more, no less.

"Hunter?" Aloysius snapped his fingers in front of Hunter's face. "I'm going. But remember what I said."

"Yeah, right."

15

"I think we'll take a cab next trip," Hunter said after Aloysius had left them. "He'd have much less chance of tracking us down."

To her surprise, Daffy laughed. Then she said, "It's just as well he did—this time. I should have apologized to him years ago." Apologizing to Aloysius had unburdened her, yet she was pretty sure it had helped her more than it had affected him. After facing down Aloysius, she was drained. Or maybe it was the lack of sleep, but suddenly she felt like collapsing on the chaise.

Hunter must have read her mind, because he caught her arm and lowered her to the same spot Aloysius had occupied. "I think I'll call that cab now. A nap would be in order, too."

She nodded, feeling a bit silly. She couldn't help but smile as Hunter lifted her legs and stretched her comfily on the chaise. He tucked a towel behind her head for a pillow and said, "Don't move. I'll go get our stuff, call a cab, and be right back."

Daffy sighed and let her arms relax by her side. It was sweet of Hunter to take care of her; it was also something she wasn't much used to, not being the clinging type.

Today, however, she let Hunter bundle her into a cab, curled up against him while he responded to the driver's chatty recommendations on where to find everything from the places with the best slot odds to roadside stands hawking bang-up and generally illegal fireworks.

Today, she drifted with Hunter through the casino surrounding their hotel, up the elevator, and to the door of their suite.

There she paused.

Hunter looked at her, somewhat quizzically.

No doubt Aloysius had told him terrible things about her. Terrible and untrue. His favorite rant had to do with her being a tease, but she'd never given herself to Aloysius and most of the other guys she dated because things had never been right for that level of intimacy.

She stood on tiptoes and kissed him on the mouth.

His lips answered hers and Daffy smiled. As she did, he smiled with her, their lips following the gesture in a lovely dance of their own.

"I want us to make love," she said.

Hunter met her gaze head-on, his eyes searching her face. Daffy knew she'd been right to stop at the door and let him know, without question, she was ready. She'd been wild for him last night, but somehow today was different, better in a way she didn't quite understand. Had they had sex the night before, it would have been good.

But today it would be special.

A maid pushing a cart rounded a corner and headed in their direction. Hunter didn't blink. The maid passed right by them and Daffy willed herself to be still, letting Hunter search for the answer he sought—that no matter what he might have heard, pursuing her would not be a mistake.

"You," he said softly, "are a remarkable woman." Then he slid the card-key into the door. The green light blinked and he added, "Thank you for the all-clear."

Then, before she knew what he was going to do, he tossed his bundled clothing past the opened door and turned and gathered her in his arms and carried her inside. He slipped the security lock closed behind them.

"This time, no interruptions."

The kiss he gave her promised that no matter who knocked on their door, the summons would go unanswered.

Held in his arms, returning his kisses, Daffy tried to shrug out of the yellow linen jacket she'd donned over her bikini for the trek through the hotel. Hunter came to her aid, freeing her from one sleeve as he waltzed them into the sitting room and down on the same sofa where they'd lain last night. Or was it only that morning?

Slightly dazed, Daffy gazed up at Hunter and traced the line of his mouth with her pinkie finger.

He grinned and sucked her finger into his mouth, sliding it in and out with one hand as he slipped the straps of her bikini top off her shoulders.

Daffy arched against him, her need driving her on boldly. He let go of her finger and turned both hands to freeing her from her bathing-suit top.

Suddenly he stopped. "Don't go anywhere," he said, rising from the sofa.

As if she would.

Daffy rolled her head against the cushions of the sofa and sighed. Her bikini top lay half on, half off. Hunter had left the room, disappearing into his side of the suite, no doubt in search of his part of their contraceptive bargain.

But perhaps she should.

Making love with Hunter might be one of the biggest mistakes of her misbegotten romantic life. She already knew he would be the best lover she'd ever had; knew that by the way he kissed her, teased her, touched her; by the way he managed to implant himself inside her mind. She'd never thought much about any of the men she'd dated. They all met socially acceptable standards, were of the intelligence quota she demanded, and would all have satisfied her family's admission requirements to the Landry family tree.

But Hunter . . . Daffy frowned and circled her belly button with the pinkie finger Hunter had sucked only minutes earlier. Hunter was smart, but he was new money and not at all what the Landrys were used to.

Realizing where her thoughts were leading, Daffy sat up on the couch and gave herself a mental shake. She was about to have sex with the guy; for Pete's sake, that was all. There were no wedding bells chiming; she wasn't the marrying kind. Unless she could meet a man who could tame the beast that rose so perversely inside her at the first sight of a possible long-term relationship, she knew she would never marry.

She sighed and wondered what was keeping Hunter. Then a terrible thought occurred to her. What if he had forgotten to pack his condoms? That would mean . . .

"Daffy?" Hunter called her name from the bedroom.

"Yes?"

"How about a bath after all that sun and chlorine?"

His head appeared around the corner.

"That's a nice idea." But so was him jumping her body right that minute, Daffy thought, just preventing a pout from showing on her kiss-swollen lips. She didn't want to be away from Hunter long enough to rinse off in the shower, let alone to take a bath.

"Chlorine being so bad for the skin," Hunter added.

Then Daffy realized he was grinning.

"Are you up to mischief?"

He stepped into the sitting room, wearing only a towel wrapped around his waist. Daffy admired his broad chest, as she'd done every moment they'd been splashing at the water park. He had exactly the amount of chest hair Daffy liked, mainly in the middle of the chest, with some scattered across his pecs, and a dusky line that led the eye down, down, down—to where her view was blocked by the luxurious bath towel.

"I sure hope so," he said, walking slowly toward her and then veering past the sofa and into the bedroom she'd occupied. This time he returned almost immediately, bearing the hotel robe.

"Let's get you out of that suit and into something more comfortable," he said, dropping the robe on the back of the sofa and kneeling before her, his hands on her hips above her bikini bottom.

Eager to cooperate with that suggestion, Daffy lifted her hips and let him slip the fabric off her. He never once took his eyes from her face, which actually surprised her. On that very same couch he'd brought her to passionate release just by touching her. And right now, she was so on edge that all he'd have to do was look at her intimately and she'd come.

Poised above Daffy, Hunter paused to appreciate the open way she was offering herself to him. He felt a lot like he had as a kid on Christmas morning. Even in their worst of times, his mother always had at least one present for him. His hands on Daffy's slender hips, easing off her bikini bottom, he remembered those intense conflicting feelings of wanting to plunge in and unwrap his one and only present. Yet at the same time he wanted the process to take forever.

"I plan to savor you," he murmured, feasting on her eyes, pupils so enlarged her eyes appeared wide enough and dark enough for him to get lost in. But rather than frightening him, the idea excited him. God help him, but Hunter wanted to lose himself in Daffodil Landry.

He dropped the bikini bottom to the floor and then slid his hands around her shoulders and down to unfasten the clasp of the bikini top. Still he kept his eyes mated with hers. He felt her breasts rise and fall, more rapidly as he freed the last scrap of fabric from her body. Her lips were parted slightly and she was reaching her arms up to him, tugging on him, pulling him down to her.

Resisting the urgent impulse to take her immediately, Hunter tucked her into the plush bathrobe and said, "At your service. Your bath is waiting, ma'am."

He realized she would have headed into her side of the suite if he hadn't checked her gently. Putting his arm around her, he said, "Bathing together is so much nicer than bathing alone."

She actually looked shocked.

Hunter kept propelling her forward. "I take it you usually bathe alone," he said, ushering her

through the doorway that led to the master bedroom of the suite.

"Don't most people?"

"You and I, Daffy," Hunter said softly, stopping
beside the bedroom's huge sunken and mirrored
tub and turning them face-to-face, "are not most
people."

He slipped his hands beneath her robe, drawing her to him, cupping a breast with one hand,
her derriere with the other. She surrendered to his
kiss and arched against him. As she did, his towel
worked loose and slid to the floor. He edged
Daffy's robe off her. Fabric joined fabric, and then
at last, flesh met only flesh.

He breathed deeply and fused her body
against his. Too much more savoring would be
the end of him.

His heated arousal pushed against the soft skin
beneath her belly button and just above where he
wanted to sink himself into her core. She uttered
a breathy gasp and Hunter let her feel the effect
she had on him as he gave free rein to his greedy
need of her.

Circling her thatch of hair, he teased her. He felt
her own moisture mingle with the bead of lubri-
cation escaping from him and he almost bent her
over the bathtub he'd been letting fill with water.

Catching himself, he pulled back and turned
off the taps. He'd put only the smallest amount of
Caesar's bath gel into the water, but bubbles covered the surface of the oversize tub. He flicked the

jets on with his toe and almost immediately the bubbles frothed to gigantic proportions.

Daffy laughed and, reaching into the tub, scooped up a handful of lather and spread it on his chest. He followed her example and crowned her breasts with bubbles.

After testing the water temperature with his hand, he guided her in, then followed. He noticed she would stare at his body, then glance away, almost shyly. Again he was struck by her innocence, so much in contrast with what he'd been led to expect.

But there was nothing innocent about the way she was leaning forward now, her breasts just above the water line, beckoning him toward her.

She slid onto his lap and Hunter groaned.

"I may never have bathed with a man before," Daffy said, "but I've always been a pretty quick learner."

Straddling him in the water, her legs tucked around his back, Daffy marveled at just how free she felt with Hunter. Shyly, she said, not quite meeting his gaze, "You know, in some ways being together like this is a lot more intimate than sex under the sheets."

"I know what you mean," Hunter said, just before he brushed away the frothy bubbles from her breast and took the nipple gently between his lips.

Daffy arched against him, rising slightly from the water, and as she settled back, she found herself nudging against, then riding, his arousal, and slowly, slowly taking the length of him into her. As the jets of the tub swirled the water around them, Daffy lost all sense of anything but the feel of Hunter possessing her.

Eyes closed, back arched, she realized Hunter was holding her around the waist and guiding her lower. When he'd filled her completely, he grasped her in his arms and rose from the water, their bodies still joined.

"Let's finish this bath later," he said in a voice gone even deeper and huskier.

Daffy fluttered her eyelids open, squeezed him even more deeply into her, and smiled as he reacted with a pleased gasp. Slowly he withdrew from her, and Daffy bit her lip to keep from crying out. He belonged inside her.

He reached for a towel and started to dry her. She tugged it from him and threw it on the floor, drawing him down on top of her. "I'll lick you dry," she said.

And Hunter never doubted her.

Wild with desire, bent on pleasing this man in a way she'd never wanted to please another, Daffy rolled over so she half leaned on Hunter's chest. She did towel most of him dry, but saved the best for what she'd promised.

The hot water of the bath had had absolutely no calming effects on his body.

"I hope you like this," Daffy said, kneeling beside him and lapping ever so lightly at the base of his arousal. Giggling just a bit, she said, "It's a special kind of towel."

"You nut," he said, his voice somewhere between a pant and a growl as she turned with serious attention and a much firmer touch to her technique.

She took him into her mouth and Hunter said, in a voice that sounded like it came from somewhere deep inside him, "What's not to like?"

Tasting him, pleasuring him, driving him to a place beyond himself, Daffy reveled in the sensuality he'd set loose in her. She'd always enjoyed sex, but never really concentrated on the gift of giving pleasure to a man. Glancing up at Hunter, his head thrown back, his expression a blend of intense ecstasy, Daffy felt a sense of power she'd never known.

A power she would use only for good.

Slowly she realized Hunter had his hands on her shoulders and he was drawing her up to his chest.

"You're incredible," he said, smoothing her damp hair back from her face. "But right now, I want more of you."

Daffy didn't know how Hunter could hold out much longer. The way he'd thrust against the full kisses of her mouth, seeking her throat as if seeking her feminine core, she knew he was on the edge of sweet, explosive release.

This time he rolled above her and, parting her legs, tasted her. She was more than ready, lifting her hips to meet his kiss. He lapped, then suckled her, first softly, then with an urgency to which she responded in kind, crying out as she pulsed against him.

Hunter lifted his head and she saw through the haze of her satisfaction that he was looking quite pleased with himself.

And then he was moving over her and into her and Daffy forgot everything she'd ever known or ever experienced. Forgot they lay on the floor midst the scattered towels, forgot she'd vowed not to give in to his pursuit of her, forgot she'd ever said she'd never let herself need any man.

Hunter caught his breath and Daffy felt him slow his possessive movements. He pulled out of her and jumped up, grabbed his overnight bag, and said, "I knew if any woman could make me forget myself, it would be you."

Daffy smiled and remained on the floor, her body open and waiting for Hunter's return. He found the packet he sought, tore it open, tugged the condom on his beautifully aroused manhood, and in one swoop, bent down and caught her up.

He lowered her to the massive bed and said, "Now you're mine."

Daffy didn't know what felt better: his possessive words or the slow way he reentered her body, exploring, withdrawing, then plunging inward until she cried out yet again in ecstasy.

Crying and laughing, she held tight as Hunter at last found the release he sought, deep within her body, deep within her soul.

* * *

Hunter came back to his senses slowly, drifting like a leaf in a torpid September breeze. He'd shifted his weight off Daffy and the two of them curled side by side, still on top of the covers of the king-size bed. He'd wrapped the condom in a tissue from the bedside table and tossed it in the general direction of the wastebasket. Thank God he'd remembered himself at the last minute.

Glancing up, he mused how ironic it was he hadn't thought once about the mirrored ceiling, one of his favorite features of Caesar's more adult-oriented rooms. No. His every thought had been possession of Daffy and splendid release within her entrancing body.

She stirred and he fitted her more closely against his chest. He liked looking up and seeing the reflection of the two of them, naked and cuddled close. Funny, but he'd never been much for hugging. He liked his sex hot and heavy and passionate, after which he liked to move on, back to the business of life. At the moment, however, he didn't feel like scooting one inch away from Daffodil Landry.

He frowned.

"Don't," Daffy said, reaching back to smooth his brow.

"It's not really a frown," he said.

"Good." She wriggled her derriere against him and pointed a finger toward the ceiling. "The mirror tells all, you know."

"Ah, you noticed it."

She smiled and he could have sworn she also blushed slightly.

"Something else you've never done before?" Hunter let one hand roam over her breasts and found her nipples budded, tight, amazingly ready for more.

"Not exactly," she said.

"What does that mean?" He trailed one finger lightly down the side of her hip; the other was busy exploring her breast.

"It means I've never made love beneath a mirror before, but I'm embarrassed to admit to such inexperience," she said.

"Don't be." Hunter turned them so they lay face-to-face. He kissed the tip of her nose. "Call it the cave man in me, but I'm glad I'm your first."

"First?"

He grinned and slipped lower on the bed. "Watch the mirror and see how it feels."

"How what feels?" Her voice had gone all breathy.

Hunter lifted one slender ankle and, watching her reaction, suckled her big toe.

She squirmed and cried out, half laughing, half panting.

"You like that?"

"Yes," Daffy whispered, her eyes on the ceiling.

"You make a beautiful picture," Hunter said, acknowledging the view she had of them reflected above.

"You amaze me," she said.

He bowed his head and lowered her foot, then

worked his way up until he reached her inner thighs. "Keep watching," he said, and tasted her again. She was wet and hot and swollen from their lovemaking. He licked her gently and wasn't at all surprised when she came almost at once.

She clung to him, then said, "That mirror is very naughty."

He grinned. "Want to finish that bath now?"

She nodded, but didn't move. Hunter was about to rise and help her off the bed when she said, "Would you mind if I did one other thing I've never done before?"

Checking her expression, carefully neutral but given away by the quirk of her lips, Hunter leaned back against the pillows. This was going to be good. "No, not at all."

She knelt beside him and said, much like a schoolteacher, "Now watch the mirror, and let me know what you think."

When she took his manhood into her mouth, Hunter groaned. The double impact of Daffy pleasuring him and at the same time watching her in the mirror suspended over the bed almost did him in. He gasped and reached out for a handful of her hair. She turned her face toward him for just a moment, and, minx that she was, she was grinning.

Then he gave himself up to the pleasure she was creating with the magic of her touch, and this time he didn't have to disturb the delicious sensations to leap up and run for a condom.

16

They fell asleep together and it was the sweetest sleep Daffy had ever known.

When they awoke, Hunter was obviously hungry again for her, but he turned over, grabbed the clock, and said, "Damn. We've got to go."

Daffy snuggled against him. Surely it couldn't be time to leave this cocoon. "I'm not hungry. For dinner."

"Plane," he said, drawing her close and kissing her as if he intended for them to spend the night exactly where they were.

But then he said, "I have a meeting in New Orleans first thing in the morning, so we have to catch our flight."

Daffy blinked and stretched. "We must have been asleep a long time."

Hunter stroked her thigh, then said, "Hours

and hours. If it were any other meeting, I'd cancel it, but this one I can't. I scheduled the latest plane out tonight."

She smiled and leaned up to kiss him. "That's okay. I'm a working girl myself, remember?"

He nodded and sat up, brushing a hand across his eyes. "Daffy . . ."

"Yes?"

"I know I said this before, but thank you for coming to Vegas with me."

She nodded, noting her own reflection once again in the mirror. She'd given herself so completely to him, she had a pretty good idea he meant more than the words he spoke. "Thanks for asking me," she said, and rose from the bed.

He eyed the tub, then shook his head. "That water's going to be ice-cold. How about a shower?"

"Okay," she said. "But we might miss the plane."

He smiled and said, "I can resist when I have to."

But she made it as hard as she could for him, dropping the soap and bending over to retrieve it, then sliding the slippery bar up his legs and across his groin. At last he caught her hands and said, "Shower or I'll bend you over and take you now."

Blushing, Daffy asked him to pass the shampoo. She'd never wanted a man as much as she wanted Hunter; never felt as free to express her desire. And that freedom made her want to open up in a way she found exhilarating.

But it was time to head for home.

Back to reality.

As they dried, then dressed, then rushed to pack their belongings, Daffy couldn't help but wonder if the magic they had found would survive their return to everyday life.

But she promised herself, standing next to Hunter as they waited for the limousine to collect them for the ride to the airport, that she would do her best to achieve that goal.

Three days later, Daffy was beginning to wonder whether she'd dreamed the whole thing up. They'd returned on the red-eye Sunday evening, Hunter had dropped her at her house, kissed her good night, and disappeared.

Now, loitering outside the Gretna courthouse, Daffy felt two-times foolish. First, for missing so intensely a man she scarcely knew. And second, for having stood around outside her brother-in-law's office to spy on his assignation with the sweetly helpless intern—only to have the two of them leave together and head straight to the courthouse.

Well, Daffy, how unusual for a lawyer and a paralegal to go to court.

And, Daffy, how unlike you to mope over some guy not calling you.

Daffy reminded herself not to blame Hunter.

She, too, had been busy, occupied by Jazzfest-related social events that required the presence of her camera. Beginning to be annoyed at the way so many otherwise sensible people behaved once they saw the chance of making the Social Scene column, Daffy was tempted to bequeath the job to someone else and get a real journalism job.

Or become a private investigator, she thought, suppressing the urge to utter a humorless giggle. As she watched David and Nina approach the security checkpoint, David put his arm around the intern. Daffy frowned. For her sister's sake, she was determined to find out the truth. No man was going to cheat on her sister and get away with it.

Anyway, worrying about Jonni kept her from worrying whether she'd made a fool of herself with Hunter. Though even as she followed the pair, her thoughts were full of him.

Was she simply his latest conquest? Was he even at this moment in some locker room, swapping stories of which chick he'd boffed last weekend? Daffy shuddered at the very idea, but she wasn't so naive that she didn't recognize the possibility. Guys would be guys, after all.

But Hunter wasn't like that. He'd sent her flowers and left her several messages, the latest one saying that he'd had to fly to Salt Lake City for more merger talks.

She sighed, wishing he'd invited her along, but then realized how silly that was. They barely knew each other.

Yet she'd given herself to him. Completely. No holding back.

Had Nina done the same? David had dropped

his arm from the woman's shoulders and now the two walked side by side down the hallway. Daffy moved through the metal detector, considering the situation. Johnnie Cochran had probably been photographed with his arm around O. J. Simpson. Attorneys were allowed to comfort their clients. Nina could be here as a client, not a colleague. A good detective didn't jump to conclusions.

Thankful for the several niches and doorways along the hall, Daffy kept out of sight. She got close enough to hear David say, "Don't worry. I'll do all the talking."

That, Daffy could believe. It seemed to her that ever since he'd met her sister he'd been their voice, to such an extent that Jonni had become more and more silent.

Still, Jonni said she was happy. So perhaps she didn't mind David's high-handed ways.

Daffy slipped from her hiding place and shadowed the two of them down the hall, hoping David wouldn't turn around and catch her at her Columbo act. If he did, she had a story all prepared. She was en route to pay a ticket. It was a bit of a stretch, because as a dyed-in-the-wool Uptown girl, who thought of the west bank of the Mississippi River as a province in China, Daffy didn't spend enough time on the other side of the river to get a ticket there, but would David think of that?

Not as long as he was engrossed in little Miss Nina, Daffy thought, watching the way he couldn't take his eyes off her. She doubted if he looked at all his clients or co-workers like that.

The two of them halted before a door, which David held open. They entered and Daffy approached, noting it appeared to be a courtroom. She hesitated, but her journalistic training stood her in good stead and she sailed on in.

The press, she knew, always belonged.

She pictured the rows of reporters surrounding her at Hunter's keynote speech and, of course, that image led to Hunter. And, of course, that thought led to their lovemaking.

Only the staccato banging of the gavel brought her up short. She slipped into the first seat she spotted and glanced around her.

David was at one of the tables in the front, Nina beside him. Opposite them sat a stern-faced woman in an ill-fitting navy suit and a bear of a man Daffy disliked on sight. The judge sat behind her raised bench, flipping through sheaths of papers and looking as if she'd rather be on the ninth hole at English Turn than in the stuffy courtroom.

As she glanced around at the clusters of anxious and grim-faced men and women, Daffy wished herself elsewhere. Right now, she'd give more than her eyeteeth to be in Salt Lake City with Hunter James.

Not just having sex.

Making love.

She sighed and circled her ankle, spelling out his name.

The gavel cracked again and she heard some-one call the case of West vs. West.

David and his paralegal intern rose, as did Navy Suit and her client. Daffy quit thinking about Hunter and sat at attention.

She had to hand it to her brother-in-law. He outtalked, outcharmed, and outsmarted the other side. Before Daffy could say "Dear Love Doctor," the judge had ordered Nina's ex-husband to cough up alimony and child support, and put into effect a restraining order so he couldn't go anywhere near her.

The gavel slammed again and David whisked Nina toward the door.

Daffy stared after them, impressed despite her-self. The other attorney swept her client, who made Daffy think of a summer storm menacing the Gulf, from the courtroom, and Daffy shivered as she caught sight of the look in the man's eyes.

Bravo for David, she thought. He was doing a good deed, helping a woman in need. Perhaps he was innocent of all the crimes Daffy had already convicted him of. And perhaps it was time for Daffy to make peace with her sister's choice of spouse.

Just to make sure, she hurried outside and tailed the two of them as they left the courthouse. No by-the-hour motel stops, no lingering after-noon luncheon.

They drove straight back to work, leaving Daffy to return to the contemplation of her own problems.

* * *

Hunter paced his hotel room, clutching his phone. Using the tiny hand-held device, he could buy and sell stock, troll the Internet, call up any of his employees.

But he couldn't locate Daffy.

He wasn't sure why, but he needed to talk to her. Needed to hear her voice.

It made no sense at all.

Sure, they'd had a terrific fling in Vegas. He'd had sex he'd never dreamed would be so good. He'd been shaken to his very core by her responses to him. He'd wanted more, not less, and he'd only begun to explore what lay between them.

And now he couldn't even talk to her on the goddamn telephone.

No swearing. Not in my house. He heard his mother's voice ringing in his head and he had to smile. Maybe if he quit swearing, he'd find her.

Bemused by the thought, he redialed her home number.

And sure enough, she answered!

He made a mental note to send a dozen roses to the long-suffering and oh-so-wise Thelma James of Ponchatoula, Louisiana, as he said, "Daffy, what's happening?" just as if she'd called him rather than the other way around.

"Hunter, what a surprise."

Surprise. Dammit, he'd sent her flowers. Called her at least three times in two days. What was the surprise?

"The connection is breaking up," she said.

No swearing. Hunter gripped the phone and said, "I'm going to be stuck in Salt Lake for at least another day or so."

"I can hear you now. This merger must be complicated."

"Very," he said, wondering whether he should tell her how much he missed her. And how much that amazed him.

"Business is like that," Daffy said.

Hunter nodded. He was doing a pretty poor job of this phone-conversation thing.

Silence hung over the lines, plumping the pockets of his phone carrier but doing nothing for Hunter's interests. Finally he said, "Daffy?"

"Yes?" Her voice leapt a bit, which gave Hunter hope.

"If you're not busy this weekend . . ."

"Yes?" This time the question was much more reserved and Hunter almost lost his nerve. But not for nothing had he earned his way out of the gutter.

"Want to go up to Ponchatoula with me?"

"Ponchatoula?"

Right. Daffy the consummate Uptown girl had to think he was pulling her leg. She probably thought City Park was a suburb of New Orleans. Well, for some things Hunter refused to apologize. "My hometown," he said.

Silence ticked away yet again. Hunter stared across the lonely sitting room of his suite in Salt Lake's finest hotel, picturing Daffy beneath him on the bed in Vegas, her face a symphony of ecstasy as he brought her to the heights of pleasure. But other images overlapped, particularly the rancid memory of Emily ridiculing him for having the nerve to ask out the homecoming queen.

"I'd love to go with you," she said softly.

Hunter stared at the receiver. Had she really said yes? And why did it matter so much? "Great," he said. "I'll pick you up early Saturday morning. I'm afraid I may not be in until late Friday."

"Sounds good," Daffy said. "I have an event I have to cover Friday night anyway."

"Oh," Hunter said. Had he expected her to be sitting by the phone, nothing else going on in her life?

"Hunter?"

It was his turn to utter the "Yes?" that drove him crazy when she'd said it.

A beep sounded on the line and Daffy, to his extreme frustration, said, "See you Saturday. I've got to get this call."

And there he was, alone in his suite, left hanging.

At least Saturday was only three days away.

Daffy felt compelled to take the other call, knowing that if she stayed on the line much longer, she'd break down and shout out her need for Hunter like a silly teenager suffering her first crush.

And Daffy Landry had never needed any man.

Right. So, chicken that she was, she took the other call rather than acknowledge that maybe, just maybe, things were changing. Why else did she feel as if the lights in her room had dimmed the moment he hung up?

Jonni repeated her greeting and Daffy blinked and managed to respond.

"You left me a message to call you," Jonni said in her usual self-contained and quiet way.

"That's right. I did." But the only person she wanted to talk to was Hunter. No, that wasn't true. She had asked Jonni to phone her. "There's something I wanted to tell you," Daffy began.

"If it's about David, I don't want to hear it," Jonni said.

Daffy held the receiver out and stared at the beige plastic. "Excuse me?"

"I know you've been thinking the worst of him, and if you've gone and done something to try to prove it, I simply do not want to know."

Wow. "Well, it's a good thing I don't have bad news," Daffy said.

"So you did do something."

"I only followed him."

"Daffy!"

"I was trying to help."

"I don't need any help." Her sister's voice was firm.

"But if he were seeing someone else, wouldn't you want to know?"

"What difference would it make?"

"What difference?" Daffy knew her voice shot up. "Only about a day-and-night difference."

"I married David and I'm not leaving him," her sister said softly, but in a determined voice that raised the small hairs on Daffy's neck.

"Even if he were cheating on you?" Daffy knew how strongly Jonni felt about the fidelity she expected of herself; how could she make an exception for her husband? Why, one of the reasons Daffy doubted that she would ever marry was because she wasn't sure she wasn't too much of her mother's daughter not to stray.

"No matter what," Jonni said.

"Why?"

The silence stretched long over the phone and Daffy, for once, kept her silence, waiting for her sister to find the words she sought.

At last Jonni said, "Daddy stood by Mother."

"Wow," Daffy whispered. She repeated the word, noting in a most detached way that her vocabulary had dwindled to that single word.

She wanted to argue with her sister, line up the logical reasons that their parents' relationship should not determine the fate of her own life. But what was the point? Jonni wasn't open to reason, and if David truly was only assisting the intern with her legal needs, her sister had nothing to worry about anyway.

"I've got to go," Jonni said, her voice firm. "The nanny's bringing Erika in from her walk. I do appreciate your trying to help, but let it go, okay?"

"Sure," Daffy said. The phone buzzed in her ear after her sister hung up.

She continued to grip the receiver, mulling over Jonni's attitude and kicking herself for not having asked Hunter what hotel he was staying in. She should at least have gotten his phone number before she'd taken the other call.

Daffy couldn't remember when she'd felt more lonesome.

17

Saturday morning arrived cool and clear, more like spring than early summer in Louisiana. Daffy snuggled under the covers, then threw them off as she remembered just what day it was.

Hunter was picking her up at nine to drive to Ponchatoula.

And the clock read 8:45!

Vaulting from her four-poster bed, Daffy grabbed for the peignoir draped across the foot of the bed and then paused, the frothy fabric clutched to her bare breasts. Despite the number of times both her mother and her sister had admonished her, Daffy still slept in the nude.

Fifteen minutes. That gave her time to put on a quick cup of coffee before jumping into the shower. She did love her morning java. And before embarking on a day with Hunter, she needed her wits about her.

At that moment the doorbell rang, chiming clearly all the way through the raised Creole cottage to her bedroom near the back of the house.

Not Hunter! Not yet.

She wasn't ready to face him, not after the stilted phone conversations and the week's gap since their fantasy trip to Las Vegas. She, for once, had no idea what to say.

The bell rang again. Apparently Hunter was not feeling awkward. Daffy slipped into the robe, ran a comb through her hair, and swished a mouthful of Scope. One did like to be prepared for happy outcomes.

She was almost to the door when she remembered just how sheer her peignoir was. She considered, one foot in midair, then sailed forward.

Good. Shake him up a bit, she thought, and swung the door open wide.

Looking every inch as gorgeous as she remembered him, Hunter stood on her porch, two steaming cups of PJ's coffee in his hands and a paper bag tucked under one elbow.

"Room service," he said, a look of what Daffy could only think of as wolfish admiration on his face as he surveyed her from the top of her tousled head to the tips of her bare toes.

She stood in the open doorway, reveling in the way he was soaking in the sight of her, and did the same. He wore khaki shorts, a polo shirt, tennis shoes, and the ancient Timex. Nothing fancy.

Certainly nothing to indicate his substantial bank balance.

Not that Daffy cared. It was the curve of his mouth and the light in his eyes and that searing, so-direct way he had of seeing into her soul that mattered to her.

A clip-clip-snip noise penetrated her bemused brain and Daffy dragged her attention away from Hunter. Her next-door neighbor, wealthy enough to hire a staff of gardeners, was out early, clipping her bushes and checking the quiet street for any tidbits worthy of repeating to her circle of afternoon-tea lady friends.

Daffy lifted a hand in a friendly salute. Her peignoir gapped and her neighbor pursed her lips, resuming her clipping with even greater vehemence.

Biting back a gurgle of laughter, Daffy said, "Maybe you should come inside."

"Good idea." After bestowing a friendly smile on the neighbor, Hunter followed Daffy in. As he stepped into her house, he said, "One look at you in that robe—if you can call it that—and the entire neighborhood will be banging down your door."

Daffy blushed, but made no move to close the drifting fabric together. "Coffee!" She held out a hand, but Hunter shook his head.

"First things first," he said, turning to set the cups and the paper bag on a side table.

Then he opened his arms and advanced on her even as she flung herself against him, all self-constraint vanished.

"This was the longest week," he murmured, smoothing her hair and kissing her all over her face and neck.

"Oh, for me, too." Daffy clung to him, her pride evaporated, her misgivings forgotten. Last night she'd told herself she'd keep him at arm's distance. Be friendly, but clearly not swept away by him. She'd planned to show him it took more than one fab date and the most incredible love-making she'd ever known to woo and win Daffodil Landry.

"Where's your bedroom?" Hunter nibbled at her mouth and worked at the sash of her peignoir as he asked the question.

His eyes had that dark and smoky look she'd seen so often last weekend. Her body was responding already. She was damp with wanting him to fill her, possess her, and travel with her to the paradise of passionate release.

With a grin, she pulled her sash free, roped it around his waist, and, beckoning with one finger, said, "Come with me."

"Just try escaping me," Hunter said, wondering why he'd bothered asking directions to the bedroom. One flick of a finger and that see-through scrap of cloth would dissolve onto the floor, and they'd never make it there. "God, I missed you," he said, though he was pretty sure he was repeating himself.

Daffy smiled, slipped the sash off him, and stretched out her arms to him. Hunter took one delicate hand into his and marveled that a week away from a woman he'd really only just met could make such a difference in his whole outlook on life.

They were passing down a broad hallway. Any other time Hunter might have been interested in his surroundings; he was naturally curious as to the kind of life Daffy lived. But today nothing mattered but this overpowering sense that his world would not be all right until the two of them lay exhausted in a sweaty tangle of limbs.

Funny, he'd stopped for the coffee thinking to use it as a bridge, a means of reconnecting by bringing a gift that also served as a topic of conversation. But to his delight, she'd welcomed him with open arms. Could life get much better?

Daffy led him into a large room dominated by a massive four-poster. Standing beside the bed, she let that sexy concoction of a robe slip to the ground.

Oh, yeah, Hunter thought, life had just gotten even better.

She reached for his belt, but he got there first, stripping himself of his clothing and kicking free his shoes, all the while staring at her body like a man starved.

Still standing, he pulled her to him. She arched against him and he caught one breast in his mouth, reveling in the feel and the taste. "Don't ever go away for so long," he said.

She laughed, a breathy sound that was as much a sensual moan as a sound of humor. "You went away, not me."

"Yeah, right. But don't." He lifted his mouth from her breast and said, "It's possible I'm addicted to you."

She stroked the line of his jaw with a very naughty gleam in her eyes. "Then maybe you ought to score a quick fix." As if to accentuate her comment, her hips performed a wild dance of desire and she pulled him onto the bed amidst the rumpled silky-soft sheets and lacy pillows.

"I've gone to heaven," Hunter said, and slid into her slick warmth, joining her body with his, the two of them so perfectly in sync it seemed they must have been doing so for more than one lifetime.

He moved over her, cupping her hips up to better answer his hunger for her. And she drove him on, her body speeding his tempo, the breathy moans and sweet senseless things she was saying enveloping them in a heated world in which only the two of them existed.

He thought he called her name, but couldn't say for sure. The blood roaring in his ears mingled with her own cry of ecstasy. Hunter clasped her even more tightly to him, and with a shout, lost himself in her.

He didn't move at all for the longest moments; then slowly, through the afterglow of his release, he realized he was probably crushing her. Lifting his weight off her, he drank in the sight of Daffy, glowing, satisfied, smiling.

"Wow," she murmured.

"Wow," he echoed with a grin, shifting to the

side of her and stroking her belly lightly. "If I'd known coffee was an aphrodisiac . . ."

"Silly, *you*'re the aphrodisiac." She rolled onto her side and they lay face-to-face.

"Why, thank you, ma'am," he said. "I've been called a lot of names in my day, but that's a first."

"Then you hang around with a lot of nonobservant people." She kissed him on the shoulder, then lay back with a sigh.

"Ready for another great weekend?" Funny, but he'd asked her to go with him to Ponchatoula as a test to see how the Uptown girl would react to the true world of Hunter James. He'd impressed her with Las Vegas, but he'd thought to shock her with his past poverty, probably to see whether or not she'd run screaming from his side. Now he couldn't imagine why he'd thought such a measure necessary. He couldn't imagine spending the weekend—or any day—without her.

"Ready when you are." Daffy pushed up until she sat back against the mound of pillows.

He couldn't say he was ready to move. Spending the day right there in Daffy's bedroom appealed mightily to him. If he hadn't told his mother he was coming for a visit and bringing a friend, he'd heat things up all over again. But this time he'd do it nice and slow . . .

Daffy was staring at her legs and had one hand pressed to her inner thigh.

"What's wrong?" Hunter sat up. "Did I hurt you?" He'd thrash himself if he had.

A funny, almost curious expression flitted

across her face as she lifted her hand. "I'm okay," she said rather ruefully, "but we were in such a rush we skipped a detail or two."

Hunter looked from her hand, where a streak of moisture glistened, to her thigh and slapped himself on the forehead. "No condom."

She nodded.

"Never in my life," he said, watching her to see if she was upset with him for not taking the responsibility he'd preached so pointedly only last week. He'd known that if any woman could cause him to forget his rules, it would be Daffy. She had the power to mesmerize him he'd never found in any other woman. "We-ell," he said slowly, dragging the word out a syllable or two, "we-ell. I apologize. It is my fault."

Daffy just sat there, her hand back between her thighs, an odd look on her face.

"Are you upset?"

She shook her head. Ducking her chin, she said, "It feels . . . kind of good, actually. I mean, this is the first time in my life I've ever had sex without a condom."

Hunter sensed her embarrassment at the intimacy of the discussion. He pushed back against the pillows and put an arm around her. Only then did she glance up and meet his eyes. Instead of upset, though, she looked happy. He tightened his hold around her and said, "It's my first time, too. And man, did it feel great!"

She blushed and nodded.

"Hey, marry me and we'll do it like this always."

Daffy stilled. He could feel her withdraw from his embrace.

"Very funny," she said, slipping free from his arm and sliding off the side of the bed. "Why don't you heat up the coffee and I'll take a quick shower?"

So he wasn't invited to the shower? Hunter got off the bed, kissed the top of her head, and said, "I was only joking."

She nodded and gave him a smile that was a shadow of her usual happy one. "Yes, I know," she said, and picked up her robe.

Hunter stood there as she flitted into the bathroom and pulled the door closed. Man, even speaking the verb "to marry" sent Daffy scuttling.

He'd have to find out why.

And he'd have to remember his condoms. From their most recent discussion, he was pretty sure they had nothing to worry about healthwise, but a rule was a rule.

Besides, a guy could get spoiled.

He pulled on his shorts and headed to the front of the house to collect the coffee. That was when the thought struck him. He looked around for the voice that must have spoken, 'cause surely it hadn't come from inside his own head. But there it was again: "So why not marry Daffy?"

Marry?

Shaking his head the way he did to clear water

from his ears after swimming, Hunter entered the kitchen and put the cups into the microwave. The pale yellow walls reminded him of the dress Daffy had worn to the TekWare convention—and shed in the limousine.

Never before had he paired a particular woman with the verb "to marry."

He stirred the heated coffee and considered that a weekend in Ponchatoula would probably settle his senses back to normal and also do a good job of chasing Daffy away. Once she realized the gap in their backgrounds, no doubt she'd decline to date him again.

For someone who'd invited her with just that idea in mind, he felt absolutely zero satisfaction.

Safe behind the bathroom door, Daffy leaned against its solid surface and took a breath that reached deep down to her toes. Perhaps it had been unsociable of her not to invite Hunter to share her shower. Perhaps she had retreated like a bug coming face-to-face with a flashlight. Perhaps she had overreacted to his joking "marry me."

She pushed away from the door and, facing the vanity mirror, forced herself to admit what had sent her fleeing.

Naturally, he'd been joking.

But for the most fleeting micromoment, she'd wished he'd spoken in earnest.

"Get a grip," she said to her image in the mirror. "You're not the marrying kind, remember?"

And neither was Hunter James, Mr. "Give me

thirty days and I can make any woman fall for me." His whole relationship style was that of Julius Caesar invading Gaul, or was it Britain? *Veni, vidi, vici;* I came, I saw, I conquered.

Or perhaps, Daffy thought, amused despite her bafflement at her own reaction, for Hunter James the English translation should more accurately be ordered as: I saw, I conquered, I came.

And then he'd be on his way.

With a sigh she turned on the taps and stepped into the shower. As much as she sensed Hunter was a love-'em-and-leave-'em kind of guy, she certainly couldn't fault his technique or his generosity. None of her lovers came close to his ability to give her as satisfying an experience as he had for himself.

Well, sad to say, Daffy thought, dumping shampoo onto her hair, but she and Hunter were two of a kind. Both in their own ways fickle, unsettled, and racing as fast as they could away from the demons of their past.

Thinking of running away led to the idea of avoiding the trip. Maybe she'd tell Hunter she'd changed her mind.

Considering this option, she began to carefully shave one leg.

A leg she'd wrapped around Hunter's body during the most intense intercourse she'd ever experienced.

"Chicken."

She shaved the other leg, then washed away the last traces of their intimacy.

Pausing, she relived the moment he'd pulled her so close to him she'd felt their bodies merge and then he'd filled her with his seed.

Nah, she wasn't staying home. For better or worse, she was going to Ponchatoula.

18

Hunter almost passed up the exit to Poncha-toula, turned the car around, and headed back to New Orleans.

New Orleans, where women like Daffy be-longed.

The drive was less than an hour, all interstate, but Daffy had chattered so brightly, so gaily, and in such a well-mannered and meaningless way, Hunter almost didn't recognize the woman he'd bedded only a short time earlier.

Almost.

She had to be nervous, no other reason for her to dither on like that. Why, she'd told him stories about half the people she'd photographed for her column, and never once had she relaxed and been the Daffy he'd spent the weekend with in Las Vegas.

His mother was going to think he'd lost his mind.

He could see her wise eyes now, moving over Daffy, taking in the linen shift with the matching sandals and handbag, the diamond bracelet dangling casually from her wrist. He could almost read Thelma's mind, hear her thinking, "Lovely, but has that money gone to your head, son?"

And what would Daffy see when she looked at his mother? Would she see the hands worn by years of framing work and the lines etched in her face by a lifetime of struggling to provide for her family? Or would she see the hands that had held him safe and the bright mind and loving heart that had always looked out for his best interests?

Why, oh, why, had he invited Daffy?

"That sign says Ponchatoula," Daffy said, pointing to the exit marker.

"Oh, right," Hunter muttered, and peeled off just in time to careen into the turn and to annoy an eighteen-wheeler close on his rear. The big rig laid on its air horn and Hunter shrugged. Let the driver complain. He couldn't be any less happy than Hunter right at this moment.

"Do you drive back and forth a lot?" Daffy was sitting half facing him, but her attention seemed fixated on anything that passed by outside the car, rather than on him.

"Lately I've spent a lot more time in the city," he answered.

"Which one?" After she asked the question, she

trilled a bit of a laugh, then stopped abruptly, her hand clamping over her chin.

"Am I making you nervous, Daffy?" He had to ask. And it was hard, pressing those words out from behind his teeth. He wasn't one to ask a woman what was going on in her mind. If he didn't connect easily with someone, he'd just shrug and move on. But damn it, he couldn't do that. Not now, when he'd invited her to Ponchatoula. Not after how great last weekend had been.

Not now.

Not ever.

Hunter glanced over his right shoulder, then his left. Now, who had said that?

Daffy was gazing out the window as if she'd never seen a Sonic drive-up or a Chevron station or a washateria crammed into a two-story lean-to. Hell, she'd probably never stepped inside a laundromat in her life. She was playing with the diamond bracelet on her wrist but her lips weren't moving, so hers hadn't been the voice that uttered, "Not ever."

Must be your subconscious, he said to himself. Daffy sure had a way of getting to him. First he'd invited her to dissuade her from being interested in him, then to test her interest, then to drive her away, then to see if just maybe she'd care to hang out with a guy who had a stellar future but not so pretty a past.

"Nervous?" She shook her head as he asked the

question. "I'm rarely nervous," she said. "Where does the name Ponchatoula come from?"

There it was again, that calm sort of question that held no flesh-and-blood life to it. Who cared what the meaning was of the name of the town? What Hunter cared about was . . .

"Daffy."

"Yes?"

He pulled off the main drag, filled with antiques shops and restaurants that catered mainly to the tourists who strayed into town in search of a great buy they could trumpet to their friends back home.

Turning in the seat, he lay his arm over the back of her headrest and saw to his dismay that she in no way leaned closer in response to his overture. "Are you upset with me because I forgot to use protection?"

Her eyes widened. He watched the beautiful column of her throat as she swallowed, hard, and stared back at him. Her hair swung gently against the tops of her shoulders when she replied, "Oh, no, not at all."

He brushed a hand over the crown of her hair. "Are you sure?"

She nodded, and blinked.

"Anything else?" Surprised at himself for asking, Hunter waited for her reaction. Why did he care if she was upset? Hadn't he wanted her to be? Hadn't he wanted her to see she wasn't hanging out with a millionaire, but rather with the bad seed of a small town, the bastard son of a woman who'd left the space for "father" blank on the birth certificate?

"I'm fine," she said. "What are we going to see first?"

He moved his arm back to his side of the car and faced the steering wheel. It was funny, this wanting to understand her mood and her not letting him in. He was used to things being the other way around, like when Lucy pestered him about what he was feeling and he never wanted to share with her, assuming she wouldn't understand.

Was that how Daffy felt? That he, Hunter James, wouldn't understand her, so what was the use of explaining it to him?

He drove back to the main street, moving into the left lane for the turn just before the railroad tracks. If Daffy felt like that, he promised himself, before this weekend was out, he would unlock the secret to understanding her. He didn't want her to shield herself from him, to close him out. Damn it, for reasons he couldn't explain at all, it mattered too much to him. No matter what, he'd get a closer glimpse inside that beautiful head of hers.

"I thought we'd stop by the house first," Hunter was saying.

Daffy nodded, wishing she hadn't denied being nervous. "Great," she said. "That's a charming train station. It looks like it belongs on a postcard."

"It's another antiques store now," Hunter said, "like almost every shop along the main street. It's better than being a ghost town with all the life sucked to the edge of the town by the Wal-Marts and Kmarts, but I don't quite get the antiques thing."

"I love antiques. I found my bed . . ." She blushed and let her sentence trail off.

Hunter was staring at her with a curious expression on his face. "It's a beautiful bed," he said, pulling off the road that paralleled the railroad tracks and stopping in front of a rambling yellow house with a tin roof. "Where did you get it?"

"In an out-of-the-way shop in Charleston. It was on consignment and I was visiting one of my sorority sisters and she mentioned it to me. I fell in love with it the moment I saw it."

"I can understand that," Hunter replied, making no move to turn off the ignition even though he'd parked the car.

"You can?"

He nodded. "I may not be into antiques, but I know a thing of beauty when I see it."

Daffy toyed with her bracelet and glanced at him, almost shyly. "Me, too," she said softly.

He leaned over, placed a hand over her hand. "Thanks for coming with me, Daffy."

"You said that about Las Vegas, too."

"I hope I always say it."

Daffy didn't move. She scarcely breathed. Why was he saying all these things? He sounded like a man who'd found the woman he'd been searching for the world over, yet she knew him to be a flirt and a rambler. And why did she savor every sweet word he said? Why not smile and laugh and flutter her lashes and let them slide right past her? She'd done exactly that with every other man she'd ever dated.

"Ready?" Hunter lifted her hand and brushed his lips over her knuckles.

She wasn't, but she wasn't going to admit to that. "Yes," she said, reaching for the door handle.

Hunter jumped out and zipped around to open her door for her. Daffy liked that he did that. "Thanks," she said, stepping out. "Your mother taught you right."

"Oh, yeah." Hunter grinned. "There's no one quite like Thelma."

"That's what you call her?" Daffy walked side by side with Hunter along a stone pathway toward the one-story house. A porch traveled along the two sides she could see and wicker chairs and a swing invited visitors to dawdle there.

"Pretty much." Hunter paused on the porch. "How about you?"

"I call my parents Dad and Mother."

"Interesting contrast." He led her to the swing and she joined him there. "You don't talk about your parents much."

"No, I guess I don't. So is this where you grew up?"

"Daffy and her defenses," Hunter said. "You don't let anyone get in too close, do you?"

She started to object, but what was the point? Jonni knew her best; her father accepted and loved her, but he accepted everyone. Her mother pretty much ignored her except on socially essential family occasions, and all her friends accepted her as the fun-loving social butterfly she portrayed herself to be. "I guess I don't," she said once more.

He leaned against the back of the swing and rocked them gently by pushing his foot against the floor. Didn't say a thing, though, for which Daffy was thankful. And appreciative. She stole a sideways glance at him, then slipped one hand into his.

"I'm not trying to shut you out," she said. "I'm just cautious by nature."

And if someone was going to get hurt in this thing between them, Daffy wasn't volunteering to be "it."

"Ah," he said, and held on to her hand.

A large yellow cat poked its head around the corner of the porch. "Meet Mr. Pickle," Hunter said. "Now, there's a cat who used to jump if anyone said boo to him."

The cat strolled forward and paused to rub his chin against Hunter's calf. Hunter scratched the top of the cat's head and the feline sat back and meowed a loud complaint.

"He's pretty trusting now," Daffy said.

Hunter fixed her with a look Daffy couldn't—or didn't want to—interpret. "Come on," he said, rising, her hand still tucked in his. "Mr. Pickle wants his swing."

Sure enough, as soon as they headed for the

front door, the cat leapt into the swing and applied his tongue and one front paw to the task of washing his face.

Hunter unlocked the front door and held it open for Daffy. She walked into a large living-dining room with casual furniture that invited one to sprawl comfortably, either on the deep chairs beside the fireplace or on the sofa in front of the television. The end tables were cluttered with baskets of yarn and needlepoint projects; the coffee table held a partially completed jigsaw puzzle. Hindering more than helping solve the puzzle was another cat, this one streaked in tones of chocolate and caramel and stretched out asleep atop the puzzle pieces.

"How homey," Daffy remarked.

"Thanks," Hunter said somewhat dryly.

"That," Daffy said primly, "is a major compliment."

He dropped her hand, but only to catch her by the shoulders and draw her close. "I'm glad you like it."

She tilted her mouth to meet his kiss and as his warm lips captured hers, she sighed softly, parting her lips to let him in more fully.

Hunter accepted the invitation and pulled her soft body to his own aching, hard one. He didn't want to care what she thought; yet he did. He didn't want to need her, yet he craved her. He didn't want to love her, yet he—

He broke off the kiss, stunned by the thought he'd almost formed.

Almost. Not quite.

"Don't stop," Daffy murmured, guiding his head back down.

"Better make sure no one's home," he said, stalling for some recovery time.

"Oh, of course!" Daffy backed up, one hand over her rosy lips.

"Thelma will be at the shop," Hunter said over his shoulder as he strode down the hall that led to the kitchen, "but it's hard to say who else might be here. She adopts people the way she does cats."

Hunter was an only child and Thelma a single parent. Curious, Daffy followed him out of the cozy room, down a hallway hung with lots and lots of pictures. She halted in front of an array of what had to be Hunter's grade school pictures.

The bright-eyed boy, with a grin full of mischief, changed little from photo to photo. Though, leaning closer, Daffy noted what looked like a black eye on the picture marked "fifth grade." Intent on her study, she didn't hear Hunter walk up behind her.

He put his arms around her and covered her eyes with his palms. "Not the baby pictures!"

Laughing, Daffy pulled his hands down and tucked them around her waist. Holding on to him, she said, "Oh, yes, the baby pictures. You were adorable. How'd you get the black eye?"

She felt him stiffen; then his shoulders moved in a shrug. "Fight."

Tit for tat. She'd closed up on him and now he was doing the same. Feeling braver, possibly because they weren't face-to-face, she said, "Tell me what you were fighting over and I'll tell you why I call my dad Dad and my mother Mother."

"You're good," he said, nuzzling his chin against the top of her hair. "Some snot-nosed kid called my mother a bad name and I socked him. He hit me back."

"And was his shiner worse than yours?"

"How'd you know?"

"A good guess."

He kissed the side of her ear and tightened his hold around her waist, his fingers drifting lower. Daffy sighed and snuggled against him. She clearly had no willpower where this man was concerned.

"Well?" Hunter said, his fingers moving in circles over the surface of her tummy.

"My mother," she said slowly, trying not to sound bitter or like a spoiled child who, no matter what, would condemn her parent, "is one of those women who should never have had children. She's incapable of giving selflessly of herself."

"And is that what it takes to be a mother?"

"I think perhaps it is."

"And your dad wasn't like that?"

"Wasn't and isn't." Daffy heard the emphatic way she answered and wished she could forgive her mother. Or maybe she had forgiven her but what she really wished was that she had a mother whom she could turn to, laugh with, shop with, cry with.

The only means of communication her mother knew was criticism, followed by ostracism.

"My dad has always been my friend," she said. "Even when being my friend wasn't such a popular position to take."

"You mean, after you messed with Aloysius's best man and screwed up your wedding?"

Daffy caught her breath. "Did I tell you that?" Perhaps she had, but she hadn't meant to reveal that side of her.

"Let's just say I've heard the story."

Daffy wriggled around till she faced Hunter. He kept his arms around her. Looking him square in the eye, she said, "As sick as it sounds, I had my reasons. I wanted to punish Aloysius to get back at his father. My mother . . ." Her voice faltered.

"Yes?" Hunter brushed a strand away from her cheek and the tender gesture almost did her in.

"My mother was with Aloysius's father, in our house, and Jonni walked in on them. It was for that reason I wanted to punish them. For hurting my sister."

"And for hurting you."

She nodded and, to her dismay, realized her chin was trembling. "After that day, my world was never a safe place. I never knew whom to trust or whom to believe in."

He bent and kissed her gently and held her closer, running soothing hands over her back and shoulders and saying silly things like, "Shush, my baby, everything's gonna be all right."

And Daffy believed him.

Because when Hunter had his arms around her, her world was safe again.

19

Maybe she was all wrong for him, but if she was, holding her sure felt right.

"Everything's gonna be okay," he murmured again, between kisses, reveling in the taste of her, touched by the way she'd opened up emotionally. Standing there in the hallway beside the rogue's gallery his mother insisted on maintaining, he pressed her against him. He savored her with his mouth and let the rest of his body speak to the dramatic effect she had on him. But he needed to address some of the fears she'd shared.

"Your mother is your mother, but you are you," Hunter said softly. "And you are a very special and wonderful woman."

Daffy had had her eyes closed, but at that, she opened them and said shyly, "You understand that I'm afraid of being like her?"

He nodded. Given his own fears that he'd turn out to be as big a jerk as his old man when it came to relationships, it was a pretty safe guess.

"Wow," she said.

"Wow," he repeated, kissing her throat. "And do you understand you turn me into a wild man?"

"Want to show me just how wild?"

"It's a good thing no one else is in the house," he said, cupping her breasts with his hands.

She uttered a shaky laugh and tossed her head back, offering herself to him.

He reached around for the zipper of her dress, then paused. The bedroom he called his when he was in town had a lock on the door. "Maybe we'd better get out of the hall," he said, scooping her into his arms.

"Whatever you say," Daffy murmured, snuggling sweetly against his shoulder at the same time that she reached with one hand to enclose his arousal through his shorts.

He almost dropped her.

She laughed, a throaty gurgle of desire that set his fire for her raging. "She-devil," he whispered, moving past the kitchen doorway.

The phone on the kitchen wall shrilled.

He paused.

Daffy's deep kisses and naughty handwork urged him down the hall.

He moved his feet.

The phone machine clicked on and a voice Hunter could have gone all day without hearing sounded throughout the house. Lucy.

"Hey, Hunter, it's me. I saw your Jeep go past Robo's. I'm glad you didn't stay away so long this time. Can't wait to see you. Call me."

Daffy's lips had screeched to a halt after the "it's me." At least she hadn't jumped free of his embrace or demanded he put her down.

Before either one of them could say anything, the phone rang again. He stepped quickly toward the bedroom.

"Don't you want to know who's calling?" She asked the question in what he could only call a voice of fake innocence.

"No." He gripped her tighter. "I have everyone I need right here."

"That's sweet, but what if it's your ... mother?"

"Won't be."

"Hi, honey. Lucy told me you're here. There's fresh lemonade in the fridge and peanut butter cookies. Come by the shop after you get settled in."

Hunter stared at Daffy. "That's completely out of character. And Thelma never bakes cookies."

"Really?" Daffy wrinkled her nose. "I had this image of her with an apron on, bustling about. And her house looks so homey."

"Oh, she bakes," Hunter said, "but pies and cakes. She says cookies aren't enough of a challenge."

"Thank goodness. The only thing my mother makes is reservations." She sounded wistful.

He kissed the tip of her nose.

"Hunter?"

"Yes?" He'd made it almost to the door of the bedroom. He said a silent prayer for the phone to remain quiet. It would be just like Lucy to call Emily and for Emily to call him at home. He didn't want any more interruptions. And he didn't want cookies or lemonade.

He wanted Daffodil Landry.

He lowered her to the bed. To his surprise, Daffy sat with her knees together, smoothing her skirt and her hair.

"Maybe we should go to the shop now," she said, looking more at her pretty pink fingernails than at him.

"Now?" He knelt beside her and took her hand. Considering what he wanted to be doing, that gentle touch evidenced pretty strong self-restraint. Then he noticed she was blushing slightly. "What is it, sweetheart?"

She lifted her head, her eyes wide and inquiring, no doubt at the endearment. "It's just that if your mother knows we're here and we show up an hour or so from now, she'll guess . . . well, won't she guess what we've been doing?"

He rocked back on his heels. "I see your point. One look at the smile on my face and the glow on yours and it won't be a guess, either."

She smiled and he offered a hand, pulling her lightly to her feet. "Okay, to the Berry Best Frame Shop we go."

"Berry Best?"

"One of the consequences of Ponchatoula being

the strawberry capital of the world is that almost every business has 'berry' somewhere in its name." Hunter led the way back through the house, trying to adjust both mentally and physically to the change of plans. He couldn't say he blamed Daffy; as a guest, she didn't want Thelma thinking the first thing she'd done was go to bed with her hostess's son. But damn, he wanted her.

He held open the front door for her. "By the way, the answer to your earlier question, the name Ponchatoula comes from the local Indian name for hair to hang, inspired by all the Spanish moss draped from the trees."

"Oh." Daffy knew that during her earlier nervous chatter she'd asked the question, but at the moment, the last thing she cared about was the Facts on File chapter on Ponchatoula.

Hunter was the most wonderful man she'd ever met.

And unless she'd missed her mark, he had a girlfriend in Ponchatoula. Who else called up and said casually, "It's me"?

The phone started ringing again and Hunter pulled the door shut behind them, but not before Daffy heard yet another female voice.

Casting a sideways glance at his profile, the high forehead, the vivid, dark eyes, the beautifully formed nose, the generous mouth that curved upward in the expression of a man at peace with his world, Daffy sighed. What woman wouldn't find him irresistible?

A girlfriend? More than likely, he possessed a harem.

The yellow cat glanced up from the swing, twitched his tail, and settled down again.

"This is a peaceful house," Daffy said. "A nice place to grow up."

Hunter nodded, some of the sunniness gone from his expression. He hesitated; then, instead of walking straight ahead to the car, he steered her to a path that ran around the side of the house.

The porch followed the house, with another set of wicker chairs and two small tables welcoming visitors. Next to the house stood a small outbuilding of sorts, possibly a tiny garage converted to an apartment.

Hunter, hands on his hips, stared at that small building. Daffy watched as his expression fluctuated from neutral to sad and then back to the more self-assured Hunter she was more used to seeing.

"I bought the front house for my mother with the first real money I earned," he said. "I wanted to buy her a big, new house, but she wouldn't let me. She said she had her roots planted on this block and there was no moving her." He cleared his throat. "The little place in back is where I grew up."

He turned and, mesmerized, Daffy followed him around the path toward his Jeep.

How could anyone live in a place that small? Even for a mother and a growing boy, there wasn't room to turn around in. Daffy honestly couldn't get her mind around it, but at least she kept her mouth shut. She was pretty sure the last thing Hunter wanted was sympathy.

Especially from a woman who'd grown up in a mansion on St. Charles Avenue.

"Cat got your tongue?" Hunter stopped at the side of his Jeep, arms crossed, looking down at her with a fierce expression.

"Mr. Pickle?" Daffy put a finger to her lips and said, "No, I don't think so."

Hunter laughed, a bit grudgingly, but at least it chased the chill away from his features.

Daffy met his gaze and said, "I don't care if you grew up in a sharecropper's shack or the governor's mansion. To quote what a pretty wise guy said to me only recently, 'You're you.' "

His jaw worked and after a moment he said, "Thank you, Daffy."

"You're welcome, sir."

He caught her mouth in a sweet, gentle kiss, and Daffy almost wished she hadn't shied away from making love with him in his mother's house. She wasn't the only one nervous about this visit.

Lifting his head, he said huskily, "We'd better go if we're going."

During the few minutes it took to drive to his mother's shop, Daffy tried not to visualize Hunter's other girlfriends. They were probably all much more like his mother, more of the marry-settle down-raise a family sort. They probably won blue ribbons at the county fair for their strawberry pie recipes. Probably not a one of his hometown girlfriends could compete with her record of disastrous relationships. Probably not a one of them had been caught with her fiancé's best man.

She sighed and wondered why the competition mattered.

What a great question for the Love Doctor. She laughed, and Hunter looked at her with a question in his eyes. Shaking her head slightly, she said, "Just thinking."

"Hope they're good thoughts," he said with a smile.

Daffy could think of no rejoinder. So she merely nodded, meanwhile mentally composing a letter that followed the salutation with:

I met this really great guy, but I'm not the only woman who thinks he's great. As a matter of fact, he told me point-blank that, given thirty days, he can make any woman fall in love with him, and I've known him less than a month, and, Dear Love Doctor, he's right!

She gasped and Hunter hit the brakes.

"What's wrong?" He looked truly concerned.

She rubbed her forehead. "A teeny touch of a migraine," she mumbled, trying to sort out what had gone wrong in her brain. She might be smitten with the guy, but no way was she in love with him! Impossible. She was too jaded and too worldly-wise to let that sort of silliness happen to her. Besides, everyone knew that the minute Daffy Landry even imagined herself in love with a guy, nothing but trouble followed.

"Do you want to stop at the drugstore?"

"For what?"

"Migraine medicine."

"Oh, no, thanks. It was only a twinge. I'm better now." She mustered what she hoped was a convincing smile and wondered how to escape his charm, his magnetism, his sweet solicitude over her faked headache. Darn it. Hunter James was too good.

Too good not to fall in love with.

He parked in front of a row of shops. "Feel like going in?"

Daffy nodded. "Absolutely."

"I could take you back to the house. No tricks," he said, grinning slightly. "Just so you could rest."

Daffy reached over and patted his thigh, a gesture of comfort intended as much for herself as for him. "I am perfectly fine," she said. "And I want to meet your mother."

Hunter hoped both of Daffy's statements were true. He got out of the car, opened the door for Daffy, and led the way across the sidewalk to the Berry Best Frame Shop, all the while wondering what he was doing that Saturday in Ponchatoula.

He'd turned down two invitations that only a few weeks ago he would have jumped at. He'd declined not only a day lazing on a sailboat but a weekend skiing in Salt Lake (to rush home to see Daffy). He'd also ignored a call from Tiffany Phipps about a pair of tickets she just happened to have to a hot sold-out concert in New Orleans, but Hunter hoped he would have had the sense to do so even if he'd never met Daffy.

It was funny, he thought wryly, pausing at the door of his mother's shop, but Tiffany was the sort of woman he'd feared Daffy would turn out to be. And yet here he was, about to introduce Daffy to Thelma.

"Here goes," Hunter said, somewhat under his breath, but Daffy's nervous smile told him she'd heard.

"Don't worry," she said as he opened the door and the bell tied to it clanged, "I won't embarrass you."

"You couldn't," he said.

"Be with you in a minute." His mother's voice floated from the back of the shop.

Hunter glanced around the small store, its floor crowded with bins of photographs and prints available to be framed, the walls nearly solid with paintings, lithographs, and prints. His mother had an eye for the striking and unique, but she also carried the usual suspects. Jazzfest posters, Mardi Gras memorabilia, strawberry festival posters, and, of course, anything and everything else ever done with a strawberry on it—you name it, Berry Best could frame it, sell it, and wrap it to go.

Daffy also was glancing around, surveying

what probably looked to a first-time visitor like an art-supply store hit by a hurricane that was at least a four on the Saffir-Simpson scale. But Hunter had grown up in the artistic clutter and he knew his mother could unerringly locate every piece of inventory.

"Hello," Thelma said, advancing from the back of the shop. Then she caught sight of him and said, "Hunter!"

He nodded and smiled and cocked his head slightly sideways to indicate Daffy's very obvious presence.

Thelma moved forward. "And you must be Hunter's friend from the city," she said, a smile on her lips but a searching look worthy of Hercule Poirot solving a whodunit in her eyes.

"I'm Daffy," Daffy said, holding out her hand. "From Daffodil."

Thelma shook hands, very businesslike, and said, "How nice of Hunter to bring you by for a visit."

Hunter couldn't believe his ears. The woman who had given birth to him was acting like one of those characters on a *Twilight Zone* episode taken over by a creature from another dimension. Who had kidnapped Thelma and replaced her with this automaton of socially correct behavior? What had happened to the woman who had stood-in as mother, confidante, companion, and tutor for his friends for as long as he could remember?

"I thought so, too," Daffy said. She moved toward Thelma as she spoke, placing herself closer to his mother than to him. "Hunter said you're quite the baker."

"He did?" Thelma shot Hunter a look that would have withered a less valiant son. Hunter gave it right back. Damn it, he wanted his mother to like Daffy. She doted on Lucy, and Lucy was all wrong. No matter how many times she threw herself at him, Hunter would resist.

"Oh, yes." Daffy toyed with her bracelet and said, "That's something I'm quite in awe of."

"Baking?" Thelma made a sweeping, dismissive gesture with her hands. "There's nothing to it. At least, if you know what you're doing."

Daffy nodded in all seriousness.

After having heard Daffy tell him that everything she knew about cooking she'd learned from her mother—as in how to make reservations—Hunter couldn't believe his ears. The two of them had to be playing some woman's game. Kind of like two guys outbluffing each other on how many babes they'd laid or how low their golf score was on the back nine.

But why would Daffy bother? Why try to win his mother over?

The bell on the door of the shop clanged just as the siren sounded in Hunter's mind.

Daffy cared.

And she cared enough to try to get his mother to like her.

Hunter swallowed and stared at his size-twelve deck shoes. He'd only intended to flirt with her. He'd actually intended to use Daffy to

find out the identity of that dratted Love Doctor.
But so much had happened since his visit to the
offices of *The Crescent*, he'd almost forgotten he'd
ever cared about that mission. Daffy had turned
his world on its head and now all he thought
about, cared about, worried about, was Daffodil
Landry. Well, that and his business, to be quite
honest, but somehow the two of them went hand
in hand. The two of them, he realized, were the
future as he wanted it to be.

"Why, Hunter, what a surprise!"

He turned, his mind in a whirl, and slowly, he
registered Emily standing there, a slight pout,
hurt yet somehow simultaneously suggestive,
curving her lips downward.

Unfortunately, Daffy turned, too, as did his
mom.

Well, nothing like a negative force to make the
positive ones join together.

As Emily advanced, her arms outstretched,
both Daffy and Thelma seemed to bond. They
moved closer together and exchanged glances.

Suddenly Emily was smothering Hunter in a
hug of greeting accompanied by dramatic kisses
on his cheeks—while Thelma and Daffy both
leaned back against the counter, arms folded in
almost identical postures.

Hunter would have laughed if he could have
caught his breath. As it was, it took him a few
minutes to disentangle himself from the voracious Emily. When he did, he said, "Hello, Emily.
You remember my mother, Mrs. James?"

Playing the gracious lady, Emily dipped her chin the barest of centimeters. "Of course I remember your mother, Hunter."

"And this is Daffodil Landry."

Daffy nodded, a perfect mimicry of Emily's motion. "I believe we met at Jazzfest. You were there with your husband, as I recall."

Thelma actually sniggered.

Hunter wouldn't have believed it of his own mother if he hadn't heard it with his own ears. Thelma had no use for Emily and never had. But then, neither did Hunter.

Glancing warmly at Daffy, Hunter said, "That's right. You and Roger were at Jazzfest the afternoon Daffy and I were there. How is old Rog?"

"He's fine," Emily said, her shoulders stiffening and her prissy little nose taking a vertical turn. "He's away at a banking convention."

"You must be lonely," Daffy said.

"With all the friends I have?" Emily tittered, a noise Hunter had always hated, especially when she accompanied it with a sweeping flutter of her lashes, as she did now. "I'm having a little party tonight, as a matter of fact. No point in letting the grass grow under my feet. Why don't you come?"

"Is that what fidelity is called nowadays?" Thelma still hadn't uncrossed her arms.

Emily's mouth formed a shocked "O." Daffy looked from her to Thelma and over to Hunter. Hunter merely shook his head, and said, "Daffy and I have to get back to New Orleans tonight."

"You do?" Thelma actually sounded disappointed, but to Hunter's relief, she also sounded a lot more like her normal, stolid, and dependable self.

"Daffy's a reporter," Hunter said, not sure why he didn't say "social columnist," unless it was to protect her from Emily's pretensions. "She works a lot of weekends."

Daffy nodded, but didn't elaborate.

"You know, Hunter," Emily said, still with that pout on her face, "you keep avoiding my parties and Roger and I will think you don't like us anymore."

Hunter studied her face, remembering those days in high school and how he'd suffered from wanting her to say yes to a date with him, remembering how crudely she'd rejected him. He took a deep breath. "Roger's not a bad sort, Emily, but just to set the record straight, I've never actually liked either one of you."

He didn't know whose gasp was louder. All three women stared and clasped hands over their mouths. Emily, two spots of color in her cheeks, said, "Trash will always be trash." Then she flounced out of the shop, slamming the door so hard the bell fell off and landed on the floor with a thunk.

"Good riddance to bad rubbish," Thelma said, walking over and collecting the bell.

Daffy looked the most shocked. Hunter watched her, stung by Emily's harsh words, yet somehow not minding them the way he would have at so many points in his past.

"Sticks and stones may break my bones, but words can never hurt me?" Daffy murmured the question under her breath, a look of caring and concern clear in her eyes.

Hunter reached out a hand and joined it with hers. She squeezed his fingers gently and he smiled deep into her eyes. "You're a treasure," he said.

Thelma dropped the bell and it hit the floor with a protesting clang. "Well, I never," she said.

"There's always a first," Hunter said, stroking the back of Daffy's hand and wondering if she'd think he'd lost his mind if he told her he couldn't live without her in his life.

20

Thelma tied the bell back onto the door and turned around, her face much more welcoming than it had been when Daffy and Hunter had first entered. That was a relief, Daffy thought, retrieving her hand from Hunter's.

She caught his look of disappointment when she pulled away from him, but she couldn't hang all over him with his mother present. She might have a wild reputation, but Daffy followed her own set of social strictures.

"So," Hunter said, stuffing his hands in his pockets.

"Don't let her bother you," Thelma said. "You know quite well she only started sniffing around after you made a pot of money. Fortune hunters!"

She crossed to a large layout table that stood near the cash register counter. "Hunter, why don't you run down to Paul's Café and get us some coffee? And tell whoever's behind the counter to make a fresh pot, not to send me any sludge."

"Coffee? But you don't like—"

His mother's stare could have pierced a stack of picture frames.

"Sure. Be right back." Looking as if he'd rather do anything other than leave the two of them alone in the shop, Hunter left the store.

Thelma patted a stool next to the one she occupied. "Join me?"

She might have asked, but Daffy didn't hear it as much of a question. Curious, she took the seat and smoothed the short skirt of her summer shift. Her bracelet caught the light and Daffy felt Thelma's eyes on her.

"At least you don't look like you're after Hunter's money," his mother said.

Daffy smiled. Her own mother never managed to speak a forthright sentence to her. Why, even the time she'd taken them to the doctor to be put on the pill, her mother had left them alone with the doctor for what passed as an explanation. "Oh, no," she said. "I have plenty of my own."

"Inherited or earned?"

"Both. I'm a photojournalist."

Thelma's eyes sharpened under her fluffy graying hair. "You make your living with a camera."

Daffy nodded. "And you make yours providing pictures and art their very best setting."

Thelma said, "Berry best." And then she smiled

and Daffy saw the softer side of her coming through.

"You must be proud of Hunter."

"That I am, but life is about being happy as much as it is about being wealthy."

"And he's not happy?" Daffy considered his mother's statement.

"There's happy and there's happy." Thelma picked up an Exacto knife and toyed with it. "Hunter's never brought a girlfriend here to visit. Not in the whole time he's lived in New Orleans."

"I'm not really his girlfriend," Daffy said, thinking she ought to set the record straight. "We haven't known each other very long."

Thelma snorted, a quite inelegant noise that said a lot about what she thought of Daffy's protestations.

"Every girl in Ponchatoula, even that married slut Emily, is after Hunter. He's had his pick of the sweet ones any time now and never settled down. If anything, he plays the field a lot more than a mother likes to see. But he's charming and good-looking . . ."

Her voice trailed off and Daffy guessed Thelma's thoughts had turned to the man who had fathered the son.

Thelma cut a stray strip of paper free from a matting frame with the Exacto knife. Chop. Slice. The wisp of paper curled and she flicked it away. "Well, I want him to find that level of happiness we all seek."

Daffy wasn't sure what to say. So she sat there

in silence, pretty sure Hunter's mother wanted her to say just the right words to reassure her that she, Daffodil Landry, was that source of happiness that Hunter needed.

But Daffy couldn't say that. For one thing, it was too presumptuous. She might know in her heart that she'd fallen oh-so-hard for Hunter James, but it took more than one half of a couple to dance a waltz. And she wasn't too certain Hunter was at a point in his life that he'd consider partnering anyone—let alone a woman he'd been warned away from.

"Well," Thelma said, putting down the knife, "maybe you two haven't known each other long, as you say. But when a customer walks in here with a piece of artwork and suggests this kind of frame and that type of matting, it doesn't take me more than a few seconds to know whether it's a match or not." She rose from her stool. "You're a photographer. Trust your instincts."

The doorbell clanged and Hunter entered, a cardboard tray of drinks in his hands.

In a far less gentle voice, Thelma said, "Just don't break his heart."

"Room service," Hunter announced, exchanging smiles with Daffy. Only that morning he'd arrived at her house and used the same line. Only that morning, but it seemed like a lifetime ago.

He set the tray on the cash register counter and handed a cup to Thelma, who said, without a trace of embarrassment, "Daffy and I have been having a get-acquainted talk."

Hunter carried a cup to Daffy. She took it and he was relieved to see a twinkle in her eyes. Thelma could be hard on people she didn't cotton to, as she phrased it, but it seemed from Daffy's unruffled expression that she'd passed whatever test Thelma had constructed.

"Good," Hunter said, popping open the Coke he'd bought for himself. "And I guess that was something you couldn't do with me?"

Thelma gave him one of her looks. "Of course not. Women don't talk the same when there's a man around."

"That's true," Daffy said. "Just like men talk differently when it's just the guys."

"Sports and locker-room jock talk, you mean," Thelma said as she moved back to her layout table, the coffee carefully located away from her work area on a side shelf. She began arranging a print, trying first one mat color, then another. Hunter had always liked watching his mother work. When she had been the employee and not the owner of Berry Best, he'd done his homework there, under the sharp eyes of Thelma and old Mr. and Mrs. Farmer, the former owners.

"So how long are you two staying?"

"It's just a day trip," Hunter said, wishing he could get Daffy alone again. And soon. There was so much he wanted to say to her, so much he wanted to know about her. Funny, but with all the other women he'd dated, he'd focused so much on the chase that once he caught them he was pretty much bored, except for the initial rush of the sex, of course. But the more he saw Daffy, the more he wanted to get to know her.

"Come back next week," Thelma said, "and stay over. We'll go out to the river. Do you like water-skiing?"

Daffy jumped like a kid caught daydreaming in class. Hunter wondered where her mind had wandered to, and hoped she was thinking the same sort of thoughts about him that he was having about her. "I'm not sure," she said, sipping her coffee.

"That means you've never done it," Thelma said.

"I'm afraid that's true."

"I'll teach you, if you'd like to learn," Hunter said, moving over to stand beside Daffy. He'd figured out she was being very reserved and lady-like around his mother, which he appreciated—to a point. He could barely keep his hands off her and if he couldn't hold on to her, at least he could stand close by.

It was crazy, this way he needed her. Physically. Mentally. Sexually. Crazy. It was like some software virus had infiltrated his operating system and everything read DAFFY.

"I'm game," Daffy said, smiling up at him with a hungry expression in her eyes.

That did it. They had to leave. She wanted him. He wanted her. Enough of the social chatter. Hunter glanced at his watch and said, "As a matter of fact, this is more like a half-day trip than a day trip. We're going to have to be going."

"So soon?" Thelma, to Hunter's chagrin, sounded more amused than surprised. Sometimes his mother read him a little too well. "Then would you stop by the house on your way out of town?"

"Sure," Hunter said. "You want me to deliver something?"

"No." Thelma studied the print in front of her. "There's a roast in the freezer and I forgot to put it into the refrigerator to defrost. Would you mind doing that for me so I don't have to leave the shop?"

An innocent-enough request, Hunter knew, but Thelma was up to something. "Sure, we can do that."

"A roast?" Daffy's eyes had lit up. "You mean you cook it from scratch?"

Thelma looked amused. "How else do you fix a pot roast?"

Daffy blushed slightly and said, "Pick it up at Langenstein's?"

Hunter laughed, but with her, not at her. "That's a New Orleans deli," he explained. "Daffy's the queen of takeout and reservations."

"Come back next week and I'll give you a lesson or two."

Hunter almost dropped his Coke. That invitation was clearly a stamp of approval from Thelma. He wished he'd been a fly on the wall when he'd been out of the shop, to hear what the two of them had discussed.

Well, Daffy would probably tell him. "Ready?"

She nodded and crossed over to Thelma. "It was a pleasure to meet you," she said, sounding as if she sincerely meant what she said.

Hunter watched as Thelma put down her work, then stared Daffy in the eye. "Next week. Pot roast. And maybe I'll show you how to make a pie crust. I bet you've never even seen a ball of pie dough."

"I wouldn't know one if it bit me," Daffy told her.

"Figured as much." Thelma waved a hand at them. "You two run along, but don't forget to stop by the house."

Daffy stepped toward the door. Hunter leaned over and kissed Thelma on the cheek. She rubbed a worn hand on the top of his head and said, "Be happy, son."

For Thelma, that was a highly sentimental thing to say. "I'll try," he replied lightly.

Her expression grew fierce. "Don't just try. Do it."

So his mother didn't think Daffy was all wrong for him. Hunter sketched a salute, and said so only Thelma could hear, "I'm going to do my damn—darndest."

"Get along with both of you. I've got a shop to run here."

Hunter had just helped Daffy into the Jeep when he caught sight of Lucy's car out of the corner of his eye. She was cruising the main drag slowly, looking for a parking place.

Looking for Hunter.

He leapt into the Jeep and, gunning the engine, sped off. Given Thelma's approval of Daffy, perhaps his mother would turn her efforts to dissuading Lucy from thinking Hunter would come home to her.

Home, Hunter thought with a rare sense of contentment, sat next to him.

Lost in his reverie, he went straight at the light.

"Isn't that the turn to your mother's house?"

"You catch on fast." Hunter made a U-turn just past Paul's Café and said, "If you look to your right, in that wired-off area, you'll see the town's mascot."

She peered out the window. "Is that an alligator in there?"

"Yep. Poor schmuck. Years ago, or so legend has it, someone caught an alligator here in the center of town, so they penned him up and made him a home. When he died, the town gave him a funeral, complete with a fire truck procession. And then someone had to go and catch a replacement."

"You don't approve, do you?"

Hunter shook his head. "How would you like to spend your days in a cage? That poor gator should be out in the swamps, killing birds and fish and lazing around with the other gators."

"You don't like to feel trapped, do you?" Daffy asked the question just as Hunter pulled up in front of his mother's house.

"Never," he said.

She climbed out of the car, a thoughtful expression on her face. Funny, Hunter reflected, but that was one of his own fears of marriage. Being trapped and unable to move freely, unable even, in some sense, to change and grow as a person without threatening the other half of the couple. So why didn't he worry about that with Daffy?

Go figure, he said to himself, walking side by side with Daffy to the front door.

"That cat hasn't moved," Daffy said, sounding amused.

"He can sleep for hours," Hunter said, thinking he could, too, in bed with Daffy. But then again, he'd keep waking up to taste her, take her, possess her, surrender to her.

Surrender to her? *No guy in his right mind thinks like that, Hunter*. He told himself to get a grip and led the way to the kitchen.

He opened the freezer compartment, searching for the cut of beef. His mother liked to buy in bulk from a local butcher, so there were several choices to sort through. At last he found the one labeled "chuck roast" and took it out.

Daffy was leaning against the counter, arms at her sides, staring hungrily at him as if she wanted to put him into a slow cooker.

Hunter switched the package into the lower compartment of the refrigerator. Be happy, his mother had said.

He let go of the leash he'd been holding on his desire for Daffy and advanced across the kitchen, holding her gaze with his. When he stood right before her, he said softly, "So you want to learn your way around the kitchen?"

He could tell by her puzzled reaction that she'd expected a different sort of comment. A sexual come-on, a "Hey, let's hop in bed together before we head back to New Orleans."

But who needed a bed?

"I'm interested," Daffy said at last.

"Good." Hunter brushed his fingertips up one side of her neck. "Because we're going to start with a lesson on appetizers."

"Appetizers." She was breathing a bit faster. Her blue eyes had gone even bluer.

"You know," Hunter said, removing her purse from her shoulder and setting it on the floor, "a delicious mouthful or two you eat before the main course."

"Right."

Hunter took one of her hands and, lifting it, feathered a kiss over the inside of her elbow. Then he did the same on her other arm.

The pulse in her throat was racing, so Hunter kissed her there, too, suckling her neck with just enough pressure to cause her to throw her head back and clutch the back of his hair.

He grinned. "So far, what do you think of the appetizer lesson?"

She moaned and reached for the buttons on his shirt. He caught her hands gently and said, "Oh, no, you're the apprentice and I am the master chef."

"What does that mean?"

"It's a bit like being my slave," Hunter said. "If you want to learn, you have to do everything as I explain it."

"We're in your mother's kitchen," Daffy said, half protesting, but more for form than with any real conviction.

"What better place to take a cooking lesson? It'll get you ready for next week."

She closed her eyes and Hunter kissed her on both lowered lids. They quivered under the touch of his lips and she said, "I'm ready for you. Now. Here." She placed her hands on his belt.

He almost ripped his own clothing off and took her on the spot.

But that, he concluded, would lack finesse. And Daffy wasn't a woman to be wooed once and won for life. No, Daffy needed special handling.

And he, Hunter James, wanted to be that man. Today, tomorrow, and the day after that.

"An appetizer," Hunter explained, glancing around Daffy's shoulder to the counter behind her and satisfying himself he had plenty of room clear for what he had in mind, explained, "may also be called a canapé, or crudités, or an hors d'oeuvre." With each term, he kissed his way down her neck, closer to her breasts.

Her eyes opened and she said, "I know all the words, I just don't know how to make them."

"The idea of an appetizer," Hunter went on without pausing, except to slip her dress off one shoulder and tug the wispy lace of her bra free to expose one breast to his full and very appreciative view, "is to whet one's appetite for the main course."

He kissed the very tip of her aroused nipple. She wriggled against him and murmured, "Maybe we should skip the cooking lesson and find that bedroom with the lock on it."

He stepped back, raking her with his eyes, fixating on that one breast.

At first she squirmed, but as he continued to stare, she played along, leaning against the counter in a languid pose, her head tipped to give him a maximum view. "Like what you see, oh, Master Chef?" She asked the question in a sultry voice, then giggled.

"Oh, yeah," he said and, moving forward, took her breast in his mouth. He suckled, he kissed circles around her nipple, he flicked his tongue across the pebbled flesh.

Daffy moaned and laughed and arched her back, urging him on. He knew she was wet and wanting him. He could have taken her standing right there in the kitchen. Instead, he stopped, abruptly, and lifted his head.

"Now that, my apprentice, is how one whips up an appetizer."

She stared at him, her eyes glazed with desire, her mouth a round pout of surprise. "Don't stop. Not now."

"No?"

She shook her head. "I'm on fire. I'm consumed." She glanced down where her one breast was exposed. "The rest of me wants you, too."

"Well, there is more than one variety of appetizer." Hunter wasn't sure how long he could play this game. His arousal was threatening to bust through the front of his pants. All of him wanted her, too, but perhaps he could hold out for a few more delicious minutes.

With a gentle hand, he put her bra back into place and pulled her dress back onto her shoulders. She was looking pretty disappointed, obviously assuming he really was going to stop. Just then he lifted her by the waist and set her on the counter, hiking up her skirt before her fanny touched the counter.

"Hunter!" She gasped his name. This time he'd shocked her.

He grinned and placed her right arm to the side, then her left. Tugging her slightly forward, he bent his head between her thighs.

She clutched the top of his head and said, "This seems awfully . . ."

Her voice dwindled as he palmed her damp panties, then flicked his tongue in an echoing touch. "I knew you'd be wet," he said, pushing aside the silky fabric and tasting her.

"Oh, my goodness gracious," Daffy said in one long breath. "I can't believe we're doing this." And she couldn't. But she didn't stop him. Instead, she lifted her hips to meet his greedy, seeking, all-too-knowing tongue.

"I'll never be able to take a real cooking lesson

here," she said in her last moment of sanity before she gave herself over completely to reveling in Hunter's hot kisses.

He spread her legs even more widely apart and Daffy had never been so exposed and so open. She might be fully dressed, but to Hunter, she was transparent, her soul and heart and mind accessible, vulnerable. He was spinning crazy circles of heated desire through her body with every magical move of his tongue and lips. He was murmuring, too, words Daffy wasn't sure she understood.

But as she quit trying to think and arched her back and cried out, he caught her close and, through the shimmering beauty of the sweet release, she thought she heard him say, "My appetizer. My main course. My dessert. Mine. All mine."

21

He took her there, in Thelma's cheery yellow kitchen. Simply yanked out a condom from his back pocket, unzipped, and without a word, holding her half off the counter, dove into her still pulsing body.

If he'd been in his right mind, he would at least have made tracks for the bedroom. But Daffy drove him from sanity, whipped him to frenzied desire the likes of which he'd never known.

And he was a pretty randy guy.

When he exploded, it was a damn good thing she was clinging to his shoulders. Staggering slightly, Hunter lowered her feet to the floor. Her panties tangled around her ankles, her once pristine dress crumpled above her waist.

Neither one of them said a word.

Reaching for his shorts, Hunter pulled them up

his legs and yanked off a paper towel to disguise
the used condom, all the while wondering what
she must think of him. So much for finesse. More
like a graduate of the cave-man school.

Moving almost in slow motion, Daffy rearranged her clothing. Her lips curved into that
dreamy smile he loved to see. Then she leaned
on tiptoes and kissed him, a gentle blending of
her lips with his that told him he had nothing to
fear.

He clasped her to him, held her long enough to
feel her heart beating against his chest, and then
said, "We'd better skeedaddle."

"That's a funny word," she said, not moving.

"It's Jamesian for if we don't want to be caught
red-handed, we'd better blow this joint."

She laughed, this time the blush far from faint.
"We are outrageous."

But she didn't sound at all offended.

Hunter reached under the sink, found a bottle
of cleaning spray, grabbed another paper towel
began swabbing the counter.

Daffy watched, an amused expression on her
face, as he shined the surface where he'd pounded
into her as if his life depended on it. Nah, he argued back while he made one more go-round
with the paper towel, just horny, that was all. Any
guy would be after all that breast teasing and oral
sex. It didn't mean she had any hold on him.

"I like being your appetizer," Daffy said,
pulling out the wastebasket for him. "And your
main course . . ."

He tossed the towels into the trash, removed the plastic bag, and replaced it with another. No point in leaving the condom in the house, no matter how open-minded and realistic Thelma was. Hunter paused, trash bag in his hand, a funny thought in his mind. Hell, she'd set them up by asking him to defrost the roast! Maybe it was better for Daffy not to realize that, given how shy she'd been prior to their visit to the shop, worrying that his mother would think they'd dallied at the house to, well, to dally.

"What's wrong?" Daffy studied his face and Hunter thought for a silly moment that he'd spoken his thoughts aloud.

He started to keep his musings to himself, but realized he didn't want to. With Daffy, he wanted to share everything. "Come out the back door," he said, "and I'll tell you on our way to the car."

"Is someone after us?"

Hunter smiled. "In a small town, you never know who might be knocking on your door." Once outside, he tossed the garbage sack into the garbage can. "But being pursued is the least of my concerns." Man, he managed to sound unconcerned, which, considering he figured Lucy was hot on their heels, was a pretty cool accomplishment.

"Oh?" Daffy wasn't buying it. Not at all.

"Actually," Hunter said, opening the door of the Jeep for Daffy, "what I was wondering was what you and my mom talked about."

Daffy climbed into her seat and Hunter dashed

around to the driver's side. As he slid behind the wheel, Daffy raised one hand, her fingers spread wide. "One," she said, a grin peeking out around her full, kissable mouth, "whether I was wealthy. Two, whether I'd inherited my money or earned it the old-fashioned way. Three, how I had earned my money, and four, did I know that every female in Ponchatoula over twelve and under ninety is out to snare you."

"You two talk fast."

Daffy's grin blossomed. "She talked. I listened."

"That happens a lot with Thelma."

Hunter zipped around the corner to head back to the interstate. As he made the turn, he caught sight of Lucy's car. He said a silent prayer to the god of lovers that she hadn't knocked on the door while he and Daffy had been lost to the world in Thelma's kitchen. As generous as Thelma was, and as fond as she was of Lucy, she just might have given Lucy a key to the house at some point in the past.

And Lucy, Hunter knew, would have no hesitation in using it. She might have cried and pouted after confessing to having written that ridiculous letter to that quack love doctor and then agreed not to carry the torch for him, but Hunter wasn't convinced she wouldn't keep trying.

And even though he knew she didn't have a snowball's chance in a Louisiana summer of winning his heart, he would never want to hurt her the way finding him in flagrante delicto with Daffy would hurt her.

Hunter pressed the accelerator and surged onto Interstate 55, a fist grabbing his gut.

Daffy had hurt someone in exactly that way.

On purpose.

Had she changed from the girl who had engineered that injury to Aloysius?

"You've gone off in a thinking trance," Daffy said, bringing him gently back to his surroundings, to her warm and comforting presence next to him in the car.

She placed a soft hand on his thigh. "May I join you?" Her tone was wistful, not complaining. She sat half turned toward him, completely opposite to her distant and nervous body language during the drive up. Her eyes were shining, and she watched him with what smacked awfully close to adoration.

Forget Aloysius.

Daffy had changed, matured from the hurt child she'd been. He squeezed her hand. Thinking of what Thelma had said about her not breaking his heart, he said, "I hope you take Thelma's advice."

Daffy lifted her other hand and sketched a circle on his chest. "Don't worry," she said. "This is one heart I am not going to wound."

Her lashes lowered and her head dropped to the back of her headrest. And just like that, exactly as she'd warned him she always did in a car if she let herself relax, she fell asleep.

Hunter drove toward New Orleans, his hand over hers, his heart at her mercies.

* * *

Four days and half a lifetime later, Daffy sat in front of her dressing table fiddling with a silver bobby pin, unsure whether to wear it or leave it out of her hair. No matter which decision she made, she could hear her mother's voice commenting on its unsuitability.

She wished Hunter were there. He'd place one gentle hand over the pin, read her mind, smile reassuringly, toss it back on the table, take her in his arms, and kiss away any worries about the forthcoming dinner party in honor of her mother's birthday.

Daffy faced the mirror, picturing Hunter, his body close and warm and so very male, standing so that his body brushed hers.

She blinked and focused and tried, but all she saw in the mirror was her own face, blue eyes too serious, wide mouth perhaps a trifle discontented on this evening, skin clear as always, hair swirling just below her chin. On the outside, Daffodil Landry was the same woman she'd been, oh, say a month ago.

On the inside, now *that* was the kicker.

The past four days, she and Hunter had been inseparable. He'd gone to several of the charity events and social functions she covered for the paper; she'd accompanied him one day to his suite of offices, where fellow and sister designers created the next generation of software legerdemain.

And Daffy had broken one of her firmest rules: she'd let him sleep over, not once but twice.

If the two of them hadn't been lying arm in arm yesterday morning, flushed from sweet good-morning sex, Hunter wouldn't have been there when Jonni called to remind her about the birth-day party. And if he hadn't been there, Daffy wouldn't have invited him.

But the invitation had slipped out and he'd ac-cepted.

Daffy placed the silver pin in her hair and stud-ied the effect.

Too childish.

She eased it from her hair, then lowered both it and her head to the dressing table. Closing her eyes, she tried to alleviate the tension in her shoulders, tried to deny her mother the power to turn her into such a wreck.

Her mother always had this effect on her.

Nothing was ever right for Marianne Livaudais Landry. As she'd been known to say more than once, she might have married a Landry, but she'd always be a Livaudais. And everyone in New Or-leans who knew what was what understood that statement.

Daffy had warned Hunter the evening might well be rocky. One never knew with Marianne. She might be charming or she might be waspish; always with a smile on her lips but never in her heart.

At her dressing table, lost in her thoughts, Daffy was surprised to feel the kinks in her shoul-ders beginning to soften. Strong hands kneaded the hurt, freeing her body of the wounding pain.

"Mmm," she murmured, wondering when she'd fallen asleep and begun to dream of Hunter.

The sweet treatment moved up her neck, parting her hair. Warm lips kissed the top of her head.

Daffy's eyes opened abruptly.

She lifted her head.

"I didn't conjure you," she said, gazing at Hunter's reflection in the mirror.

The head gave a gentle shake.

Daffy turned and threw her arms around him. She didn't care, for that moment, just how needy she appeared. "I thought you were meeting us at the restaurant."

He smoothed her hair. "I finished earlier than I expected."

She lifted her head. "Hey, how did you get in?" She might have broken the rule about no sleep-overs, but she sure hadn't given him a key.

"I think your housekeeper likes me," he said, grinning slightly and lifting her up from the dressing-table bench so that she nestled full-length against his body. "Now if only your parents do."

Wrapping her arms around his neck, she said, "What's not to like?"

Hunter returned her hug and then guided her back to the seat. Sensing his mood had sobered, Daffy watched his reflection in the mirror as he rested his hands on her shoulders.

"Seriously, Daffy," he said, "don't your parents expect you to socialize with a certain type?"

"Don't you mean pedigree?" Daffy leapt up

and faced Hunter. "You're the one who's worried about who you are and who you're not. You're the one carrying that baggage, Hunter."

"Hey," he said, backing away a step, "no need to attack."

"And I didn't mean to." Daffy's outburst had surprised her. She gave him a little smile. "Just trying to get my point across."

"It's a sore spot," he said, "but maybe I do make too much of it."

Daffy picked up the silver barrette she'd been fiddling with earlier. "A lot of people judge me by my supposedly wild reputation without ever seeking to get to know who I am. *You* haven't done that, Hunter, which leads me to suspect it's not my family's supposed social prejudice you fear, but your own insecurity that's bothering you." There, she'd said it. Glancing up from the barrette, she checked for his reaction.

Surprisingly, he was smiling. He lowered his body to the dressing-table bench. "Have I ever told you that you remind me of Thelma?"

"What?" Daffy dropped the hairpin on the dressing table.

"Wise, witty, and perceptive." He flashed her a grin. "And you both give right-on lectures."

"Thank you. I think."

He drew her onto his lap and put one arm around her. "I almost didn't go into business with Aloysius because I didn't see how the fatherless kid from Ponchatoula could handle breathing the same air as the rich city guy."

"It would have been easier to run away than to face your insecurities, wouldn't it?" Daffy asked, smoothing her hand over his hair.

"Yep."

"I bet Thelma kicked your butt at the very idea."

Hunter laughed. "Exactly." He ruffled her hair and gave her a hug.

They sat there, silent for a long moment.

"I run away," Daffy said softly.

Hunter stroked the back of her neck. "How?"

"From my fear that I'll cheat the same way my mother did." There, saying it out loud was a relief. "Instead of facing the issue, I create chaos and drive men off to spare them the pain I fear I'll inflict—the way my mom hurt my dad. And that's crazy."

"Not crazy. Simply protective," Hunter said. "Have you ever talked with your parents about what happened?"

"Are you kidding?" Daffy's shoulders tensed as she responded, the very idea making her nervous. "Ask my mother why she did what she did? I couldn't!"

Hunter kept stroking her neck. "Sometimes it helps to clear the air. I remember the day I ran home from grade school and yelled at my mom for not giving me a dad."

"You did that?" Daffy searched his expression but saw only love, no residual hurt. "You and Thelma seem so easygoing with each other."

He nodded. "But if I'd let all that worry and

anger build up and fester inside me without letting it out, we'd never have gotten to that state."

She looked at him in awe. "And just how old were you when you figured all this out?"

He laughed. "I was eight going on forty, but you know good and well it was Thelma who had the smarts to let me be angry. And eventually, I realized she was there for me, no matter what, and having a mom who did that was better than a dad who ran away."

"You're fortunate to have such a wonderful mother," Daffy said somewhat wistfully.

"I know," Hunter said. "And she gave me an example I plan to follow. When I marry, I'll be there for my family—solid, forever, the way my mom was for me. Even when I'm afraid of my father's bad blood, I hold on to that ideal."

Still on his lap, cuddled in his embrace, Daffy glanced shyly at Hunter. The woman Hunter married would be lucky indeed. She sighed, wishing for a future she could almost, but not quite, picture. "I need to accept that running away isn't the answer."

Lifting her as he stood, Hunter set her on her feet and kissed her gently on the mouth. "I think you're already learning that lesson, Daffy."

Daffy hugged him and he tightened his hold. His mouth against her throat, he murmured, "What time is dinner?"

"Twenty minutes from now," she said, circling one hand over his heart.

"Ten minutes from here to Delmonico's. That

leaves time for ten minutes of heaven." He nuz-
zled her neck and reached around to the back of
her dress.

Daffy smiled. He'd find no zipper in this cleverly designed outfit. She put a hand on each slender shoulder strap and smiled. After a gentle tug
on the bows, the silk confection slid to the floor.

Hunter whistled and stepped back, kicking off
his shoes and tearing at his tie. "That dress is a
man's best friend."

And those were the last words either of them
spoke for nine minutes and fifty-nine seconds,
until, flushed with passion and satisfaction,
Hunter lifted Daffy off him and said with a smile,
"Time to go!"

Other people's families had always fascinated
Hunter. When he was a child, other kids' fathers
had been his most intense source of interest. He'd
imagine himself the son of first this one and then
another. At some point before he reached his
teens, he concluded not having a father wasn't
such a bad thing. That was after he got to know
Lucy and she told him how her father came home
drunk once a month and with the same regularity
beat up her mom.

Leaving his Jeep in the care of the none-
too-impressed valet at the restaurant, Hunter held
the door open for Daffy, gave her a reassuring
smile, and prepared himself to meet the Landrys.

The maître d' fell over himself greeting Daffy.
Several heads turned and Hunter caught more

than one well-dressed couple staring openly at Daffy. The stir didn't seem to phase Daffy at all. She reacted with regal cordiality, a side of her new to Hunter.

He'd seen her splashed with water from head to foot and laughing like a child. He'd devoured the sight of her in sexual ecstasy, murmuring in breathy gasps that drove him wild. He'd admired her holding her own with Thelma, and watched somewhat nervously as she exchanged barbs with Aloysius, but this polite and I'm-better-than-thou side of her he'd never seen.

It was a side that nettled him, that reminded him of Emily, the queen holding court.

And then Daffy turned and smiled at him, a smile so sweet and sincere it chased every doubt from his mind. So that only he could hear, she whispered, "Everyone's nice to the society photographer."

It was as if she'd read his mind, detected his doubts. And answered them.

Hunter brushed the back of her hand as they headed for the table. Of course Daffy had had to learn to discourage zest for publicity in all forms and fashions. He'd noticed the other day, when he'd gone along to some charity dinner dance, that several of the women preened openly when they caught sight of Daffy and her camera.

Wishing he still didn't care quite so much about those wounds of the past, Hunter glanced around at the well-fed and pampered diners in this expensive restaurant and wondered how much money and time it would take before he felt like someone who belonged.

The maître d' paused before a table that held center stage in the dining room. Two couples, one older, one younger, were already seated. Hunter recognized Jonni, of course, and her husband. And he didn't have to be told the other fair flower was the woman who'd given birth to the twins. If there'd been a little dimmer light, she might have been mistaken for their only slightly older sister.

Daffy, under her breath, said, "It's show time, folks," and to the silver-haired man rising from his chair, she said, "Hi, Daddy."

The two exchanged hugs. When Daffy stepped back, she said, "Happy birthday, Mother," before taking the chair Hunter pulled out for her. To the table at large, she said, "Meet Hunter James."

Hunter said his hellos and sat down, vaguely surprised Daffy had added no description after his name. What was his role here? Business associate? Friend? Casual acquaintance? Date for the evening to round out the numbers?

Jonni, seated to his right, turned and touched his forearm. "We're so glad you could come tonight. I've wanted to get to know you better. Daffy says such wonderful things about you."

Daffy was talking to her father, which left David to pay court to the birthday honoree. "You do know how to set a guy's mind at ease," Hunter told Jonni half jokingly.

Jonni smiled. "These family affairs make Daffy

nervous. She'll be fine once she settles into the rhythm."

"Thanks," he said. "And remind me to thank you again for that first meeting."

"You two keep up that whispering and Daffy and David are going to get jealous."

Hunter turned his head. Mrs. Landry was glaring at him, yet her lips were smiling. Nice. Less than five minutes and he'd alienated Daffy's mother.

"I never get jealous," David pronounced, signaling the sommelier to his side.

"That's true," Daffy said. "I do, but not of Jonni."

Mr. Landry glanced up from his menu. "Shall we start with one of each of the appetizers?"

"Darling, that's so much food," Mrs. Landry said.

"Great," Daffy said.

Everyone else nodded, so Hunter did, too.

Mr. Landry gave an instruction to a hovering waiter, as did David to the wine waiter. Drinks appeared on the table, as did a beautifully wrapped small package, quickly joined by another.

Daffy stared at the gifts beside her mother's place and Hunter realized from her expression she'd never even thought of bringing a present.

"For me?" Mrs. Landry pretended surprise. She patted her husband's hand and bestowed a dazzling smile on Jonni. She never once glanced in Daffy's direction, until Jonni said, "That's from both of us, Mother."

"Why, how nice. Two of you and one present. Now, why didn't I think of that?"

Daffy put her hands into her lap and Hunter saw her fold them tightly together. He wouldn't be surprised if she left nail marks in her palms, as hard as she was squeezing.

Without thinking, he reached over and eased one hand free from that grip, covering her hand with his own, resting there in her lap. Let them think whatever they wanted. His mission was to protect Daffy.

The thought gentled him, and he smiled into her eyes. She looked surprised and slightly wary. Hunter could understand that; Mrs. Landry was a far cry from his mother. Thelma spoke her mind, but always in love. Even when she had a sharp word to say, Hunter knew she spoke with reasoned judgment, because she wanted what was best for him. Daffy's mother, on the other hand, struck him as someone who would compete with her own daughter over a man, and if she lost the contest, would prove herself a poor sport.

Daffy shifted her hand. Hunter kept his hold and after a long moment he felt her hand relax in his. And then she smiled back at him.

Which made the world an all-right place as far as Hunter was concerned.

22

With Hunter by her side, Daffy found dinner with her parents a much more manageable experience. Sure, her mother needled and annoyed her, and her father doted fondly on everyone, and David spouted facts and figures, and Jonni agreed with her usual sweet smile. All in all, they accepted Hunter's presence without any overt curiosity and, to her relief, the anticipated criticism.

All the while, through the appetizers, the main course, the decisions over dessert, Hunter was there beside her.

Since the moment he'd taken her hand, she'd felt safe. Watching Jonni nodding as David explained why something the city council had just done was utter foolishness, Daffy wondered if that was how Jonni felt with David.

Safe.

Hunter brushed the back of her hand and she looked up. Everyone else at the table stared at her, including the hovering waiter.

"Something sweet?" Hunter said, then added, "For dessert?"

She must have been lost in her thoughts for some time. "I feel like indulging myself," she said. "Crème brûlée, please."

Her mother made a face Daffy knew indicated disapproval but didn't press it. Her mother never had anything but fresh fruit for dessert. Well, she had the figure to prove the wisdom of that, but Daffy had the metabolism to eat anything she wanted. So she smiled at her mother, for the first time that evening, and said, "I adore crème brûlée."

Her dad, ever the peacemaker, turned to Hunter. "So how did you and my daughter meet?"

Daffy looked from Hunter to Jonni and back.

Hunter placed his arm on the back of Daffy's chair, for all appearances a man at ease with his surroundings. Impressed by his composure in facing the Landrys, Daffy waited to see how he would describe their "blind date" arranged by Jonni.

"Actually, it was by accident. I was pretty hot under the collar over some silly column and I went to *The Crescent* to see if I couldn't figure out just which meddling busybody called themselves the Love Doctor."

Daffy froze. She didn't move even her eyelashes. She held her breath and her toes quit wiggling around inside her shoes.

Her mother, in a way only Marianne Livaudais Landry was capable of, given that Hunter had his arm around her own daughter, leaned forward and, with that breathless come-hither expression of hers, said, "And why were you upset with the columnist?"

Hunter hesitated and Daffy noticed that and wondered why, even in her shocked state. Finally he replied, "Over something written about a friend."

Which column? Trying to remember some of her pithier replies, Daffy realized it could have been almost any one of them. Forcing her lips to move, she said, in what she hoped was a casual voice, "It must have been pretty strong."

Hunter laughed, a laugh with a hard edge to it. Jonni's expression revealed her concern. Daffy waited for her own smart-mouth words to be cited.

"Well, let's just say," Hunter continued, "that to have one's relationship potential described as Diagnosis Terminal is insulting, let alone coming from someone who has no idea what she's talking about."

Oh, my goodness gracious. Daffy's coffee cup, halfway to her lips, stalled in midair. She managed to guide the cup back to the saucer and then she yanked her hand down to her lap. The words swam in her mind. She saw the signature line and she gulped for air, hoping everyone else was too riveted by the discussion to notice she was about to go into cardiac arrest.

Loyal But Lonesome in Ponchatoula.

Daffy blinked, trying to conjure the rest of the letter. Her readers used initials for the people they wrote about. What initial had been in that letter? J? L? No . . .

H.

He was always popular . . . he goes out with other women in New Orleans . . .

Diagnosis Terminal.

She'd written those words—words that she'd really intended for herself—about Hunter. Ever since her first relationship, she'd done crazy things to scare away her suitor of the month, and now she'd orchestrated one of her worst stunts—without even meaning to.

"How do you know the doctor's a she?" Her dear, logical dad asked that question.

Hunter shrugged. "I can just see her, some prune-faced spinster who's never found love on her own, setting herself up as an expert on everyone else's love life."

David nodded. "I agree with Hunter."

"Well, prune-faced or not," Marianne said, "everyone reads that column. And not because the author is nice. The doctor just does such a lovely job of skewering silly people who don't have the good manners to keep their problems to themselves."

"I don't think it's meant to be mean," Jonni

said. "It's meant to be common sense, realistic advice."

"Yes, for people who don't have anything more meaningful to read," David pronounced, looking as bored as Daffy was shocked. Any conversation he didn't control bored him, though.

"But no one knows who the author is," Marianne said, "so why did you think you could find out?"

Good question. Daffy eyed her mother with some respect.

Hunter shrugged.

It was Jonni who said, "You thought you'd get someone who worked there to divulge the identity."

Hunter nodded, looking somewhat embarrassed.

The waiter delivered the plates.

Daffy stared down at the beautifully browned crème brûlée, the gingery brown sugar gleaming from the pass under the broiler. She made no move to reach for her fork.

Hunter had charmed her to find out the identity of the columnist so he could wreak revenge.

Sure, he'd remembered her from the Orphan's Club fund-raiser, but that alone might never have prompted him to ask her—or Jonni, who he *thought* was her—out. And that first meeting at the coffee shop, with that bet that he could win any woman in thirty days—why, oh, why hadn't she listened to her own warning systems then?

Daffy never cried.

But at that moment she was experiencing a very blurred view of her crème brûlée.

"Tell us, Daffodil, do you know who writes that column?" Marianne toyed with her fresh raspberries, her eyes alight.

Wouldn't she just love to know. Daffy shook her head.

"So, Hunter, what's your plan to discover the author's identity?" David chimed in.

Daffy realized Hunter had moved his arm from the back of her chair to around her shoulders.

"I really don't care anymore," he said. "Now that I've met Daffy, who cares about some dumb love doctor?"

"Now *that's* romantic," Jonni said.

David looked at his wife. He set down his brandy snifter and put his arm around her.

Daffy couldn't meet Hunter's eyes. He said all the right things, but did he really mean them? And even if he was as sincere as a priest professing his calling, how could she tell him the truth about that column?

"Daffy, what a pleasure to see you."

She had to look up then, as she recognized the dear and familiar voice of her childhood friend Oliver Gotho. Close beside him stood his wife, Barbara, whose hand was tucked snugly in his. And if Daffy wasn't mistaken, the glowing and gorgeous Barbara looked a little bit pregnant.

At that moment Daffy couldn't have wished for a better sight—or for a better-timed interruption.

Scattering Hunter's hand from her shoulder, she rose and hugged both Oliver and Barbara, then turned to introduce them to Hunter. Everyone else, of course, they'd met.

Hunter stood, too, and shook hands.

Grateful for the diversion, he exchanged a few words of greeting with the obviously happy couple. With a touch of envy that caught him by surprise, he noted the way they held hands and finished sentences for each other.

He and Daffy sat back down. Oliver and Barbara looked at each other as if exchanging silent questions and agreeing on the answers. Intrigued by the smoothness of their silent communication, Hunter wondered how they achieved that miracle, a miracle he craved for himself.

Correction. For Daffy and himself.

He reached for her hand. She didn't seem as willing to receive his touch as she had earlier, but she rested her hand in his.

"We won't keep you from your dessert," Oliver said, "but Barbara and I would like to share our wonderful news." He glanced at his wife and said, "We're not only celebrating our anniversary, but we recently found out we're going to be parents."

A round of congratulations came from everyone at the table. Daffy's words were a bit more subdued than Hunter would have expected and he wondered whether the long dinner with her parents had taken its toll on her. Best to whisk her away as soon as possible. Oddly enough, in his concern for Daffy, he'd forgotten his own misgivings about fitting in with her family.

The happy couple said their good-byes and wound their way through the tables toward the door.

Hunter stared after them.

He wanted what they had.

And he wanted it with Daffy.

He didn't want to pursue and bed and win Daffy, then move on to the next challenge. He wanted to win her and keep her. Loving Daffy would be one of the greatest challenges of his life, of that he had no doubt. And he had no doubt that loving her would be the smartest and best decision he'd ever made.

Because he did love her.

Hunter stared down at his untouched dessert, his favorite chocolate cake. How had it happened? He'd meant to enjoy the chase, to flirt and pursue and tantalize.

He hadn't meant to make it forever.

But somehow she'd changed all that.

He noticed Daffy's crème brûlée, as perfectly arranged as it had been when the waiter delivered it. She, too, had lost her appetite. It was funny in how many ways the two of them were alike, even while they were so different. They'd grown up on opposite sides of the social tracks. If he hadn't made his fortune, no doubt the two of them never would have crossed paths. But they had, and that circumstance had changed his life.

Oh, yes, she'd changed him—but would she choose him?

For the first time that week, Hunter didn't spend the night at Daffy's. He had some of his designers working all night on a special feature that had experienced some bugs. He wanted to check on their progress and he had to fly to Salt Lake City the next morning.

Hoping she'd say, "Come over no matter what time it is," he broke the news as they waited for the valet to bring around his Jeep. Her parents had driven off in their Mercedes and David and Jonni had just pulled away in their more Americanized wealth wagon, the latest-model Cadillac. Obviously he had a lot to learn about behaving like a rich guy. But then, he thought with a glance at his watch, he'd always followed his own path.

As his Jeep appeared from around the corner, Hunter waited to see if Daffy would respond as he hoped, but instead, she only nodded.

"Dinner wasn't so bad, was it?" She'd withdrawn and he didn't know why. Here he was again, facing those uncharted waters of communication between a man and a woman. Well, he'd tried it once before with Daffy and it hadn't been so scary.

She gave him a brief smile. "It wasn't nearly as bad as usual, thanks to your support, and to Jonni pretending her present was from both of us."

The valet jumped out, then ran around and

opened the passenger door. Across the way, a streetcar rumbled down St. Charles Avenue and with a screech of brakes drowned out whatever else Daffy was starting to say as she climbed in.

Hunter tipped the valet and slid behind the wheel. Daffy's hands were folded in her lap.

He could take only so much withdrawal from Daffy. He needed their sense of connection. Not only needed it, but welcomed it, thrived on it. After he merged into traffic and made the turn to head back uptown, he said gently, "Want to tell me what's wrong?"

Want to tell me what's wrong? As she considered Hunter's question, Daffy clasped her hands even more tightly together. How to admit to him it rankled her that he'd asked her out only to ply her for information. How to admit she wanted to trust him—wanted that more than she was comfortable acknowledging—but was simply afraid to. He'd said he'd been acting on behalf of a friend in seeking the Love Doctor, but Daffy knew the truth. He'd been the victim of that letter, not some imaginary friend.

Her thoughts raced and dove in her head. Yet she couldn't find the words, or maybe it was the courage, to share those thoughts. Before she knew it, they were in front of her house. Hunter still had his hands on the steering wheel and was looking straight ahead.

"Seeing my mother always makes me tense," she said at long last.

"Why don't you tell me the truth?"

"That *is* true."

Hunter shook his head. "Daffy, something happened between you and me from the time we left this house"—he pointed his finger toward her house—"and the time we left the restaurant."

She nibbled on the tip of her little finger.

"And maybe I should be smart enough to know what it is," he went on, "but I haven't got a clue." He scowled. "Unless you're carrying the torch for your friend Oliver and seeing him reminded you."

"Oh, that's not it at all!" Daffy shifted in the seat to face Hunter. Just because she couldn't express her fears and confess her identity didn't mean she wanted Hunter thinking she was pining for another man.

"Aha!"

"Aha, what?"

"If that's not it, that means there is something wrong you're not telling me." He looked way, way too smug.

"I hate it when logic is used against me," Daffy said, grinning despite herself.

"I hate it when I feel a wall between us," Hunter said.

"Now *that's* romantic." Daffy reached out and touched his hand. "I know you have to go to work, but do you want to come inside for a few minutes?"

His answer was a quick exit from the Jeep. As she reached for her key, Daffy remembered the evening they'd returned from Jazzfest. They'd both been hot for each other, and they'd both been playing games.

Tonight was different.

She slipped the key into her front-door lock.

She, Daffodil Landry, was different.

Inside, she led him to her favorite chairs in the back room. After a deep breath, she said, "At dinner, when you were describing how we met, I realized you only invited me—or rather, Jonni—out to use me."

Hunter leaned forward in his chair, his eyes intent. "I don't deny that."

"It, um, hurt."

He shook his head slowly. "Quite the arrogant jerk, wasn't I?"

Daffy laughed. "At least you admit it." She smoothed the skirt of her silk evening dress. "And that bet, that you could make me fall for you . . . is that . . ." She couldn't even bring herself to ask the question. It was too humiliating. Daffy Landry, who was always the one to crook her finger, nab her man of the month, and then discard him, was groveling.

Plus she was still holding back. Blurt it all out, she lectured herself. Tell him you'll die if he isn't sincere; tell him you can't live without him. And then top it off with the truth about the Love Doctor.

Hunter was out of the chair and on his knees beside her. Taking her hand, he said, "Daffy, look at me."

She met his gaze.

What she saw frightened her.

She could drown in the love and adoration she saw there. "I've never cared about another woman the way I care about you. I don't know what happened, but somewhere between Las Vegas and New Orleans, I fell and fell hard. I swear on my mother's head I am not leading you on."

Daffy caught her breath. "Wow," she murmured. She'd seen how he felt about his mother. Slowly, she said, "I believe you. It's just hard to know what to think sometimes."

He gathered her to him and whispered, "Then don't think. Just love me."

Hunter didn't realize he'd been holding his breath until Daffy relaxed into his embrace and snuggled against him. Smoothing her hair and murmuring her name, he slipped free the clever bows that held her dress together. His crew at work could manage without his motivating presence for a little bit longer. Heck, there wasn't a one of them who would walk away from a woman like Daffy at this moment.

Not that there was anyone else quite like Daffy.

They were standing and moving in dancelike circles, undressing each other as they swayed. On the rug in front of the fireplace, Hunter joined with her, slow and sweet, their passion almost a sacred ritual, rather than the wild frenzy they'd shared before they'd left for dinner.

He moved with her, loving the rhythm of her body as she found her release with him deep inside her. Clinging to him, she cried his name, and

Hunter vowed in that moment that no other man would ever touch her. Clasping her cheeks, he drove with a sense of urgency he'd never experienced in his life. She met him, thrust for thrust, and he sensed her own passion reigniting and rising free and wild all over again.

He exploded into her as she cried out and lost herself in him for the second time.

They collapsed onto the rug, arm in arm. "There's no one like Daffy," Hunter said and promptly fell asleep.

23

Hunter carried her to bed, kissed her good-bye, and promised to call her as soon as he got to Salt Lake the next morning. Curled up on her side, feeling more satisfied than she'd ever felt in her life, Daffy said a sleepy good night.

Five minutes later, she sat bolt upright in bed, the covers clutched against her naked breasts.

Hunter was leaving town and she hadn't told him that she was the Love Doctor.

It wasn't something she could say on the telephone.

She threw herself against her mounds of pillows and slapped one hand against her forehead. Boy, did she know how to mess things up.

But it was hard to feel too bad after making love with Hunter. She snuggled down under the covers and relived every moment, beginning not when he'd slipped her dress free from her body, but when he'd cared enough to get her to tell him what was wrong.

If she could make a relationship work with any man, Hunter was the guy.

If . . .

She sighed and decided not to worry about the answer. She'd tell him, she'd apologize, and that would be that.

Or would it? Hunter had Aloysius and goodness knows who else warning him away from her. Don't trust Daffy—she's, well, daffy. And sometimes that daffiness skirted on cruelty, according to her enemies. Given the truth, would Hunter decide she was not his type of woman?

She frowned and considered keeping the Love Doctor's identity to herself. She could quit writing the column, something she wanted to do anyway, and move forward with her life.

No, she couldn't do that. If she was to have a chance with Hunter, they had to be honest with each other.

Honest.

So why had Hunter said he'd been acting on behalf of a friend?

What else had Hunter said? *Don't think. Just love me.*

Beginning to feel dizzy from her thoughts, Daffy decided to sleep on things and see what they looked like in the morning.

Morning came and Daffy still didn't know what to do. But work intervened and as she hustled downtown to the Hilton to a Ladies Lunch and Fashion Show Fund-raiser, camera in hand, she considered asking her sister's advice.

She was sworn to secrecy on the Love Doctor's identity, but telling Jonni was a lot like talking things over with herself. And with her best friend, Beth, working overseas for CNN, Jonni was the natural one for Daffy to turn to. After all, if one couldn't trust a twin to keep a secret, whom could one trust?

So she shot the photographs of Junior Leaguers modeling clothing from a thrift shop they wouldn't be caught setting foot in under normal conditions, and stared down her old nemesis Tiffany Phipps, who, of course, had taken time away from her important law practice to stroll down the runway.

She delivered the film to the newspaper, then raced over to *The Crescent*'s offices. Working for both the city's daily newspaper and one of the main entertainment tabloids was driving her a little bit nuts. What she needed, Daffy realized as she screeched to a halt in the parking lot at *The Crescent*, was one real job.

One real, meaningful job.

But right now, she had a bag of mail to sort from readers seeking the wit and wisdom of the Love Doctor. Smothering a sad laugh, Daffy entered through the back door of the building and made her way to the cubicle she used.

The letters, cleverly disguised in file folders so employees not in on the identity of the doctor couldn't stumble across them, were stacked on the desk.

At least Daffy didn't have to open her own mail.

Wondering why she'd ever appointed herself to such a role, Daffy bent her head and began shuffling through the letters.

"Daffy Doc!"

Oh, no, not Marguerite. Daffy didn't think she could take such chipper energy today. All this thinking in circles was wearing her out. Plus she'd missed Hunter's call while working the fashion show. Hearing his voice on her cell-phone messages cheered her yet depressed her, too. "Hello, Marguerite," Daffy said, holding a letter and barely lifting her glance from it. Surely the editor could tell how much she had to do.

"Just the person I wanted to see." Marguerite perched on the edge of Daffy's desk and waved a hand at the stack of folders bulging with letters. "I'm thinking that we should double the column length of Dear Love Doctor beginning next week."

Daffy dropped the letter she'd been holding without really reading. "I'm not sure that's a good idea."

Marguerite looked shocked, no doubt because she thought every idea she had was terrific, and most people didn't disagree with her, at least not out loud. "Well, whyever not?" She picked up a pencil from the desk and began drumming it against her knee.

Daffy squelched the urge to grab the improvised drumstick from the editor and said, "Too much of a good thing can work against it. Think of television. There are some shows that are meant for the half-hour format. They get popular and the network gets greedy and expands them to an hour. And what happens? It doesn't work."

"I'm certainly not greedy." Marguerite snapped the pencil in two. "I'm a businesswoman."

Daffy shook her head. Debating with Marguerite was generally useless. Besides, why bother? All she had to do was resign and she was out of the discussion. And so was the Love Doctor. Daffy had insisted on a contract that said no one else could author the column should she decide to quit writing it. Marguerite had really hated that provision, but Daffy had stuck to her guns. But she wasn't ready to resign. Not yet.

"And a very good one," Daffy said, deciding to smooth things over. "Let me look at my schedule and consider the idea."

"That's more like it." Marguerite jumped off the desk and flitted away, no doubt buoyed by what she interpreted as Daffy's concession to her decision.

Wanting to be done, wondering yet again why she'd appointed herself the Dear Abby of the lost souls of love, Daffy pulled out a stack of letters and shuffled them. Closing her eyes, she stabbed one with her finger. Whatever it was, she'd answer it.

When she opened her eyes and saw how long

the letter was, Daffy almost dumped it back. But a plan was a plan.

Dear Love Doctor,

I have three best friends. I've asked two of them what to do about this situation and since it involves the third one, I can't ask her. So I'm writing to you to break the tie between my two best friends' opinions.

Daffy rubbed her eyes and wished she'd stopped at PJ's for a cappuccino on her way in.

The problem is I found out my third best friend's boyfriend is cheating on her. My two other friends disagree on whether I should tell her or not. One says she won't believe me and it will cost me our friendship. The other best friend says it's my duty and I must tell her. I'm confused and worried because if I tell her, my other friend will be upset with me, and if I don't, then the other friend will be mad at me.

Daffy had to admit she was confused, too. She eyed the letter and realized it carried on to the back of the page. And Marguerite wanted to double the column!

The way I see it, I also have a fifty-fifty chance of losing my third best friend, too. I mean, I think I should tell her 'cause I'd want to know if my boyfriend was a skunk, 'cause as I'm sure you know, guys can be skunks and hide it real well.

At that kernel of wisdom, Daffy paused. *Guys can be skunks and hide it real well.* But it wasn't just guys who did that.

So please, Dear Love Doctor, tell me what to do. Do I tell my friend or do I look the other way?

Signed,
Confused in Chalmette

Daffy turned to the computer and poised her hands over her keyboard. She wanted to dash off a quick and pithy reply to Confused so she could call Jonni and discuss her own problems. Yes, Daffy thought, the doctor needed a doctor.

As she glanced over the letter, an image of her mother filled her mind. She tried to force it away, but as she focused on the monitor, the image overtook the blank screen. And joining it came the picture of her dad, her dear, long-suffering—perhaps too much so—dad.

What would have happened if Daffy hadn't told her dad about her mother's affair? Had he wanted to know? Obviously he'd forgiven Marianne, so had Daffy done the right thing? Remembering how dramatic she'd been, she cringed. She'd driven like a bat out of hell down to his law firm and flung herself into his office. He'd excused himself from the meeting going on and taken her into another room, where she'd burst into tears and told him his wife—she couldn't bring herself to say "my mother"—had been in bed with Aloysius's father.

He hadn't acted all that shocked. He'd paled a bit, she remembered, but his attentions had been focused on calming her, rather than on expressing his own feelings.

Daffy lowered her hands to her lap. After a long moment, she began to type.

Dear Confused,

I cannot tell you what to do in this situation. I'm afraid both your friends are right, which also means both your friends are wrong. Look inside your heart and ask yourself why you would tell and why you would not. Calm and still within you is your answer. What I'm trying to say is only you can know what is right for you to do. Not even the Love Doctor can solve this riddle for you.

Daffy scanned in the letter and saved it and the reply to a disk. Never before had she not answered a reader's question. Never before had she felt humble enough to admit she didn't know right from wrong. The Daffy of a month ago would have rattled off a smart-ass response and her readers would have tittered and some of them probably would have taken the path suggested.

Certainly the Daffy of a month ago would have responded that any friend in her right mind would share her information.

Yet she hadn't called Chrissie after she'd encountered Aloysius with two hookers in Vegas. But she had been pursuing David and his intern, seeking any signs of wrongdoing.

Why one and not the other?

Because she didn't like David.

And she thought she knew what was good for her sister better than her sister did.

Guilty on two counts of arrogance.

Sobered by her realization, Daffy pushed away from the desk, took the disk, and slipped it into her purse. It wouldn't do for Marguerite to catch sight of this column until it was too late to stop the presses. She'd hand it to the production people on Friday, saying the editor had asked her to deliver it. Then they'd assume it had been signed off on, and the answer that wasn't an answer at all would appear in next week's issue.

And Daffy would probably be fired, which might not be the worst turn of events when all was said and done.

For what had to be at least the twentieth time in the past half hour, Hunter opened and shut the blue velvet ring case.

He'd known the ring he wanted for Daffy as soon as he saw it perched regally in a case by itself. Three stones commanded attention, the center a dark blue sapphire that reminded him of the color of Daffy's eyes when they were flamed with passion. On either side of the sapphire lay a perfect pear-shaped diamond in a weight and size worthy of a pharaoh's queen.

A solitaire hadn't seemed like enough, not for Daffy.

And not enough to express the depth of his feelings for her.

Hunter eased the case open one more time, picturing the ring on Daffy's hand. Jonni had supplied the ring size and the knowledge that Daffy adored sapphires.

More nervous than on the day WebWeavers' stock went public, more anxious than on the day he'd hired ten employees he could scarcely afford to pay, and more eager than he'd been when, as an eight-year-old, he'd been treated to a weekend at Disney World, Hunter headed to his Jeep.

Having returned a day earlier than anticipated, he planned to surprise Daffy at her house. And at the appropriate moment, or when he could no longer contain himself, ask her to marry him.

When the housekeeper answered the door and told him Daffy wasn't at home, his face must have telegraphed his dismay. Silly of him to expect a society photographer—and a babe of the first water—to be sitting at home on a Friday evening at six o'clock.

Fortunately, the housekeeper knew where

Daffy kept her appointment schedule, and even more fortunately, she was partial to Hunter.

"You've been away?" she asked as she opened the door and ushered him into the cool interior.

He nodded, the ring scorching his pocket.

"I thought only business could keep you from Miss Daffy."

Hunter grinned. "I'm that obvious?"

She smiled. "Yes, and it's beautiful, if you don't mind me saying so. Miss Daffy needs a man like you."

"I hope she agrees with you," Hunter said under his breath. But how could she not? They moved together, breathed together, loved as one. He'd never met a woman with whom he felt so much at peace, had never known such a state was possible. Oh, she drove him wild, but in a wonderful way.

The housekeeper left him seated in the hallway, where he'd delivered coffee to Daffy only a short time ago, the morning they'd traveled to Ponchatoula. She returned quickly with an address on a slip of paper.

Eyeing his slacks and casual shirt, she said, "At this address, it's bound to be black tie. You may want to change your clothes."

He took the paper and thanked her. She called, "Good luck," as she closed the door behind him.

Pausing on the porch, the sun slanting in his eyes, Hunter studied the address and after he had, he knew the fates were with him. The night's event was at the Opera Guild House, the house next door to where the Orphan's Club fund-raiser had taken place—the first time he had spotted Daffy across the proverbial crowded room.

She'd disappeared that evening, a little bit like Cinderella with the clock striking midnight.

But now he was on his way to claim her.

He was doubly lucky in the location, as the house next door was Aloysius's aunt's house, where he kept his rooms in the city—and where his evening gear was stashed. A quick change and he'd charm his way into whatever event was taking place.

And Daffy would be his.

The first sign of trouble Hunter encountered was the arch of pink balloons bouncing in the breeze over the entrance to the house. Everywhere he looked, he saw pink.

He made his way manfully forward, trying not to countenance the stares of several groups of women gathered on the porch of the historic house. They wore evening dresses in shades of pink.

Perhaps, Hunter thought as the door swung open and a maid in a pink uniform gazed at him, he'd made a mistake in not assessing the situation more carefully.

The maid gaped at him, then tiptoed forward and said, "Thank goodness you are here at last! But go around to the back door. Don't you know your place?"

Hunter stared at her, wondering what rabbit hole he'd fallen down.

"I'm here for the fund-raiser," he said.

"Yes, and it's about time," the maid whispered. "These ladies get really bitchy when they have to wait for their drinks."

"Drinks?"

"Oh, well, you're not too bright, but you're here, so come on in." The maid tugged on the sleeve of his thousand-dollar dinner jacket and said, "I'll show you the way."

Moved along by an inexorable force, Hunter swam through a sea of high-pitched voices issuing from every imaginable female form—all clothed in cotton-candy pink. So much for mingling with the hoi polloi and finding Daffy. He'd have to make the best of it, avoid a scene, and slip out as soon as possible. Given the hold the maid had on his sleeve, he thought it prudent to follow her.

And that was how Hunter James found himself behind a bar decked out in pink ribbons.

Daffy had to be there. He was a lot less conspicuous behind the bar than adrift in the sea of pink, so he popped champagne corks and poured bubbly for the next half hour, all the while scanning the crowd in search of her. He found it hard to believe she'd be dressed in pink to cover the event for the paper, but as he'd yet to spot any woman, no matter her age or girth, garbed in any other color, he took to checking every face he saw.

When he'd begun to despair, and was about to conclude that the helpful housekeeper had misinformed him, he spotted her.

Across a crowded room, exactly the way he'd first seen her.

Only this time she wasn't standing next to an identical blonde, a blonde he now knew to be her twin sister. And she wasn't wearing black. Her pink sheath was a deeper hue than the softer tones filling the room, and Daffy wore the dress with her unmistakable air of distinction. Rather than the inviting look she'd had in her eyes that first night, she appeared ready to do battle.

This time she was talking to . . . Hunter overfilled a champagne flute and apologized to the matron glaring at him. But surely that wasn't Tiffany with Daffy?

Preening.

Telling Daffy goodness only knew what.

Hunter threw down the bar towel he'd tucked into the cummerbund of his tux.

A silver-haired woman, glass extended, said in a schoolmarm's voice, "And just where do you think you're going, young man?"

"To save my life," Hunter said.

24

He caught up with the two women just as the bossy matron overtook him.

"Don't think you'll work one of our fund-raisers again, young man, if this is an example of your work ethic."

"Hunter?"

Daffy gasped his name and said to the irate woman pursuing him, "Mrs. Fagot, weren't you interested in a donation from Hunter James?"

The woman drew herself up and declared, "I'm interested in any donation that serves our worthy cause of providing funds for cancer research. But I'm also interested in having my glass of champagne refreshed, something this young man seems to find beneath his attention."

Daffy moved a step or two away from Tiffany, an action that Hunter applauded silently. "Mrs.

Fagot, let me get you another drink," she said, throwing a rather quelling look at Hunter.

"But what about that good-for-nothing bartender?"

"That's not the bartender," Daffy said. "That's Hunter James."

Hunter heard the woman's snort of disbelief as the two of them receded.

And, contrary to every one of his hopes and plans, he was left alone with Tiffany Phipps.

How had Daffy done that? Maneuvered herself out of his reach and left him with the last woman on earth with whom he cared to share oxygen.

"So," Tiffany said, swaying toward him in a sequined pink sheath, "coming out in support of breast research?" As she asked the question, she ran one pink-tipped fingernail down her cleavage to the point where it disappeared beneath her strapless dress.

Ten million or not, Tiffany was a disaster.

"I was looking for Daffy," Hunter said, backing away a step.

Tiffany shadowed him. "But she's too busy with Mrs. Fagot to notice that."

"Maybe. Maybe not."

Tiffany gave him a pretty seductive come-hither smile and Hunter had to acknowledge that at one point in his life, he would have been putty in her hands.

But that was B. D.

Before Daffy.

He took another step away from her, hoping to

bump into Daffy, hoping she'd see him and return to rescue him from Tiffany's clutches. But what had Tiffany told her?

"You didn't, by any chance, imply to Daffy that you and I were an item, did you?" Hunter's question was interrupted as he smashed into a small table holding a vase of flowers. Only his exceptionally quick reaction saved the vase from meeting its demise.

Tiffany purred an answer Hunter could only shudder at.

The ring in his pants pocket felt as if it had set fire to the fabric by this point. Then, out of the corner of his eye, he caught sight of Daffy making tracks toward the front door.

"Stop!" His voice rang out, far louder than he'd intended, and every pink lady in the house turned to stare at him.

Even Tiffany halted.

Hunter grabbed his moment and fled.

In record-setting time, he zoomed across the room, out the door, down the sidewalk, and straight toward the BMW about to pull away from the sidewalk.

Seeing no other course, he flung himself in front of the car and held up both hands.

Fortunately for him and for his and Daffy's offspring, she hit the brakes.

And Hunter climbed in.

Which gave him a close-up view of the storm cloud that was Daffy's face, and which pretty much signaled his second sign of serious trouble.

It sure wasn't the romantic scene he'd pictured, not with Daffy glaring daggers at him as he panted like a Saints wide receiver who'd just gone long and missed a touchdown pass.

Daffy barely gave Hunter time to close the passenger door as she thrust her car back into the traffic on Prytania. She was so upset she was speechless. She should be happy to see Hunter back in town. She should be flattered he'd sought her out at an event she was covering for the paper.

He reached a hand toward her. "Don't even think of it," she said.

"What?" The shock on his face couldn't be faked.

"Hands that touch Tiffany Phipps don't touch me." There, she'd said it. God, but it was humiliating to have the tables turned on her, especially after the way she'd used Eric, Tiffany's brother, to hurt Aloysius.

Hunter leaned so close he almost blocked her view over the steering wheel. "What are you talking about?"

"You know darn well."

"It's Tiffany, isn't it?" Hunter laughed. "She's nothing to me."

"Nothing?" Daffy couldn't believe how jealously she was reacting. "Then you and I must use different dictionaries if you call spending the night with her after we came back from Las Vegas *nothing*!"

"How could you believe that of me?"

Daffy shrugged.

"Okay, at one point in my life, it might have been true. But that was before I met you. You've changed me, Daffy. I hardly recognize my own thoughts anymore. I see a beautiful woman and I think, she's not as pretty as Daffy and not half as interesting." Hunter's voice had risen with every sentence until he was practically shouting.

Amazed, Daffy slowed the car and pulled it to the side of the street.

Hunter kept on. "Dammit, I came home from my trip a day early. And do you have any idea why?"

Daffy shook her head, her own jealous rage dissipating as quickly as a dewdrop in July.

"To ask you to marry me!"

It was a good thing she'd already stopped the car and switched into Park. Otherwise, they would have needed a tow truck to sort out the crash.

She stared at Hunter. "You didn't really say that, did you?"

He reached into his jacket, fumbled around, then pulled out a velvety jewelry case.

"Oh, no," Daffy said.

It was Hunter's turn to stare. "I guess I'm handling this all wrong, but just let me stumble through it."

He opened the case and held it toward her. The sun was just setting and as the gems caught the rays they seemed to take fire. Daffy sucked in her breath and said, "It's the most beautiful ring I've ever seen."

"It's yours."

She shook her head, slowly, reluctantly, fearing with her next words she was risking her only chance at happiness, but unable to stop her response. "I can't marry you."

"Of course you can."

"No, I can't." She should have known Hunter wouldn't accept a simple no.

"Why not? We're perfect together."

Why wasn't he using the L word? Daffy studied the ring, 'cause that was a lot easier than meeting Hunter's gaze. And the ring was stunning. She couldn't have designed anything else more perfect.

But perfection wasn't necessarily love that would last a lifetime. Love required truth and honesty and commitment and she wasn't at all sure either one of them understood those qualities well enough to make a marriage work. In the past, she would have said yes and then found a way to drive him away. At least she was getting slightly smarter. "I'm sorry," she whispered, "I truly, truly am."

Hunter couldn't grasp that she'd said no. "Can you at least explain why not?"

"We were just shouting at each other a few minutes ago," she said.

"Every couple has fights."

"We haven't known each other long enough."

"Long enough for what?" Hunter took her left hand, wondering what had gone wrong, asking himself why he wasn't about to slip that one-of-a-kind ring on her delicate finger. "To know I want to wake up every morning with you and go to sleep every night and share every success and every struggle? Long enough for that?"

Daffy blinked and Hunter studied her. Was she touched enough to cry? Surely that was a good sign. "Long enough to know you're the woman I want to make babies with and travel around the world with? Long enough to know you feel the same but you're afraid to say yes?"

"I'm not afraid."

"Yes, you are. You're afraid we'll make a mess of things and you'll cheat on me and I'll cheat on you and then we'll hate each other for what we could have kept beautiful and that will be that."

Daffy gasped. "How do you know that's what I think?"

He took the ring box back and snapped it shut. "Because we're both afraid of the same thing, but you know what? I've got the guts to face the challenge."

"And you think I don't?"

She was getting mad. Good. Hunter wanted to rile her, and rile her good. Then she'd come out with the truth and admit she loved him and couldn't live without him. Love. Hunter frowned. Had he told her he loved her?

"Daffy . . ."

"Anyway, I can't marry you because I'm the Love Doctor."

Her last sentence came out in a rush and, lost in the quandary of whether he'd committed the faux pas of not actually saying he loved her, Hunter didn't catch her words at first. And then, as they settled into his mind, he said, "What do you mean, you're the Love Doctor?"

"I write the column," Daffy said, really pretty calmly for someone making so monumental a confession.

"You?" Hunter's image of a prune-faced biddy with a bun of gray hair rose to mock him. "Oh, no, tell me it's not true."

"It is true. I invented it, I write it, and I wrote those words about you—not about any *friend* of yours."

"Okay, so I said it was for a friend." Hunter, still holding the ring box in his hand, stared at Daffy as if he were seeing her for the first time. "But you said you didn't know who the Love Doctor was."

"We both lied."

"Yep."

"And I know, now that you know the truth, you won't want to marry me, but at least I have it off my chest," Daffy said, looking pretty sad.

"What do you mean, I don't want to marry you?" Hunter was really having trouble following her logic. "If you hadn't written that column, and I hadn't gone to *The Crescent* looking for the good old Love Doc, and Jonni hadn't said you'd have coffee with me, we wouldn't be here together today."

"That's one of the most beautiful speeches I've ever heard anyone make," she said.

Her lips had parted softly. Her eyes were glistening. Hunter leaned in and kissed her on the mouth. She responded, then pulled back abruptly.

"But I still can't marry you."

"Then you *are* afraid!"

She nodded. "I promised I wouldn't break your heart, and until I know in my own soul I can be the partner you need, I can't say yes."

Hunter lost it. He saw her slipping away from him. "Daffy, don't walk away. We can face our demons together. That's what love is all about. And I love you."

She was crying. Daffy, who never cried, was sobbing openly. "You're so wonderful," she said between sniffles. "I've hurt every guy I've ever been involved with and at least now I'm wise enough to stop before I hurt you."

There was nothing else he could say. She wasn't ready to believe she'd changed from the wounded child who'd struck back because of her own pain. "Dear, sweet Daffy," he said softly, his own heart as heavy as hers, yet he wasn't about to give up on them. "Just go home and sleep on it. Call me tomorrow and we'll work through this." He caught one of her tears with his thumb and added, "Together."

Jonni didn't believe Daffy had said no.

Daffy's phone rang bright and early the next morning and her sister, obviously trying to be discreet, asked how she was.

"Fine," Daffy said, stroking her cat, who'd decided in Hunter's absence to return to her perch on Daffy's bed.

"Just fine?" Jonni sounded puzzled.

It took Daffy a second or two, but then she figured out Hunter must have gotten her ring size from Jonni. And Daffy had never even slipped the ring on her finger.

"I can't marry Hunter." She heard her own mulish tone and wondered at it. Was she just being stubborn? Or was she standing on principle here?

"Why not?" Jonni sounded truly shocked. "You're a perfect match."

There it was again, that word "perfect."

"And why is that?"

"Because you make each other so happy. I've never seen you the way you are with Hunter."

That got to Daffy. "Oh, Jonni, I love him!"

"So why not marry him?"

"But what if I screw it up? What if I hurt him or he hurts me or we realize after a few years we're not so perfect after all?"

"If everyone said that, no one would ever get married."

"So why do people do it?"

"Because it's worth it. All the working things out and compromising and trying to learn to see the world from the eyes of another person—it all comes together and you know a joy and a peace that's not possible any other way."

"Wow," Daffy said. "Is that how you feel with David?"

"Yes." Her sister sounded just a tad defensive.

"I am sorry I've been such a jerk about David," Daffy said.

"It's okay. Not everyone is meant for everyone else. I mean, I think Hunter is a great guy, but I could never imagine marrying him."

"And why not?" Now *she* sounded defensive.

"I think he'd be very exhausting. You know, always on the go and wanting you to be with him every step of the way."

"I know," Daffy said, "and it's beautiful."

"Aha!"

"Hunter said I was afraid and I am." Daffy clung to her phone, hoping against hope her sister would say some magic mantra that would change her mind. She *wanted* to marry Hunter, she really did.

"Only you will know when the time is right for you," Jonni said, sounding far wiser than she should, given that she was a twin and only fifteen minutes older than Daffy. "But listen to your heart, not just your head."

With those words of wisdom, words that oddly echoed the same advice that the Love Doctor had delivered to Confused in Chalmette, Jonni rang off.

Daffy pulled the covers over her head, only to be interrupted by a knock on her bedroom door.

Hunter? Had he come after her? He'd said to call him, but she hadn't dialed his number. She didn't know what he could do to persuade her it would be okay to marry. The permission had to come from within her. "Just a minute," she called, reaching for her hairbrush.

"No rush," her housekeeper said.

Daffy dropped her brush, got out of bed, donned her oldest and most comfortable bathrobe, and opened the door.

Almost hidden behind a massive display of spring flowers, chief among them bunches of daffodils, her housekeeper said, "I thought you might like this in your bedroom."

"Oh, why did he have to go and do that?"

Her housekeeper carried the bouquet into the room. The arrangement was so large she set it on the floor in front of the fireplace. "Maybe because he loves you."

"You, Sarah, are a hopeless romantic."

She dimpled. "I take it Mr. Hunter found you last night?"

Daffy frowned. "Oh, yes, he found me."

Fortunately, the phone rang and the housekeeper left to answer it. Daffy wasn't up to any more explanations of her own muck-ups, shortcomings, and failures. She inched toward the bouquet, searching the mass of blooms for a florist's card.

She spotted it tucked between a daffodil and an iris. Her hands a little shaky, she opened the miniature envelope, wondering what she'd find. Would he try to persuade? Charm? Lecture?

Rather than the florist's card she'd expected, Daffy found a folded square of lined paper inside the envelope. She opened it and recognized her own handwriting. That confused her, but as she focused on the words, she knew he couldn't have made a better choice of message. There on the paper was the personal ad she'd penned that first day in the coffeehouse, when he'd asked her advice on how to describe the relationship he wanted.

For Richer or Poorer, in Sickness and in Health:

Don't answer this ad unless you know what forever means.

But he'd scratched through her message and edited it to read:

Unless you're willing to discover together what forever means.

Daffy smoothed the paper and walked back to the bed, reading it over and over. Her cat looked up, blinked, and seemed to frown at her. Daffy stroked her silky fur and said, "You're the only one who doesn't want me to throw caution to the winds. And you, Mae West, are biased."

The cat kneaded her claws and purred loudly.

Daffy climbed back into bed and pulled the sheet over her head. A second knock sounded. "Come in, Sarah," she said, not even bothering to uncover her face.

She heard the door open and close. Suddenly Mae West quit purring and scrambled off the bed.

Daffy inched the sheet away from her eyes.

Hunter stood inside the doorway.

"Hunter!" She lowered the sheet; then, remembering she was naked beneath it, she clutched the sheet to her throat.

"Nice flowers," he said, advancing toward her, his gaze raking her body. "Someone must be goofy over you."

"What are you doing here?" Daffy asked, thrilled he'd come to her, but stubbornly refusing to admit to such a spineless reaction. Considering she'd said she couldn't marry him, surely she had no right to feel so happy to see him.

He stopped at the end of her four-poster bed, his expression dark and unreadable. "You haven't forgotten your water-skiing lesson, have you?"

She had. Not that it mattered. Not after last night. "Hunter, I can't go to Ponchatoula."

He moved around to the side of her bed. "Why not?"

"Because." Daffy pushed up against the pillows. She needed to get out of bed and face him eye to eye, but her bathrobe lay beyond her reach. And she didn't dare have this discussion while she was naked. If Hunter even reached for her, she knew she'd cave in. Their lovemaking was fabulous, but great sex couldn't solve her internal conflicts.

"Want this?" Hunter grabbed the very robe she'd been eyeing and dangled it beside the bed.

"That would be nice," she said, trying to speak

primly, but beginning to grin despite herself. "Honestly, Hunter, you can't expect me to visit your mother under the current circumstances."

He dropped the robe on the floor. Suddenly he loomed over her, his face serious, his voice harsh. "Oh, but I do. You agreed to learn to water-ski and to take a baking lesson from Thelma. That, Miss Daffodil Landry, constitutes a commitment."

Daffy stared up at him, dazed by the sudden attack and feeling a teeny bit guilty, too.

"You're afraid you can't commit," Hunter said. "Well, today you can practice following through with something you said you'd do."

"You don't have to shout," Daffy replied, knowing she sounded petulant.

Hunter grinned. "At least you heard me."

"I thought you wouldn't want to see me anymore."

"Are you nuts?" Hunter sat on the side of the bed, his voice softening. "What did I tell you last night?"

"To call you and we'd work through my fears together," Daffy whispered.

Hunter stroked her hair. "Daffy, people in love help each other."

Daffy caught his hand and kissed his palm. He leaned over and skimmed his lips over her forehead. Daffy lifted her arms and clasped Hunter around his neck, drawing him closer. Before she could kiss him properly, he withdrew from her grasp, vaulted off the bed, and said, "No distractions. Are you coming with me?"

She'd intended to avoid him and do battle with her demons in her own way. Yet here he was, offering to stand side by side. She wasn't sure she could face the challenge in his way, but she certainly owed him at least a major attempt to do so. Meeting his gaze directly, she said, "I'll go." And in her head, she could almost hear herself saying the words "I do."

Hours later, inside Thelma's kitchen, Daffy finished swabbing Solarcaine on the tip of her nose and the tops of her shoulders, then washed her hands. "I thought I had enough sunscreen on," she said ruefully.

Thelma pulled a bag of flour from the freezer and plopped it on the counter. "It's the reflection off the water that burns you," she said.

Whistling, Hunter entered the room. He paused as he surveyed the baking items lined up on the counter, then winked at Daffy when his mother's back was turned.

Daffy blushed as red as her sunburn. They'd made love on that same surface and Hunter didn't have to say a word for her to know that was exactly what he was picturing.

"Everyone else is coming at six," Hunter said. "What can I do to assist?"

Thelma turned and studied him, a smile softening her face. "If I do say so myself, I raised you right." She dusted some flour from her hands, then asked, "Want to help with Daffy's lesson before you fire up the grill?"

"Sure." If possible, his grin grew even more wicked. "I love giving cooking lessons. Are we having any appetizers?"

"For a barbecue?" Thelma shook her head. "You've been living the good life too much. It's ribs, corn on the cob, and potato salad. Oh, and pie, of course."

"If I don't mess it up," Daffy said.

"Don't be silly." Thelma handed her an apron that went around her neck and tied at the waist. Before Daffy could put it on, Hunter was at her side, easing it over her head so the fabric didn't scratch her sunburned shoulders.

"Nothing to making a pie," Thelma said, taking out a large mixing bowl.

"Daffy was a natural at water-skiing," Hunter said, tying the knot and then patting her on the fanny.

"That she was," Thelma said. "I'm glad you two could make it. It was a treat to shut the store and go have fun."

"You should do that more often," Hunter said, moving a big bowl of peaches over to the sink. He selected a knife and began peeling the fruit.

Thelma sighed. "I suppose I should. Now, Hunter, if you and Daffy were to spend more time up here, I just might do that."

Uh-oh. Dangerous waters. Daffy pointed to the mixing bowl. "What goes in first?"

Thelma shot her a piercing glance, and Daffy realized Hunter's mom knew she'd been trying to change the subject. One couldn't get much past any member of the James family!

"Flour. You measure dry ingredients in this type of cup and liquid in this kind." Thelma pointed to the metal and glass containers. "I was glad to see Lucy is dating that new science teacher at the high school. Makes me feel all's well that ends well."

Hunter nodded as Daffy dumped the indicated amount of flour into the bowl and followed Thelma's directions to make a well for the other ingredients.

"Daffy's pretty much a natural at anything she attempts," Hunter remarked, apparently still following his own line of thought.

"Is that so?" With two sharp knives, Thelma demonstrated dicing the cold butter into flaky pieces and then handed the knives to Daffy.

"Yep. She puts her mind to it, she does it."

"Now that's an admirable trait," Thelma said, flicking the oven on.

"Hey, I'm right here," Daffy said. "You're talking about me as if I'm not."

Hunter nodded. "You almost weren't." He began slicing the skinned peaches.

Daffy glared at him. She didn't want to discuss their private business in front of his mother.

Hunter smiled back at her and said, "We don't keep secrets in our family, do we, Thelma?"

"Now mix the butter and the flour together," Thelma instructed.

Holding the two knives at a rather awkward angle, Daffy began trying to blend the two ingredients. Hunter's mother replaced the knives with a metal utensil Daffy had never seen before and said, "Pastry blender. I never bother with it, but it might be easier for you to use. So what's going on between you two?"

"I asked Daffy to marry me," Hunter said.

Daffy gasped.

"I take it she didn't say yes?" Thelma glanced between Daffy and her son as she asked her question.

He shook his head. "Can you believe it? She turned down your son."

Thelma grinned, a reaction Daffy found surprising. Surely most mothers would leap to their sons' defense. "No doubt that'll keep you from getting too big a head."

Hunter laughed. He dried his hands on a towel and leaned over to Daffy. "Sharing isn't so hard, is it?"

She stared at him, puzzled. "Sharing? You mean talking about such personal matters in front of others?"

He nodded. "I've finally figured out that the biggest difference between your family and mine isn't money or social status. It's the way you all keep your true feelings hidden. Everything's polite, but nothing reaches beyond your emotional vests."

Daffy looked down at the bowl of pie dough beginning to form under her ministrations. Sure enough, the flour and the butter were blending and forming a whole new entity. Meeting

Hunter's gaze, she said, "Jonni and I are a little bit better at sharing, but none of us are willing to reveal ourselves too openly."

He tipped her chin up.

"Any idea why not?"

She shook her head.

"Afraid you'll get slapped down, most likely," Thelma said. "Most of us are afraid of rejection."

"Is that what you're afraid of, Daffy?" Hunter dropped his hand, but he just kept looking at her as if he could see into her soul. "If you had a frank and open discussion with your mother about that issue standing between the two of you, are you afraid she'd reject you?"

Daffy stared down at the ball of dough. "Maybe I am. And maybe she would. But you know what? She couldn't push me away any more than she does already."

"Bravo," Thelma said. "Now, sprinkle some flour on this cutting board and I'll show you how to roll out that dough."

"Bravo," Hunter echoed softly, slicing the last of the peaches and smiling at Daffy.

A week later, Hunter paced the floor of his office. He thought he'd made great progress convincing Daffy they could work through her issues together, but upon their return from Ponchatoula, she'd asked for time alone. To think, she'd said. She wanted him, of that Hunter was certain, so rather than drive her away, he'd reluctantly agreed.

Aloysius, stretched out comfortably on the leather sofa, sipping a scotch and water, shook his head.

"What if time works against me? I've done everything I can think of," Hunter said. "I've sent flowers and not just any old bouquet. Daffodils every day. The florist warned me today they might not be able to make my order."

Aloysius eyed his drink. "I think maybe I went a little heavy on the water."

"Are you listening to me?"

"I always listen to you. You made me a multi-millionaire. Why shouldn't I listen to you?"

Hunter stopped pacing. "I thought you were already rich when I met you."

Aloysius shrugged. "A common misconception."

"What do you mean?"

"I come of old stock, but the bank account had pretty much been drained dry."

"Do you mean to tell me when you were hanging around the computer lab bragging about how you could bankroll the smartest, the best, and the brightest, you didn't have the cash to do what you said you could do?"

Again his business partner shrugged. "Maybe I should have told you, but your ideas made so much sense, I figured with my name and your brains, my uncle's bank would ante up the seed money."

Hunter walked over to the leather sofa, a piece of furniture that alone must have cost several grand. "I can't believe you never mentioned this fact before."

"You thought I was wealthy. That gave me a leg up so I could hold my own with the brilliant Hunter James."

Hunter shook his head. "I'll be damned."

"I knew a good gamble when I saw one," Aloysius said, "and I can't thank you enough for coming through and making us both filthy rich." He took a long swallow of his drink. "I like being rich much better than being poor."

"What good does it do if the woman you love isn't with you?" Hunter resumed his pacing.

"Tell you what I'm going to do," Aloysius announced. "It's against my better judgment, but given how well our business has turned out, it's the least I can do."

"And what's that?" Hunter responded with only half his attention, expecting Aloysius to offer to set him up with yet another babe to take his mind off Daffy.

"I'm going to tell you how to win Daffy over."

"Yeah, yeah." He whipped around. "Does that mean you've really forgiven her?"

Aloysius shrugged. "Don't remind me of the details or I may change my mind. However, I must say it seems the two of you have met your match, so who am I to stand in the way?"

Hunter smiled as he watched Aloysius sit up and reach over to the coffee table. Sifting through several e-commerce and business magazines, he pulled out an old issue of *The Crescent*. He flipped through it, folded down a page, and handed it to Hunter.

Dear Perplexed,

What a pushover you are! You want to get a woman's attention? Try ignoring her!

He had to hand it to Aloysius. He read on:

If you want something badly enough, you have to be prepared to walk away from the table.

Hunter sighed, but took heart at the ending:

Try that. Write back and let me know your wedding date.

"That's the secret?" Given that Daffy had penned those words, it made sense for Hunter to follow her advice. Even the housekeeper wouldn't let him in the house, having informed him sorrowfully that Daffy had strictly forbidden her to give him access. Daffy, Sarah had told him that morning, was still thinking.

"Yep." Aloysius rose. "Come on, old boy, let's get some dinner."

"I'm not hungry," Hunter said. "But thank you for trying to help me out with Daffy."

"You're quite welcome. Now come keep me

company and practice ignoring Daffodil Landry."
He put an arm around Hunter, and before Hunter
knew what had happened to him, his partner had
hustled him past the suite of offices and into the
elevator.

25

It was a beautiful day for a drive across the end-less expanse of the Causeway, but Daffy wasn't in much of a mood to appreciate the blue sky, fluffy white clouds, and sailboats dotting Lake Pontchartrain. She was on her way to her parents' summer house.

Evidently, Hunter had given up on her. After they'd returned from Ponchatoula, he'd spent a week besieging her, but then all had gone quiet on his end. The flowers had stopped. The phone calls had died completely. His appearances on her doorstep had ceased.

So she'd mucked it up royally. Well, she might have driven Hunter away—without intending to, unlike her other relationship disasters—but this was the last time it was going to happen to her.

She was going to drive up to her parents' house, march inside, and confront her mother—and face her fear that she'd hurt Hunter the same way her mother had wounded her father.

Not Hunter, she corrected herself. She couldn't blame him for giving up on her. He'd been ready to work things out together and she'd insisted on time alone. So she had lost the best man she'd ever met. But someday surely she would meet someone else and want to make a go of things.

Not likely.

Daffy sighed, exhausted from her own internal arguments. She was tired of her own company and heartsick for Hunter.

Her mother was out on the patio, a beautiful deck area surrounded by trees and flowers and overlooking a sparkling swimming pool and spa.

"What a surprise," Marianne said, glancing up from a book.

Daffy nodded, realizing she had no idea how to start this conversation.

"I gather you were in the neighborhood?"

Daffy nodded, again, feeling like a marionette. Her mother had a way of doing that to her, pulling strings so that Daffy ended up reacting rather than initiating.

Well, today was going to be different.

"I've come to speak with you about something that's important to me," Daffy said, taking a chair opposite the chaise on which her mother sat.

"Wedding bells, dear?"

Daffy shook her head. Had Jonni told their mother?

"Don't tell me you drove that nice, rich Hunter James away, too?"

"I did not drive him away." She spoke from behind clenched teeth, because that was exactly what she had done.

"Well, if he's not offering marriage, that's just as well."

"He did propose," Daffy said, "and I said no."

"Most girls your age are married."

Daffy stared at her mother. "Do you have any idea why I said no?"

"I only met the young man once," Marianne said. "Were you two not compatible?"

"If you mean in bed, we were quite compatible." Daffy couldn't believe she had actually said that sentence to her mother. Her mother, who pretended sex didn't exist; her mother, who'd let the doctor explain why she and Jonni should take their little pack of pills; her mother, who'd screwed Aloysius's father right in their own house, in the bedroom she shared with Daffy's dad.

"There's no need to get personal," Marianne said.

"Why did you do it?"

"Do what?"

"Screw Mr. Carriere."

"Daffodil Landry!" Her mother sounded sincerely shocked. "That's no way for a lady to talk."

"It's okay to do it but not to say it?" Daffy jumped up, unable to contain her agitation. She was positive the key to her fear of commitment lay in her fear that she would turn out to be a mirror image of her mother. If she didn't straighten out this question, she knew she didn't have a chance of figuring out the rest of her life. Hunter had been so wise to encourage her to confront Marianne.

"Daffy, there are some things a mother shouldn't have to explain to her children, but since you ask, I'll say this, and only once will I address your question." She lay her book down. "I married when I was twenty. I'd never had relations with any man other than your father. When Pierre came over to the house that day, I was swept away by the circumstances. I love your father and he has forgiven me. That's all there is to it." She picked up her book, and then added, "Oh, and you might try to learn to forgive also."

"Oh," Daffy said, sitting back down and trying to digest her mother's words. Gone unspoken were the words "And if you hadn't told your father, things would have been so much smoother."

"So do you think I'm like you?"

Her mother sniffed. "No, Daffodil, I think you were left under the pumpkin patch. You're entirely too intense to be my daughter."

"Why do you always act like you dislike me?"

Her mother peered over her sunglasses. "What an odd notion. I don't dislike you. I don't understand you, but that's an entirely different matter. Now, why don't you run along and go make up with that rich Hunter James so all my friends will quit asking me when you are ever going to settle down and get married?"

"Right," Daffy muttered, backing off the patio and crossing through the elegant and spacious home. So much for a heart-to-heart, but at least her mother hadn't clammed up. And hearing from her lips that there'd been only one man and only one time somehow made Daffy feel better.

She sighed and got back into her car. She didn't think she'd ever understand her mother, but she did feel as if a hex had been lifted off her.

She'd made it to Mile 23 of the twenty-four-mile-long Causeway bridge when her car phone rang.

It was Jonni, crying so hard Daffy couldn't understand a word she was saying.

"Slow down," Daffy ordered. "What happened?"

"David . . . shot!" A racking sob followed.

Daffy gripped her phone. "Where are you?"

Jonni managed to convey she was on her way to the hospital. Daffy had the sense to ask which one before her sister hung up.

Jonni hadn't said how badly her husband was hurt, but as Daffy sped toward the hospital, she feared the worst. It wasn't like Jonni to be hysterical.

Normally gunshot victims were taken to Charity, so perhaps he wasn't hurt too badly. Or maybe something catastrophic had happened and they were sending the overflow to Tulane Medical Center.

No point in speculating.

Even more than concern for her sister and brother-in-law, though, one thought filled her mind as she drove too fast and too recklessly across town.

What if it were Hunter?

Visions of a world without the man she'd come to love and admire and yet had walked away from crowded her mind. Hunter, as she'd first seen him across the room at the Orphan's Club fund-raiser; and then at PJ's, when he'd been far too cocky for his own good, yet somehow disarmingly charming. And then in Las Vegas, as the two of them had discovered so much about each other . . .

Daffy braked as all the traffic on the I-10 came to a crawl. But her images of Hunter paraded on and she knew, with a finality that created in her not only immense satisfaction but a wave of anxiety, that she had to go to Hunter.

If it wasn't too late.

But first she had to answer her sister's call for support.

Finally free of the traffic, Daffy left her car at a meter, threw in the one quarter she could find, and hoped that the parking demons didn't tow her car away.

When she didn't see Jonni in the waiting room, Daffy without hesitation claimed to be the injured man's sister and was shown back to his room.

She had no idea what scene she'd find. David unconscious, battling for his life, Jonni crying at his side?

The last sight she expected to see was David propped up in bed holding court, the only sight of a wound a bandage around his upper arm.

Jonni clung to him, and to Daffy's surprise, the paralegal intern she'd suspected of being David's paramour stood on the other side of the bed. A young man with red hair had his arm possessively around the intern.

Daffy hesitated and Jonni, spying her, called her into the room. "Thanks for coming. I must have scared you silly, but look, he's going to be okay!"

"So I see," Daffy said. "What happened?"

The intern answered. "Mr. DeVries saved my life."

"Her ex-husband thought he could defy not only the restraining order," David said, "but my stubborn streak and my military training as well."

Jonni, eyes shining, said, "He took the gun away from the man and saved the day. My hero!"

The man with the intern said, "I can't thank you enough for looking after Nina. As soon as this mess is behind us and we're able to get married, I want you and your wife to dance at our wedding."

Daffy blinked. So much for her sleuthing. So David truly was innocent of all charges. Impulsively, she leaned over the bed and kissed him on the cheek.

"Daffodil, am I dreaming? What was that for?"

"For being my alive-and-well brother-in-law," Daffy said. She hugged Jonni and whispered to her, "I've got to run. There's something important I have to do."

"Are you finally going to answer Hunter?" Jonni asked, excited.

Daffy tried not to look quite so expectant. "Sometimes, sis, you know too much," she said, and made as dignified an exit as she could under the circumstances.

She had one stop to make before she could go in search of Hunter.

She drove to *The Crescent* and walked quickly toward the cubicle she used. Flipping on the computer, she began to hum and to compose the farewell column of Dear Love Doctor. No need for readers' questions this time. She typed:

Dear Love Doctor,

A man I love asked me to marry him. I was afraid of holding up my end of a long-term commitment, so, like a fool, I said no. Now I've realized that loving him is worth the risk of failure, and that the risk will keep me on my toes. But he's quit calling me and I'm afraid he's changed his mind. So how do I tell him I've changed mine?

Signed,
Willing to Learn to Love Together

Without pausing, Daffy typed the response:

Dear Willing,

So you say you're ready to face the risks and challenges of a lifetime together with the man you love? Then why are you balking now? If he's changed his mind, that means you gave him the right answer to begin with. If he still wants you, then he'll be one very happy guy when you show up on his doorstep. You speak of risks. You think he didn't take a chance when he proposed? Sure he did, and he no doubt suffered when you said no. Heck, the guy's probably still whining and licking his bruises. So go ahead, put your feet where your mouth is, and take your first risk. Go to him.

Signed,
Dear Love Doctor

P.S. To all my readers, this is the last you'll see of Dear Love Doctor. I've finally learned to focus on my own challenges rather than avoiding them by solving other people's problems.

Now I'm off to follow my own advice and take the scariest risk of my life!

Signed,
Dear Love Doctor, aka Daffodil Landry

Marguerite would have her head on a platter, but that didn't stop Daffy from saving the column to disk and printing out one advance copy of what she'd written.

To tidy things up, she dashed off her resignation letter and left it in the editor's box on her way out.

She knew where he worked and she wasted no time in zooming downtown. But as she neared the office tower that housed Hunter's company, Daffy found herself stopping at yellow lights, much to the frustration of the cars behind her.

What if he wasn't there? What if he'd gone out of town? What if he refused to see her, told his secretary the way she'd told her housekeeper to say he wasn't available? She glanced at her phone but knew she couldn't call him. She had to go to him in person.

Someone laid on a horn and Daffy realized she'd just sat through a green light. Waving a hand in apology, she stared at the light and whisked forward as soon as it changed again. She couldn't let her fears stop her now.

High above the traffic, Hunter sat at his desk, a frown on his face. The NuTech merger had been finalized and the stock market had reacted with rave reviews.

Today, he was worth a whole heck of a lot more than he'd been the day before. Aloysius had already left to celebrate with Chrissie. No doubt the two of them were off to buy a yacht or some ridiculously expensive toy.

But what was the point of celebrating alone? Shopping alone? Sleeping alone?

He pulled out the old-fashioned Rolodex his secretary kept current for him and flipped to the B's. That was where he filed the numbers of the babes. He turned the cards, wondering if he should call one of them.

That was what the old Hunter would have done. Dial a babe and have a party.

But that was B. D.

Pushing away the Rolodex, Hunter fished in his desk drawer, drew out a small box, and then rose from his chair, grabbed his laptop, and headed out of his office. Down the hall, the employees, all of whom owned substantial stock shares, were still celebrating.

Maybe Aloysius knew something about Daffy he didn't know, but Hunter was beginning to doubt that. He'd ignored her religiously for more than a week and she had yet to contact him. Just how long was he supposed to put his life on hold?

He punched the elevator button, feeling better than he had for days. Forget ignoring her, forget waiting for her to face her fears. Hunter was a man of action.

He was going after her.

He couldn't stand to think of her worrying herself sick, trying to decide whether she should have agreed to marry him and then fretting over whether she should change her mind but how could she do that? Daffy had her pride. But he knew she loved him and needed him.

And he sure as hell needed her.

The express elevator slid smoothly to a stop forty-two floors below his offices and Hunter waited impatiently as the doors opened. Now that he'd decided to go after Daffy, he didn't want to waste one more minute.

Lost in his thoughts, he stepped forward. A woman was walking into the elevator and he instinctively paused to let her enter.

"Hunter?"

He focused. "Daffy." He'd almost barged right past her!

"I guess you're on your way out . . ." she said, her eyes devouring him as hungrily as he had to be staring at her.

"No, I'm on my way up," he said. "Isn't this the Up elevator?"

She was starting to smile. "There's something I need to say to you."

Hunter punched 42 and leaned back against the wall of the elevator car. It was all he could do to keep his hands off her, but he sensed Daffy needed to say what she had to say before he swooped in on her. Communication, he was beginning to learn, was the glue that kept love together. That and great sex, he added to himself with a smile.

"Are you listening, Hunter?"

"Oh, yeah."

"I understand that you may not care about this anymore, but I've learned I don't want to run away from what might be because I'm afraid of what might be." She looked confused. "Does that make sense?"

He nodded.

But Daffy wasn't so sure. She'd let her column speak for her. She handed the sheet of paper to him. Watching Hunter from across the space of the elevator car as he read her words, she knew her world would end if he'd changed his mind.

"Come here," he said, tucking the paper into his back pocket.

Daffy forgot about pride and flung herself against him. "I've missed you so much," she whispered. "If you still want to marry me, the answer is yes."

Hunter had her in a bear hug. She tipped her chin. Their lips met, and then he said, "If?"

Daffy quit breathing. "Do you still want to marry me?"

He reached behind him and slapped the Stop

button on the elevator. The car came to a halt. He let go of her and stuck a hand in his jacket pocket. Drawing out the blue velvet ring box, he said, "I thought you'd never ask."

He slipped the ring on her finger and kissed her.

"Now that's romantic," Daffy said with a happy sigh.

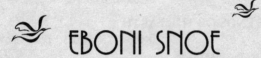

Discover Contemporary Romances
at Their Sizzling Hot Best
from Avon Books

Coming Soon from
HarperTorch

CIRCLE OF THREE

By the *New York Times* bestselling author of
THE SAVING GRACES

Patricia Gaffney

Through the interconnected lives of three generations of
women in a small town in rural Virginia, this poignant,
memorable novel reveals the layers of tradition and responsibility, commitment and passion, these women share. Wise,
moving, and heartbreakingly real, *Circle of Three* offers
women of all ages a deeper understanding of one another, of
themselves and of the perplexing and invigorating magic
that is life itself.

"Filled with insight and humor and heart,
Circle of Three reminds us what it's like
to be a woman."
Nora Roberts

"Powerful . . . Family drama that is impossible
to put down until the final page is read."
Midwest Book Review

"Through the eyes of these strong, complex women
come three uniquely insightful, emotional perspectives."
New York Daily News

0-06-109836-1/$7.50 US/$9.99 Can